T0021029

THIS THING OF DARKNESS

K. V. TURLEY and FIORELLA DE MARIA

This Thing of Darkness

A novel

IGNATIUS PRESS   SAN FRANCISCO

Cover illustration and design by John Herreid

© 2021 by Ignatius Press, San Francisco
All rights reserved
ISBN 978-1-62164-443-9 (PB)
ISBN 978-1-64229-179-7 (eBook)
Library of Congress Control Number 2021936848
Printed in the United States of America ∞

To Kitty and Edmund

This thing of darkness I acknowledge mine.
—The Tempest

AUTHORS' NOTE

This story is obviously a work of imagination about a famous actor who created an aura of mystery around himself, as was fitting for the kinds of characters he brought to life on stage and screen.

What we can say for certain, however, is that he was given a Catholic burial in his Count Dracula costume.

Requiescat in pace.

PROLOGUE

Berkshire, 1971

I come from a family of storytellers. My father was a modestly successful novelist before the creative process drove him out of his mind. He used to say that the hardest stories to commit to paper are the real ones. The old cliché "Truth is stranger than fiction" is as true as it is tedious to read. And just sometimes, we writers find ourselves hearing a life story so terrifying, so beyond the realms of normal human experience, that it is as much as our own lives are worth to believe it, let alone render such biographies credible to others. What no one expects is for such a story to be one's own.

I expect the reader to question the truth of the tale I have to tell. How could it be any different? If the years had not been so much kinder to me than to my unfortunate subject, I am not sure I would ever have had the courage to commit this man's story to paper at all. And yet I have done so. From the comfort and safety of my room, I present to you a fantastical tale of a man whose life was more fanciful than the many phantoms and tortured souls he once brought to life in the world of cinema. If some of the details appear too outrageous to be true, I should perhaps concede that my subject may not have been the most reliable of witnesses even in the recounting of his own life, his mind destroyed by years of alcohol and drug abuse. You, reader, must judge.

Often life is more frightening, more extraordinary, and therefore more difficult to accept than one can ever suspect.

How did I find myself—an English widow and jobbing writer—walking down a bustling Los Angeles street on that otherwise unremarkable day fifteen years ago? This is not my story, but I feel some need to explain myself; and if you know a little about the messenger, it may be easier for you to trust me. I want you to trust me. All I can say is that I was on assignment. Not an unusual occurrence, but on this occasion I felt a certain bitterness.

My editor had passed the file to me, thinking that he was giving me this "crazy project" only because he knew I was desperate for work and would do anything within reasonable moral boundaries to keep a roof over my head.

"Bela who?" I asked, standing in front of Mr Goldberg's desk since he never invited me to sit down when he summoned me. And it was always *Mr* Goldberg. The enigmatic Mr Goldberg; Mr Goldberg, one of the last Jews to leave Germany in the 1930s (or so he said); Mr Goldberg, with an accent that oscillated between Berlin and Burbank; Mr Goldberg, a silver-haired man with a face like an overweight frog, handed me a file bursting with what looked like old newspaper cuttings and notes. "Am I supposed to have heard of him?"

Mr Goldberg lit a cigarette, which got on my nerves more than being expected to stand to attention. "Don't pretend you're too young to remember him, Evi. Everyone your age and older has heard of Bela Lugosi. Better known as Dracula."

"A horror actor?" I could practically hear my mother's explosions of panicked rage at the very idea. *A horror film? No daughter of mine ... it's degenerate ... all those ghosts and vampires ...* "Mr Goldberg, I have never watched a horror film in my life. The first time I entered a cinema was with an unsuitable boyfriend, and even then, I had to fib to my mother that I was going to my friend's house."

"I assume you're not too pure to have heard of Dracula?" asked Mr Goldberg, giving a wry smile. "Not too lowbrow for you, is it?"

"I have read the book," I replied. "It was an enjoyable-enough read, as I recall, if one finds the notion of grown men turning into bats titillating."

Mr Goldberg scrutinized me for a moment before dissolving into laughter. "You British kill me, you know," he ventured, leaning back in his chair to enjoy the moment. "You still manage to sound polite when you're being"—he assumed a haughty posture and a British accent—"horrid."

"In this context, the English slang you are looking for is 'frightful'," I answered, "and I don't sound that posh."

Mr Goldberg finally gestured for me to sit down. "Look, Evi, you can be as hoity-toity as you like, but I know you're always desperate for work. The details are all in the file. Go interview the guy before he croaks, and get me the first instalment of 'The Life and Times of Bela Lugosi' by Monday next, and I'll give you a fat little pay cheque."

The man knew where to apply pressure, like any good torturer. That reference to my financial state was like an electric current jolting through my head; my hands reached out to take the file. "I know nothing about cinema. I know nothing about this actor," I said. It was not just procrastination—I really did know absolutely nothing about the weird and wonderful world of moving pictures and film sets and men in makeup, nor had I the slightest interest.

"There's a film guy who can help you with the history. His details are in the file. Hugo Radelle. He's a nice guy; you'll like him. Served in Korea."

I felt myself jumping to my feet like a scalded cat. "Look here, I don't think . . ."

Mr Goldberg looked nonchalantly in my direction. "It's okay," he said with feigned indifference. "If you'd rather hand the file over to someone who can be bothered, that's okay by me. I'm sure you'll find yourself some work elsewhere. Plenty of street corners in this city, even if you are past your best."

That was how it started—a little emotional blackmail, an insult or two, then the reluctant acceptance of an irksome assignment. No different from so many other projects.

Five minutes later, I was out in the blazing sunshine of the street, the file taking up unwelcome space in my bag. I told myself it was the bright light making my eyes water.

I hurried home. I needed time to get myself into a more relaxed mood, read through the file, and give this Mr Lugosi a call. A few lengthy interviews with the gentleman himself, some writing, and the job would be done.

For reasons not altogether clear, especially to me, I have written this—this "adventure"—in the only way that feels safe. I have retreated into my father's genre and written my story in the third person, like some narrative novel, as though—as if—by a disinterested observer. I give no assurances that the story you are about to read is true. Perhaps it was all the ravings of a washed-up actor struggling to come to terms with a life that proved in the end a disappointment, or better still the carefully crafted work of a fantasist, or the sad result of my own mental state, brought about by grief and years of secret addiction. Again, dear reader, I leave you to decide.

I must stop writing now if I can, though somehow it seems to help. Outside my window the sky grows dark, blotting out everything in the distance. All these years later, I still grow fearful when the shadows lengthen and darkness falls outside. I cannot bear to sleep alone.

I still need someone to watch over me in case the real darkness returns.

1956 California

There are very few people in this world who desire to have their lives snatched from them without warning. A sudden, violent death is hardly the happiest of endings, and most would prefer to have some time, even a few precious hours, to prepare for the inevitable. Not this man. He was a man withered by age and hard living who had been in the process of wasting away for so long that he looked neither living nor dead. Funny, he looked undead. Yes, undead, like the characters he had played on screen. He seemed like a man caught in a torturous hinterland from which nothing could distract him.

That afternoon, Bela sat in his chair, smoking a cigar without enthusiasm. The chair faced a window to allow him a good view of the world outside, a considerate touch by a wife attempting to distract him from his brooding, but to him it felt like the ultimate taunt: an actor condemned to the role of a bored spectator. The light hurt his eyes in any case, an ugly side effect of his previous excesses, and so he had pulled the curtains across. The semidarkness had always suited Bela, and he luxuriated in the twilight world he had created for himself.

It was this life he had promised to tell the woman who had called on him the previous afternoon. He had agreed to the meeting out of sheer vanity. It had been such a long time since anyone had been interested in him for any edifying reason—in fact, for any reason. Then, suddenly, there had been a courteous, soft-spoken voice at the end of the phone that enunciated as beautifully as the queen of

England. She had the turns of phrase to match. "Would you mind awfully if I were to come and see you?" "I trust it will be no trouble if we meet at one o'clock?" "Thank you, Mr Lugosi, that would be splendid." Even her mispronunciation of his name—which ordinarily would have riled him—endeared her to him a little.

Mrs Evangeline Kilhooley. A widow, then, but there were plenty of those around these days, a sad little army of grieving women of every age and nationality, many dragging needy children. An English widow, perhaps a GI bride? Her voice made him think of a matronly older woman, hard-bitten by years of penury but well-enough brought up to treat her elders with respect. Bela groaned at the thought. However old she was, he was sure to be a great deal older, a man deserving of respect simply by having been born in another century.

He heard the distant sound of a knock on the door, immediately followed by the chiming of the carriage clock over the fireplace. She was punctual virtually to the second. There was the sound of the door being opened and two female voices—Bela's wife and the muted tones he had heard on the telephone—followed by the creak of two sets of footsteps outside the room. Bela was astonished at how nervous he felt at the approach of this stranger who had come to write down a story of which he felt increasingly ashamed. He had never experienced stage fright as a young man, but he imagined that this must be how it felt to be overcome by paralysing uncertainty at the sight of the curtain going up.

The door opened, and there stood his soon-to-be interrogator, a petite woman swathed in soft grey, brown hair pinned carefully beneath a prim hat. Her hands were gloved in spite of the hot weather, and she carried a large, slightly battered travel bag, giving away her line of work. She hesitated in the doorway, unsettled by the poor light, which gave him time to rise to his feet to greet her. "Mrs Kilhooley?" he enquired, reaching out a hand to her. "Good afternoon."

Evangeline removed her glove and shook his hand, wincing almost imperceptibly as the cold, gnarled fingers closed around hers. "How do you do?"

"Please sit down."

She moved awkwardly to the chair across from the actor, beside a curtained window, sitting on the very edge as though she expected to have to make a run for it at any moment. "Thank you," she ventured, distracting herself by opening her bag and drawing out a notepad and silver pen. "Thank you for agreeing to see me, Mr Lug—"

"I think you should call me Bela," he said, whilst sitting down and giving her a smile intended to reassure. Her eyes darted towards the door, which seemed to have closed by itself as she had stepped inside. "There's no reason to be anxious," he added. "I don't bite."

Evangeline's vast brown eyes widened in surprise; then she seemed to get the joke and gave a nervous giggle. "I'm very glad to hear it, Mr—Bela. It's just that I thought your wife would wish to join us."

"Oh, she's heard my story before," he said airily, not taking his eyes off her. "Far more often than she could wish to hear. Is it too dark for you?"

"A little. I wonder if I might pull back the curtain a little?"

"You may switch on that light," he said, pointing to a large standard lamp beside her chair. "It will give you light enough to write by." Bela watched as she peered up at the lamp, looking to all intents and purposes as though she expected it to turn into a giant serpent if she touched it. He eased himself out of his chair with evident difficulty and switched on the lamp himself before quickly returning to his place. "What am I to call you?"

"Well …" She looked down at her papers in miserable resignation. "Well, if I am to call you Bela, you must call me Evangeline."

"Thank you, you have a beautiful name," he said in the soft, almost-growling tone he had always reserved for women. "It could almost be the name of an actress."

"I'm afraid I should have been of no use on the stage," answered Evangeline, a little pertly. "I have no ability to pretend."

Bela smiled, regarding her intently. That was the first lie. Bela knew from his long years as an actor that everybody on earth is an actor of sorts, playing the role he believes he has been allotted or the one he imagines will impress the world, or simply wearing the mask that hides any manner of fragility or sorrow.

Evangeline was playing the role of a professional woman with very little skill, he thought to himself as he watched her prepare to start taking notes. He tried to guess her age and thought that she must be over thirty, but there was a girlishness about her that made her appear much younger. Even her grey clothes belied a certain confusion as to her role—the woman widowed too young, caught between mourning dress and the demands of the world to move on with life. Or was it her own need to move on?

"Shall we begin?" he said, when she stopped moving, pen poised. "I'm an old man. Who knows, perhaps this will be my last conversation."

"I sincerely hope not," she said, and it was her turn to give him a reassuring smile. She was warming to her role now. "I will be guided by you. Take your time. Imagine I am not here if it helps."

I be able to ignore your presence? Nothing could be further from the truth, he thought, looking across the room at her bowed head as she scribbled some sort of heading in shorthand. Mina Harker would be impressed by her skill in that language of bizarre symbols. He had been alone for such a long time that the presence of an audience was of more comfort than the woman in the chair could possibly have known. And he had a story to tell before the Great Unknown came to meet him, that dreaded final curtain call when the audience leave and the lights finally fade. He had a story; and here, come at last, was this woman from misty Albion, an exile like him, waiting in respectful silence to hear his bons mots.

"You have my diary in there, do you not?" he began, pointing at her bag. "I wrote it when I was convalescing."

Evangeline raised an eyebrow. "I have read your manu-script, if that is what you mean," she answered. She was a sceptic, then, but perhaps it was not so unreasonable that an outsider should question what he had to say, thought Bela. For some reason, he felt the need to perform for her. He was not sure why, but the doubt in her voice before he had even begun to tell his tale only made him the more determined to prove that his life was as extra-ordinary as he knew it to be. It was not a good life, not a wholesome or admirable life, but he would let her know, let her understand, that it was a life unlike any other. Yes, a memorable, dream-haunted life.

2

1882 Hungary

He belonged to the old world and the old century. In his declining years, Bela would find no pivotal moment when he came of age—no childhood catastrophe that sent his world spinning out of control, no kindly mentor who guided him to greatness. His dull, uneventful childhood was played out amidst the brooding uncertainty of country folk set apart from the rest of their people by the jagged mountains—nature's prison walls.

The isolation of his people was, however, more than geographic. The sophisticated inhabitants of the cities and towns looked down upon their fellow countrymen in those far-away villages with not a little suspicion, even fear. They belonged to the cursed darkness of those deep forests and shadowy places, people of the night to be avoided by the pious men of civilisation if they wished to guard their own souls. The country folk could not resist cultivating this image of themselves, whilst deep down they feared it might be true.

"Bela, Bela!" He heard Vilma's singsong voice pleading with him in the darkness. "Father says it's a sin!"

They sat in a circle in the disused barn, Bela and his sister, Vilma, and assorted boys and girls from the village. It was midnight, of course, the witching hour, and Bela was directing the show. It was nothing more than a show, a vain boy's pretence at possession of gifts from the Prince of Darkness, but he relished every minute. "Hush!" warned

Bela, reaching forward to pick up the solitary candle flickering pathetically in the darkness. "The Dark Lord will not come to those who resist him!"

"Father will run mad if he catches us!"

Bela looked down contemptuously at Vilma's large, frightened eyes staring at him in the pale light. The candle had the glorious effect of throwing shadows everywhere, offering more horror than comfort. Swirling little figures flickered and danced across the wooden walls; spindly claws crept out of corners. "Hush! The Prince of Darkness comes!"

"Bela! I want to go home!"

But Vilma's pleas were silenced by a thundering of invisible footsteps outside. The children huddled together, shivering at the thud of gigantic feet creeping towards them and the growl of sinister voices. Bela felt his flesh crawl in spite of himself, but he stood firm, determined to greet the Darkness on his feet. The candle wavered and died in his hand, plunging the barn into pitch darkness. He heard another child give a whimper; then the door was thrown open with an almighty crash, and a mountainous figure stood before them, huge and terrible, his face glowing with hellfire.

Vilma was the first to scream, but within seconds, the circle had broken and the petrified children had begun running for cover, screaming at the tops of their voices. But not Bela. The master of ceremonies would never run from the Darkness he had summoned. He would never run ... A warm, human, flesh-and-blood hand struck him hard across the face, sending him hurtling down onto the filthy floor. He tasted his own blood in his mouth from the force of the blow and looked up at the Darkness for an explanation. The Darkness stood quite still before him, a gigantic figure of a man, carrying not a trident but a big stick and a lantern.

"On your feet, boy," came the growling voice of Bela's father. "I'll flay you alive, you little swine!"

The old man glanced at Evangeline, who was laughing softly in her chair. The story had clearly had the effect of allaying any fears she had had about their meeting, and she stared fixedly at the floor, clasping and unclasping her gloves to steady herself. "Is something funny?" he asked over her merriment when she failed to desist. "I'm not sure what's funny. My father gave me hell about that. I passed a most uncomfortable night."

"Oh, but it's all too silly!" protested Evangeline, taking out a clean handkerchief. Bela smelled the aroma of lilac water in the air and felt his temper being soothed. "Surely you didn't really imagine some demon was going to come and join the party, did you?"

"Be careful, young lady," said Bela quietly, silencing her immediately. "The Darkness does not like to be mocked. And yes, there was plenty of devilry where I grew up. The Undead stalked those fields and lonely roads looking for their prey. Our nights were plagued by nightmares of ghouls and phantoms."

"That was hardly surprising if you spent your waking hours frightening each other with ghost stories," said Evangeline. "Children have such fertile imaginations."

"There was far more to it than imagination," answered Bela, looking at her intently. It was the first time she had noticed how pale he was, his face ravaged by years of abuse. "Would it shock you to know that we used to wake up to find that our animals had been ripped to pieces, throats horribly mutilated, with the blood drained from them? We children lived in fear. At times, I felt our lives were ruled by fear and little else. It seemed to be all around us."

It was all very interesting, but Evangeline knew perfectly well that he was taking her for a ride. He told her story after story, all cut from the same cloth: terrifying creatures of the night, the dreadful Undead, zombies stalking the countryside. She had had little time to read over the file before that first meeting, but she knew his childhood had been quite different from the wild and mysterious life he wanted her to believe. He was born into a tediously ordinary lower-middle-class home, with a father who supported his family as a baker. Bela was not even born in Transylvania—as his studio's publicity had claimed to much public excitement—but fifty miles from its border.

He was a typical actor, she thought, as she walked away in search of a bus home. Fake right through, with a past he had invented to correspond with his screen persona; not even his name was real. Evi had many pet hates, but deceit filled her with particular disgust. She paused for the traffic to slow before venturing across the street. She felt grateful to be out in the fresh air, in the light again, after an hour in what seemed more a mausoleum than a home. No wonder the man was away with the fairies, she thought, fantasising about childhood adventures in barns and running away with the circus.

No matter. Evi resolved to write down the story as faithfully as she could. It was Bela's story, after all, not hers.

There are few prisons more hellish for an imaginative twelve-year-old boy than the school room. Bela remembered school as an actual hell of tedious exercises and violent schoolmasters, but whatever the precise truth of the matter, change was in the air on that sultry, sunless morning. It was simply a case of making sure that nobody noticed what a momentous day this was to be in the life of Bela Lugosi.

"Hurry now! Don't be late!" ordered Bela's mother to Bela's bowed head as he crammed the rest of his breakfast into his mouth. "If you hurry, you can catch up with the others. Where's your satchel?"

"It's by my feet, Mama; don't worry," he said quickly, picking it up as effortlessly as he could manage. It would not do for her to notice how heavy his bag was, not that he imagined she would suspect anything. He had cultivated a powerful contempt for everyone close to him over the past five years and felt no sense of regret as he watched his mother fretting about the kitchen as she had always done. He stepped towards the door, hesitating to leave. His mother was busy gathering up the empty dishes from the breakfast table; she was not going to look in his direction. "Good-bye."

"Off you go!" she answered, still not looking at him. "Be a good boy."

Bela shook his head and stepped away from the smell of bread and burnt coffee and all the warm aromas of home. It was the first morning she had failed to give him that final kiss, and the first time he craved it. He closed the door behind him and walked in the direction of the school until he was sure he was out of sight of prying eyes. Then he left the road and slipped away among the trees in search of deliverance.

"Oh, look, another runaway!" The ringmaster was as imposing in real life as he had been at the centre of the travelling stage show Bela had sneaked out to watch the night before. He was a large, portly man with a face that would have been cruelly handsome if it had not been so overcrowded by moustache and massive eyebrows and a nose and mouth that competed for room above a weak jawline. "Let me guess: you are an adventurous little boy out to make his grand fortune?"

Bela felt himself blushing. "I want to see the world," he said quietly. He cleared his throat determinedly. "I'm hardworking and honest. I'll do anything . . ."

The ringmaster roared with laughter. "I'd keep that to yourself if I were you, boy. What are you running from?"

Bela shrugged. "Nothing."

The ringmaster looked down at Bela with undisguised suspicion. He dealt with a steady stream of runaways—mostly boys of about this age—young fools he could put to work for very little. Like the others, Bela would no doubt tire of a life that would never be as exciting as it first promised, and he would leave as quickly as he had arrived. Still, there was something different about this boy. He was in rude health, with a rounded face and good complexion. His clothes were simple but of good quality, and he showed no telltale signs of mistreatment. "Are you sure, lad? We leave today, and we'll not be coming back. If you're going to start crying for your mother or missing your warm bed ..."

"I don't ever want to come back," answered Bela, but his cheeks reddened with the mention of his mother. By rights, he ought to have been mortified by the thought that, in a few short hours, Vilma would return home without him. To begin with, their mother would not miss him, thinking perhaps that he had gone off with a friend and would be back in time for supper. But then the light would fade, and his place would remain empty at the table; there would be concerned conversations and glances out the window; Vilma would be interrogated by their father about when she had seen him last. Then the process of searching for him would begin, the venturing out into the dark, the knocking on doors, the mounting panic when he could not be found. Bela knew his disappearance would cause pain to all of them, but he felt no compunction whatsoever about what he was doing. "I don't want to go home," he repeated. "I shan't cause you any trouble."

"You'd better not," the ringmaster retorted, giving him a forbidding glance. "Do as you're told. Stay out of my way." The man turned his back on Bela to indicate that the brief interview was over, only to turn back sharply. "And another thing: don't go anywhere near the sideshows."

"What are the sideshows?"

"Never you mind. Just stay away from them."

Evi paused from her typing to listen for any sound of movement outside the room. Her flat consisted of a kitchen, a bathroom, a sitting room that doubled up as her study, and an interconnecting bedroom. In spite of years alone, Evi still found herself hesitating to reach into her desk drawer, as though the ghost of her mother might appear in the room to remonstrate with her. It was the ghost of a bad conscience; she shrugged it off as she opened the drawer and took out the hip flask. Her husband's hip flask. When she drank from it, the act felt like a desecration. The urge was stronger than the shame now, that is, since the arrival of the telegram telling her he was missing.

No sound anywhere; she was safe for now to drink and write and dream. The nights were the loneliest. This was the best time to lose herself in writing. She could marvel at the misplaced courage of a young boy who walked into the unknown without a backward glance. The twelve-year-old child—just a child—clambered aboard a wagon heading he knew not where, in his thirst for the world beyond the mountains. A world of cities and towns and all that their peoples offered. And he had lied to the ring-master as he had lied to her earlier that day—he did have something to flee: those dark nights of dream-haunted childhood, that fear of the eternal darkness. That was the one threat he could never outrun.

The old man had become positively animated describing his days with the travelling show. For a few precious minutes, that dark, stifling room had been a blaze of light and colour: the glorious reds and golds of curtains opening to reveal the revelry of the show; the glittering jewellery around the Gypsy women's necks; the sumptuous costumes in a riot of silken hues. He might have had just one story in him—his own much-embroidered life story—but boy, did he know how to tell it.

"Imagine me, Evangeline!" he had exclaimed, filled with such energy that he rose from his seat, walked toward her, and clasped her hand as though he meant to lead her personally through the labyrinthine pathways of his memory, back to that time of childhood wonder. "Surrounded by those wondrous performers. Gypsy people, so strange, unique, such a fascinating race. Dark, beautiful women murmuring in their own secret language. They were unlike anyone I had ever met before." Bela's face darkened, causing Evi instinctively to slip her hand away from his. "The Darkness stole them from the face of the earth. It's true, isn't it?"

Evi shook her head. "I'm not sure I understand you."

"The Darkness took them. The harbingers of death dragged them into the death camps and gas chambers."

"I'm sorry. Yes, I'm afraid that is what happened to some."

Bela lowered his head and returned to his chair. Evi thought he would have wept if he still had the capacity for such powerful emotions. He said quietly, "We are all to blame for it. All of us."

Evi knew she ought to ask him what on earth he meant, but there had been so much soul-searching since the liberation of the camps that it was not unreasonable that he might feel burdened by some collective sense of guilt. She endeavoured to rescue the situation in the only way a nicely brought-up English girl could—she changed the subject. "What was your part in the circus? Bela, what role did you play?"

Bela looked down at his empty hands. "I was a mischief-making little boy, Evangeline. My part was to clean up after the show."

It was no good; the old energy was not there. She tried again. "Well, it must have been quite a spectacle to watch, all that drama!"

It was working; the features began to soften. "Oh yes, it was. Every night, we would pitch our tents in a field or at the edge of a village, and our auditorium would arise from nothing. Every single night! And every single night I could watch those songs and dances and feel as though I saw it all for the first time."

"And then there were the sideshows."

There could be no more enticing invitation to a young boy than a faintly threatening order to stay away, especially a boy like Bela, who naturally found himself drifting in the direction of the forbidden. And the sideshows, euphemistically labelled "exotic", were certainly not for the eyes of children.

"Oh Evangeline, imagine the excitement of sneaking into that creepy adult world! All those marvels and horrors!"

The sideshows were a theatrical world without colour and glitter or even the bright lights of the main tent. Young Bela stood stock still, taking in every detail of the spectacle before him. A woman—or was it a man? In the half-light his senses were confused. A person sat before him in a long, dark gown, with a head of luxuriant hair carefully braided in a manner that should have been sensual. A pair of tragic, green-gold eyes stared back at him intently from a thin face covered in a soft, tawny beard.

Bela felt an inexorable urge to touch her, not so much to convince himself that this bearded lady was the genuine article, but just to get a little closer to this inhabitant of life's dark corners. He reached forward, ignoring the look of panic on that face which he imagined to be caused by his looming presence. It was the first time he had felt powerful enough to be feared . . .

A second later, he was flat on his back surrounded by stars and planets. He had been too distracted to notice the ringmaster descending on him and had no chance to dodge the blow that felled him. "I thought I told you to stay away from the sideshows!" roared the ringmaster. Bela was too dazed to resist as he was hauled to his feet, and he quickly noted that trying to fight off a man of such gigantic proportions would be exhausting and futile. "Outside!"

Bela staggered out into the well-lit quarters of the main travelling show, the ringmaster swiping at his head at every step. Bela could hear the laughter of every onlooker who appeared to be inordinately amused at the sight of his inglorious exit, but he felt an unnerving sense of exhilaration nonetheless. He had conquered the sideshows! He had seen a real-life bearded lady!

"Never go near those sideshows again," warned the ringmaster, spinning Bela round to face him. "Do you understand? Stay away!"

But it was too late. Those sideshows, with all their forbidden allure, were to be Bela's first hint of the Darkness he had searched for during those childish nighttime vigils. He had tasted it, very nearly touched it, and now he craved admittance.

Evi woke up shaking. She had dozed off at her desk, her head full of giants and bearded ladies, and woken up shaking so violently she could feel the whole desk moving. She sat up painfully, her neck and back throbbing with the strain of hours crouched in such an unnatural position. Evi could taste acid at the back of her throat from falling asleep on an empty stomach, mingled with the guilty aftertaste of cheap alcohol. She attempted to stand up, but her knees gave way.

Freaks, she thought. "That's not a nice word," said Evi aloud. "Those people weren't monsters; it's just that they had an illness or a condition or something that probably could be treated quite easily these days. We're all freaks to somebody."

The word was still troubling her as she glanced into the mirror. Evi's unwashed, unpainted face in the glass stared back. Perhaps that was why she felt drawn to Bela, and he to her, in a strange way. They were both freaks. Both hiding away in the sideshows, unfit to be seen by children.

Evi would finish the instalment. She would still have time after she had handed it in to drop a line to this Hugo Radelle to ask his advice and to arrange another visit to Castle Lugosi, as she was beginning to see it. Determination. She just needed a little determination to see the job through.

A twelve-year-old boy had few weapons in his arsenal with which to fight his corner—Bela's encounter with the ringmaster had taught him that much—but what he lacked in physical strength, he compensated for in wilful determination. And he was absolutely determined that those glamorous, mysterious shows were his destiny. So, he sneaked back in and was thrown out. He returned and was thrown out again. Still, he went back, drawn as though by an enchantment ... and there were only so many times his elders could hurl him back into the light before they finally relented and let him have his way. Someone with a strong pair of legs was needed to run errands for freaks too reclusive to be seen in public, and Bela was happy to fulfil that role—*any* role at all if it kept him near them.

"I liked to call them my Dark Domain, Evangeline. My shows, my family."

Evi glanced up at him in surprise. "Your family? Were you homesick, then?"

"Why on earth should I have been homesick?" the old man answered in what was almost annoyance. "I abandoned home without a single regret."

"I hope I have not offended you. It was just an interesting choice of words. You liked them; you made friends with them. There's nothing wrong in that."

"My dear, I *loved* them. I loved them as passionately as everyone else despised them."

Evi had learnt almost immediately that her subject was at his most eloquent when his emotions were stirred a little, and she waited, pen poised, for a floodgate to open. "Tell me what they were like," she prompted. "I'm listening."

"I can tell you what they were not," he said, staring into a corner of the room. "They were not monsters. Once one was used to their deformities, the shock of their bodily forms—the lobster girl with hands and feet like pincers, the boy with an extra arm, the giant, the old woman the height of a toddler, the young man with half a face—one quickly forgot that they looked different to other people. But they had good souls."

"I'm sure they did."

Bela smiled at her curt tone. "Ah, you are a modern miss, are you not? I do not need to tell you anything. You know that the real monsters are handsome men in uniform who bomb towns and shoot women and children. The German soldiers who killed your husband were probably charming."

Evi dug her heels into the floor and looked down at her notes to avoid the temptation to flee the room. "Why don't you just tell me about your friends at the freak show?" she snapped. "And my husband died in Korea. Not that it makes much difference to me who killed him." She looked up in Bela's direction, gasping with shock to find him standing in front of her. Any man standing over her like that would have unnerved her. She felt suffocated by how much of the room he took up, having not noticed him rising from his seat. His cold, smooth hand reached out to touch her head. Dressed in black with such an authoritative presence in the room, Bela might have been an elderly priest giving her a blessing, but the comparison felt wrong in every possible way. "It's quite all right; why don't you sit down," she said, clawing back as much of her professional tone as she could muster. "Please."

Bela was in no hurry to move. His hand slipped gently down the side of her face, forcing her to acknowledge him. "Poor girl," he said. "It's not good to be all alone. Forgive poor Bela."

"No need to apologise," she said calmly, when a man her own age would have received a slap in the face for behaving so. "Just tell me about your friends, and I can finish. I mean—" Now she was appearing rude. "That is to say, I have a deadline. And I am—well, I'm interested in whatever you were interested in."

"I understand. You wish to be a closed book. And I—I wish to be read."

Excluded from the world of polite society, the freaks had none of the petty vindictiveness that had been the mainstay of Bela's childhood companions, nor did they exhibit any of the rough and random brutality of most of the travelling players and stagehands. A group of men together had a mob mentality that frightened Bela, no more so than when they had been drinking together. It never took long for a fight to break out, and a hopeless fighter like Bela could only hope to flee in time if a brawl did erupt.

Not so these people cast together by nature's strange quirks. They had been forced to transcend not only their bodily limitations but that myriad of fears and petty concerns that dominate the lives of the mass of humanity. And they always made him feel welcome, asking only that he look beyond their superficial appearances to the living, breathing persons that lay within. For a time, he had no desire for any other family, any other life, save that of being among such wondrous people.

3

Evi would one day claim that she sold her heart—the broken, mangled shards of it that she still possessed—for a pot of English tea, served by an expert on a silver tray. To the uninitiated, tea might seem like an unexceptional, not to say unpleasant, beverage poorly suited to hot weather, but to an Englishwoman abroad, it was as close to an out-of-body experience as Evi was ever going to get. Evi had had so many reasons to be unhappy since her husband had vanished into the smoke and fire of war; but it did not occur to her, until the day that she stepped into Hugo Radelle's store, just how homesick she had been for such a very, very long time.

To call Hugo's shop an Aladdin's cave of delights was to insult the wonder of the place. It was a film memorabilia store, room after room of posters and props and old costumes, autographed photographs, books beyond number about film and theatre, biographies of every actor anyone could ever want to know about—and not want to know about. There was equipment too: projectors, cameras, and the genuine article itself—canisters of films. Hundreds, perhaps thousands, of feet of celluloid.

"Thank you for replying so promptly," said Evi, seating herself at a table in Hugo's upstairs quarters. He lived simply, she thought, in a flat above a shop, but he still had style. The table was covered in a starched damask tablecloth that would not have disgraced a London teashop, or a London séance, and the Earl Grey tea was served in a teapot covered in primroses with matching milk jug, sugar bowl, cups, and saucers. There was also a tiered cake stand stacked with scones. "This is splendid. I haven't had a proper afternoon tea since before the war."

"As soon as I heard your voice down the phone, I knew you would be in want of a good cup of tea," said Hugo, pouring milk followed by tea into a cup. "Sugar?"

Her hand went unsteadily to the silver tongs in the sugar bowl. In spite of years without the burden of rationing, Evi still felt uncomfortable about taking someone else's sugar in case he was forced to go without. "How ... how long have you been over here?"

"I arrived when I was eighteen," said Hugo, gesturing to the scones. "Do help yourself. I'm afraid I rather fancied myself as the next David Niven. But then, after two years of working in bars and being an extra on this and that, war broke out. Of course, I went back home to enlist. Strange as it may seem, army life rather suited me, so I stayed on."

"That was how you found yourself in Korea," Evi put in.

"Yes." Hugo paused, sensing an undercurrent he could not quite identify. "Well, needless to say, by the end I was left rather the worse for wear, and that was that. I was already a little on the old side for the army. By then, there was nothing much left for me in England. Since I'd been fighting alongside the Yanks, I returned here." He glanced across at Evi, who was putting up a good show of being absorbed in her tea drinking. "You came over after the war, I suppose?"

"I was a GI bride," answered Evi quietly. "Widowed now." She paused. "But I don't have much to take me back home now."

An awkward silence descended, punctuated only by the soft sounds of eating and drinking. "I'm sorry," said Hugo finally. "Korea took the best of them." He looked down at the magazine he had left out on the coffee table as Evi glanced uneasily at him. "I did enjoy reading your piece on Bela Lugosi."

"Thank you, it's to be the first of a number of instalments," she replied. "Who knows, it might finish up as a book."

"Marvellous. I hope you don't mind my saying this, but I rather wish you had come to see me before this was published."

"Is something wrong?"

"No, no, not exactly." Hugo had some morbid fear that she might burst into tears if he were too negative. "It's beautifully written, of course—you really are a frightfully good journalist and everything—but, it's, well ..."

"Yes?"

"Well, I don't know what he told you, but I suspect that none of this is true."

Evi felt herself blushing, not sure whether it was anger or embarrassment. Being called a fiction writer when she was a journalist was about as low as it got for her. "I assure you, Mr Radelle, when I interviewed Bela Lugosi, he was adamant that this was his story."

Hugo laughed nervously. "I have no doubt he did ... Hugo, please. I'm not doubting your word at all, but actors are notoriously imaginative when it comes to their own life stories." He picked up a pencil and indicated the offending article. "May I?"

"Of course," answered Evi, trying very hard not to sound as though she were sulking.

Hugo began circling paragraph after paragraph—so many, in fact, that Evi wondered why he did not just circle the few sentences that were accurate. "He wasn't born in Transylvania; he was born fifty miles away from the border, as it happens. It just sounded good when Universal was promoting *Dracula*."

"Yes, I know that. A minor point."

"And I've no idea where all this circus stuff comes from. It's true enough to say that he became enthralled with acting when he watched a passing troupe of actors and was very young indeed when he headed to the cities looking for acting jobs."

"So, no bearded ladies, then."

"I fear not. He worked down a coal mine and in a factory. Then on the railways." He stopped at the sound of Evi's cup being set down with a clatter on the table. "Why don't you have a scone?" he suggested, trying to sound helpful rather than concerned. "I baked them myself."

"I'll be coming begging at your door for scones if I lose my job. My editor will go bananas about this."

Hugo chuckled, setting a scone on a plate for her by way of compensation. "You won't lose your job over this. When he entered the world of theatre, he reinvented himself. All actors do. Lugosi must have told that same story to dozens of journalists and fans over the years. Ironically, he stopped drifting and got his first break only when his terribly respectable married sister put in a good word for him."

"What a pity," said Evi with a sigh. "He said he fell in love with a beautiful bearded lady who had run away from a monstrous father."

Hugo shrugged. "Well, who knows, I suppose it's possible there was a bearded lady in his life at some point, but I'd like to see the evidence."

"I suppose the job running errands for a theatre in Budapest wasn't true either?" Evi persisted. "The kindly old theatre owner who took to him and offered him a job?"

"Sadly, no. He became a jobbing actor in the provinces. Bit parts in repertory, that sort of thing. Budapest would have been much more fun. Oh dear." Hugo couldn't help noticing how childlike his guest looked, sitting primly at his table nibbling delicately at the food he had prepared, the naive little thing taken in by an elderly actor's fantasies.

"I'm awfully sorry. I feel as though I've told you Father Christmas doesn't exist."

Evi glared at him with a ferocity that shocked Hugo. There was a passion underneath all that etiquette after all, he thought. "Thanks," she said.

Hugo sat forward in his chair. "You know, I hope this isn't impertinent of me, but perhaps you should come and see me more often?" He tried to think of a way to make the idea not sound as though he were propositioning her. "I mean about old Bela. We could look over the details together before you go to press. Look, I'll even provide the tea."

"That's awfully decent of you ... Hugo."

The pleasure will be entirely mine, he thought, before changing the subject to the weather.

Whatever Hugo had said, Evi wanted desperately to believe Bela's nostalgic descriptions of his new life amid the noise and movement and excitement of the travelling theatre. It worked on him like a narcotic, drawing him into its hypnotic spell, one that never quite released him.

Even at his most wistful, Bela admitted that the tasks he performed were as simple and humdrum as they had been at the travelling show, and his quarters at the back of the theatre were nothing more than a small, cell-like room. It made no difference. To Bela, his new home was a suite in a mythical palace, and he a young prince striding upon the stage. He would dazzle the world of the theatre as no one had ever done before. Or so he thought as he cleaned the stalls each morning and lay awake at night in that tiny, bare room. Each moment he nurtured his ambition to be an actor; and more than anything, he dreamed.

As he spoke of this land of enchantment, he was there—no longer a frail, sick man caught in the battle between life and death but a young boy, impressionable, prone to obsessions, tucked away out of sight whilst the actors rehearsed. Not quite out of sight, though.

"Boy!"

Bela scrambled to his feet, aware that the group of minor deities he had been watching so intently had all turned to look at him. The director was at his side. "Sorry, sir," Bela began, but like all good actors, he knew it was futile to perform for a hostile audience. "I was only looking."

The director had the same build as the ringmaster, but his features and manner were softer—almost effeminate, though Bela would not have understood the notion— and Bela felt a nasty sense of déjà vu overtaking him. He was in the wrong place, looking at the wrong spectacle again. "Don't be angry," came a voice in his defence. It was a low, sensuous female voice that made Bela's heart flutter. It was Anna, the loveliest of leading ladies, standing before him like Beatrice at the gates of Paradiso. "He's no trouble. You like a good show, don't you, my little friend?"

Now here was a bonus greater than Bela could have hoped for: a golden, ethereal beauty with that aura of majesty and nobility all actors seemed to share—taking his part in a scrap with the director. "Rehearsals should not have an audience," said the director. His manner was amiable enough. "You don't want to spoil the magic, do you, boy?"

Emboldened by the friendly atmosphere and the assistance of a most gracious advocate, Bela took his courage in both hands. "Let me act, then," he said breathlessly. "Then I shan't be the audience anymore."

He was not sure what sort of a reaction he had expected, but the gales of laughter that swept through the room felt a good deal crueller than anyone had likely intended. The director made to remove him from the auditorium with the words, "Nice try, Bela. I'm sure you have better things to do with your time on a sunny afternoon."

Bela shook himself free and turned to face his opponent. "*Is* there anything better to do?"

The director looked intently at him, caught between amusement and genuine surprise. "Bela, I have seen plenty of starstruck boys convinced that they were called to be actors, but do you know anything about what it involves? You see them rehearsing and performing, but you do not see the hours and hours of work they have to go through. You don't see them sitting alone learning their lines; you don't see them struggling to feed themselves when they cannot get work. And anyway, no one simply chooses to be an actor."

Bela knew that. Like the others, he was star-struck; he longed to act on the stage with lights and an audience, with laughter and tears, applause and ovations. But he knew he could not choose to be an actor. So he said it, out loud for the first time: "Acting has chosen me." He said it simply, without any intended pretentiousness.

That was the crossroads—the moment in Bela's life when the whole course of his years would be different. The director could have laughed at him or reprimanded him for his lofty notions, and Bela would have had no choice but to go back to being invisible, sweeping and cleaning the theatre. But the director was a thoughtful man who perhaps saw in the young Bela a glimpse of the impetuous youth he had once been, or he remembered a kindness done to him at the same age by a similarly greying director keen to help an ambitious young man on his way. "There's no such thing as destiny," said the director quietly. "There is talent, and there is hard work, and there is opportunity. If you can provide the first two qualities on that list, then I may be willing to provide the third."

Bela had his first part as an extra by the end of the week. It led to being regularly called to "fill in" with the other extras. Soon, bit parts followed, and then slowly, ever so slowly, real parts—with a real character to play, with lines to learn and perhaps an accent to mimic just as the Bird Man at the freak show had taught him.

Bela would never forget the kindness shown to him by the director who gave him his first break. *There is such a thing as destiny*, thought Bela; if only the director knew! The magic of the theatre could be explained only within that realm of Darkness and Light—the never-ending battle for the soul.

Evi's eyes drifted to the bookcase near her chair. The maddening twilight world of Bela's home made it difficult to make out the titles on the spines of the books, but one of them jumped out at her—more because of its size than anything else, in large, embossed gold letters: *The Complete Works of William Shakespeare*. It was her second visit to the old man, and she still felt an old-fashioned awkwardness in his presence, but a brief absence of his from the room allowed her to find a distraction for her nerves by looking at Bela's book collection. Her hand reached out to pick it up, but the volume was so heavy that she was forced to take it in both hands to drag it free from the others.

It was an old copy of the Bard's works, beautifully illustrated with hand-painted pictures and embellishments to the text and margins. Evi leafed through the soft, fine-quality pages with the reverence with which she might have treated a Bible, pausing at Macbeth's famous soliloquy: "Life's but a walking shadow, a poor player that struts and frets his hour upon the stage and then is heard no more—"

"You are an admirer of Shakespeare, then?" interrupted Bela's voice from the doorway.

"Do forgive me; I couldn't help myself," said Evi as she awkwardly closed the book.

"And why should you?" asked Bela with a smile, sweeping into his chair with an air of melodrama perfected over years. "The words of the great man are a comfort to anyone, even a poor player like me."

"Mr Lugosi, if you were a poor player, I should hardly be interviewing you now, should I?" Evi responded. She did not intend to sound so curt, but she sensed that he was looking for a compliment, and she was not sure how best to respond without either confirming the man's worst fears or indulging his even worse self-pity. "I think you keep this book so close to you because it reminds you that you are not a poor player at all."

Bela nodded nobly as though to concede the point. "Indeed. I owe everything to an English playwright from hundreds of years ago." He reached out for the book, and Evi handed it to him, watching as he traced his fingers across the soft Moroccan leather cover. He might have been a sorcerer preparing an incantation. "The theatre was always a magical realm, so far above the drabness of life with all its rules and petty regulations. It is a magical world, and so it must have a magician to control it—and Shakespeare was the ultimate magician."

Evi sat down and busied herself scribbling down some notes. "Yes, if you say so."

"Ah, you are a sceptic," answered Bela, sadly. "I had forgotten. The young are so cynical these days. It's not the way it was meant to be."

"Hardly so young," said Evi, her eyes fixed on the page to avoid looking at Bela's hurt face. "I'm thirty-two years old."

"I think I believed myself old at that age too," said Bela. "It's no age at all!"

"I'm a thirty-four-year-old widow. I came of age in the middle of a war, and my husband vanished when I was still in my twenties. I don't see what age has to do with it. Anyway"—her tone was immediately businesslike—"you were telling me something about the magical realm of the theatre."

"Oh dear, you are so angry with life, no?" Bela persisted, refusing to take the hint and start talking about himself again. "I did not have such reasons, but I think I, too, was angry with life once. But then, that is what acting is all about, isn't it? To leave the world behind."

I thought it was about grown men dressing up in silly costumes, thought Evi, bracing herself for what she felt might be a short lecture. Steady, she thought, and endeavoured to be a good girl and listen attentively.

There were many lofty ways the young Bela might have described his profession, but in later life, he would see it for what it was—an experiment in altered reality. He was not suffering, nor was he angry or unhappy at his lot in life, but acting drew him into a new world that took him far away from the drudgery of the banal and everyday. He would have understood the words "The devil makes work for idle hands" better than most, because it was the sheer tedium of human existence that made him so crave that glorious unreality of the theatre and all its works. He took to it like a drug, and learnt how addictive it was only when he was so completely imprisoned in that alternative reality he had created that there was no way out.

Ah, William Shakespeare! The greatest magician of them all, the mentor, the muse of every actor who has ever strutted and fretted his hour upon the stage for over three hundred years. Oh, the thrill of speaking those words for the first time! There were so many ways in which innocence could be measured, but what greater proof of innocence was there than to enunciate those lines and feel a breathless shudder of ecstasy, never to be felt again?

> We are such stuff as dreams are made on,
> And our little life is rounded with a sleep.

With the words of the world's greatest playwright on his tongue, Bela felt he had become a magician himself, towering above the other players in his magical kingdom. He looked at his reflection in the mirror, admiring his own ruggedly handsome face. He was a man now, a young prince, and the theatre was *his* world; those utterances of Shakespeare's sounded so like his own now: *the gorgeous palaces, the cloud-capped towers, the great globe itself* ... Many years later in the twilight of his life, those words would still possess Bela, and he would still fail to heed their warning.

A man with a face like a young Valentino paced the quiet, empty streets by the Danube in a state of ecstasy. It had been such a magnificent performance that, through a side door, he had fled the theatre and its adoring audience in search of solitude. The sound of the applause was still ringing in his ears as he walked on, though he convinced himself that it was not the audience's reaction which thrilled him so much as the words themselves—the whole transcendent experience. His father would have warned him that it was dangerous to have one's soul so captured by anything, even poetry, but the words of the play—so intangible, and yet seemingly so much more real than life itself—seemed to course through his own veins like a drug as he walked and walked through the night. Completely captured.

Bela became aware that he had wandered too far. He was in the poor quarter of the city, walking down a narrow, grimy street surrounded by ramshackle dwellings he knew would be crowded with the hungry. He did not feel any fear in spite of finding himself in the wrong place; he knew already that he was a forbidding-enough figure to be left alone if he kept striding purposefully without giving any indication to anyone that he was lost.

An old woman stared at him through a lighted window. The light on an otherwise-sleeping street caught his attention, and he glanced in her direction, unexpectedly making eye contact. A pair of magnetic brown eyes looked steadily at him from an impossibly lined face that was both young and ancient at the same time. "*Sastipe!*" said Bela, raising a hand in greeting.

The Gypsy nodded in acknowledgement, apparently unsurprised by the Roma greeting. "You have travelled among my people," she said quietly, beckoning for him to come closer, but he hesitated. The woman opened the door and said, "Come now, Bela, enter my home and I shall tell your fortune."

This is nonsense, he thought, but he was in a trance already. He felt his feet moving towards this stranger who knew his name, the feverish excitement and energy draining away at the first touch of her hand on his. He told himself again that this was nonsense, a mad old lady preying on a lost young man—Bela was not such an unusual name in his country, after all—but he found himself shivering as he sat down with her and she turned his hand over to examine his palm. He did not believe anything she said, and yet, to this day, so many years later, he never forgot a single word she uttered that night.

The fortune-teller began chanting as though reciting a message she was reading mysteriously in the lines of his hand. Bela knew the way it worked—he had seen fortune-tellers plying their trade hundreds of times when he worked for the travelling show: the closing of the eyes for dramatic effect; the whispered, dreamlike tone; the faint scent of incense in the room to make him believe he was being transported to some hinterland of wonder and mystery. Now he inhabited his own hinterland; he needed no other. Bela tried to stand, but those bony fingers closed over his wrist with an extraordinary strength that paralysed him.

"How you are destined to suffer!" she exclaimed, staring directly into his eyes with an unexpected intensity. "My poor child, your life is tragedy; I see only darkness, death, and the deepest of despairs." He made a final attempt to pull his arm away, but he was stunned—he could not move. "Like Lucifer, the brightest of angels who fell into the depths of hell, so you, too, shall fall from the heights to a depth of misery beyond your imagination. Beware, dear Bela, beware!"

Another man might have laughed at the clumsy melodrama of the scene, but Bela sat spellbound, mesmerized by her every word. He felt no hint of the absurd, no warning that his rational faculties were being broken down; he was aware of the chill silence in the room as a strange presence seemed to enter with them. In his trancelike state, Bela thought he heard the secrets of eternity whispering around him, and all the time his own poor part in them was being expounded. His destiny revealed! The destiny his father would have mocked him for speaking about, that his kindly director had tried to persuade him was a superstitious fiction—it was laid out before him in a series of tableaux, fixed and rigid in its doomed certainty.

"Has no one ever told your fortune before?" asked Bela quietly. Evi sensed that he was enjoying her hostility, almost as though he imagined her manner was yet another act, a way to entice him rather than an expression of sincere exasperation. "Come now, my dear, have you never been tempted to step into a Gypsy's tent and let her unravel the mysteries of your future?"

Evi groaned. "Yes, if you must know. I was at the fair with a group of girls once, and we went to see the fortune-teller. Just a bit of fun, you understand." He nodded, knowing perfectly well that an imaginative child would have taken it much more seriously than that. "She had the pretty scarf, the huge earrings, the crystal ball in the middle of a table. You get the idea. She said—after much hemming and hawing—that I would marry a man whose name began with the letter *J*."

"And did you?"

"No, his name is—was—Christopher." She felt her fists closing together. "I went dancing home to tell my mother, who shook her head and then slapped my face, pointing out that John, James, and Joseph are some of the common-est names in the English language."

Bela looked genuinely shocked. "That seems a little harsh. I would never have struck a girl."

"Look, I was brought up to be a good atheist. My parents were rationalists. There were no mysteries in their lives whatsoever. There was no God, there was no heaven, no hell. That being the case, they were hardly going to have any sympathy with the gibbering of a batty old lady." Evi took a deep breath through the pain of yet another childhood humiliation. "I'm only glad they never met Christopher. Not sure how they would have tolerated an Irish-American Papist."

"They never met him?"

"No, they were killed in the—" She recollected herself just in time. "There were plenty of deaths. Anyway, I'm just saying that it didn't come true. Anyone can sound a bit spooky and come out with some mystical utterance or other."

"But mine, alas, did come true. All of it came true."

4

"You're going to get awkward with me again, aren't you?" demanded Evi as she seated herself at Hugo's table. The tea was already neatly arranged in the centre, the teapot protected by a blue-and-pink tea cosy that brought back memories of sitting in her grandma's kitchen whilst she baked. It helped that there was a delicious smell of baking coming from the back kitchen, which Evi suspected had been set up to impress her. "Sorry, I suppose it's your job."

Hugo smiled. "It's an entertaining read, and apart from the fortune-teller, it is not so far from the truth."

"I don't see why we can't take his word for it. There's no chance of an independent witness to an incident like that, particularly as it happened so long ago." Evi's eyes drifted to the cake stand. "Gosh, you have been busy. I do hope this was not for my benefit." The cake stand was packed with the most delectable of English treats: fairy cakes she remembered from childhood with pink icing over the top, Eccles cakes, several generous slices of a Victoria sponge, jam tarts. She hardly knew where to begin. "I can't quite imagine you in a kitchen with your pinny on, somehow," she said, helping herself to the Victoria sponge. It was the first time she had felt the urge to eat for pleasure in months. The problem with drinking to excess was that it inevitably suppressed her appetite, and she felt so little need to look after herself that she missed meals on a regular basis, often without even noticing.

"Ah, for once I'm glad to have been rumbled," admitted Hugo, throwing up his hands in mock surrender. "I'm afraid I couldn't find my way around a kitchen if my life depended on it. There's an old Welsh lady two blocks away who cooks for me. She's the closest I can afford to a housekeeper. She comes from a family of bakers, so learning a few new recipes was no great struggle for her."

Evi fought off a fit of the giggles, afraid to scatter crumbs everywhere, but she only succeeded in making herself choke instead and began coughing alarmingly. By the time Hugo had finished slapping her on the back, it no longer seemed to matter whether he moved his chair next to her, even if propriety suggested he sit with the table between them. "Sorry," she said between gasps, "but I haven't laughed like that in ages! Did you really want me to think you spend your life baking scones?"

One of the many advantages to sitting so close to her was that Hugo was not obliged to look at her directly. "Not entirely, I suppose, but you have no idea how your face lit up when you saw the tea laid out last time. I wanted you to think I had done it especially for you."

Evi took out a handkerchief to dab her eyes. "That's lovely, but you did, in a way. You just didn't sift the flour yourself."

Hugo topped up her teacup. "Here, have a little more to drink. Your throat will be sore after all that coughing." She obediently lifted the cup to her lips. "It's nice to hear you laugh."

"Thank you. Did I get most of the facts right this time?"

"Oh, enough of them for readers, I assure you. The one thing you might point out is that he played his first horror roles whilst touring in theatre companies. It didn't all start with Dracula. The horror roles started before he fell in love with Shakespeare."

"Good grief, I didn't realise the genre was that old."

"Oh yes, by 1903 he was playing Svengali's evil servant in *Trilby*." Hugo knew without glancing at her that she had no clue what he was talking about, and he stood up slowly. "Let me show you these. I dug them out last night."

Hugo walked across to a bookcase heaving with files and books of all sizes, some smaller tomes jammed sideways across the top through lack of space. He brought out what looked like a large photo album or book of keepsakes. "This looks interesting," said Evi.

Hugo sat back on the sofa with her, telling himself it was the easiest way for the two of them to look at the newspaper clippings he had found. "Bela was highly successful, even as a young man. I daresay it must have gone to his head a little—it's hard to imagine how that could have been avoided." He pointed at a yellowing article, the small, heavy print arranged around a monochrome photograph of a young man gazing into the camera, almost in disapproval. He was unmistakably the same man Evi had interviewed, down to that slightly haunted look he would use to such effect on the flickering screen.

"Can you read any of this?" asked Evi. "My Hungarian is not too good, I'm afraid."

"Nor mine," admitted Hugo. "I'm afraid I can't read it, but it is quite clear from the sheer volume of press he received and the headlines he made that he was quite a sensation. He was the sort of actor people talked about, a young man touched by greatness. That sort of thing."

"A man with the world at his feet." She let out a long sigh. "Now, there's a thought."

Evi had aged so prematurely that she was not sure she could remember a time when she believed the world to be her oyster. Wars had a way of shattering dreams and hopes, not building them, but it was hard even for her to be left cold by Bela's flights of fancy back to a time in his life when nothing could go wrong for him. He had wanted her to imagine it; like all good actors, he tried to draw her in, to peel away that fourth wall and allow her to view his life as he acted it out for her: those intense, sublime performances; the stunned audiences; the increasingly obsequious theatre managers ... and, of course, the money. Such huge sums of money, more than Evi had ever earned.

"Would you believe me if I were to tell you that the money meant nothing to me?" said Bela. "I was never driven by the need for money, and it was spent easily enough. The wild life of a young man with money and success is just a less frustrating version than that of a young man without money and success."

"It's easy enough for money to mean nothing when one has it," Evi could not help commenting, hoping she did not sound as sour as she felt. The subject of money rarely left her mind, the need to pay rent, to keep body and soul together to nurture her own unfortunate habits. So much of life seemed to be caught up in the miserable race to earn enough money to stay alive and continue the race that it was almost an insult to hear that it did not matter.

"Remember, my dear, that there was a time when I had no money either," he reminded her, "but truly the performances meant everything. Absolutely everything. I lived only for the stage. Even the applause of the audience meant nothing to me. It was all the performance, the entry point into an altered reality: this was what I craved. Living solely to be somewhere else, not just someone else."

Evi hurried to take down every word he said. He spoke very quickly when he was excited, and even with shorthand, she struggled to keep up. "What was wrong with who you really were?" asked Evi, looking up at him. "It must have been such a dangerous way to live."

Bela looked at her darkly; he was being Dracula again, almost as though he could never quite shake off a role that had consumed him once. "It was horribly dangerous.

That was why I succumbed to it. I let it seep into my being like a strange toxin, into my mind, my heart, my will—it was as powerful as any narcotic I later discovered. But I think you know how powerful an addiction can be, is that not so?"

Evi felt her face becoming hot. She looked past him, determined not to engage with the question at all. "Why don't you tell me a little about your theatre career? I'm sure it is more interesting than my personal habits."

"Please do not think I was accusing you, my dear Evangeline. I know what you have been through."

"You have no idea," she said in little more than a whisper. "You have absolutely no idea. You fell because you were already in an elevated place. Most of us simply sink further and further into the darkness." She felt her hands trembling and realised why he had known she had a drink problem. It was of no consequence anyhow. Let him know. A man who had battled the demon drink and drugs—and something deeper—seemed to be trying to confess to her without ever finding the words. "Tell me about your tours. Tell me about how it felt to be the toast of Vienna's literati."

"Don't be bitter," he said gently. "You are still young; you have time to find whatever you are looking for. I do not need to tell you I was gifted or successful, because you know I was. I can tell you how it felt to be lost, if you prefer, since I was lost by then. I can tell you how it felt to be young and arrogant, the lord of an unreal world—with Mephistopheles opening every door for me."

Evi sat back in her chair, too bewildered to resent the sound of his voice anymore. "Tell me whatever you want," she said. "I'm lost."

Bela shook his head firmly. "You are no such thing. You have your soul. I can see that much. You can lose everything, but it is wrong to speak of losing your soul. A person does not so much lose it as give it away. And you are too attracted to the light to do that."

"It's no good, Mr Lugosi; I am still lost. I have no idea what you are talking about."

Bela would never have thought at the time in terms of losing his soul. He was far too busy throwing himself into each and every theatrical performance to notice what a price he was paying, but there were others who had fears of their own about the young Bela's welfare. One evening, after one of Bela's scintillating performances, a white-haired couple turned up at the stage door with their prematurely middle-aged daughter, Vilma. They looked so quaintly out of place among the sophisticated literati of the city that the theatre manager granted them admittance out of sheer curiosity more than anything else. They were dressed like peasants—ridiculously so, neat and tidy, almost a little well-to-do in a way—and to a city dweller they looked as though they belonged to another century, which, of course, they did.

The theatre manager would not have dared turn them away anyhow, as the old man had the look of a person who was quite used to getting his own way. "I wish to see my son," he had said abruptly as they stepped inside, with such clear misgivings about the place that Vilma actually crossed herself. "He goes by the name of Bela Lugosi. Some nonsense he's made up."

They were swiftly shown into Bela's dressing room, which fortunately was vacant; Bela was still taking curtain calls. "I shall inform him of your arrival," said the manager, backing out of the room.

"Do no such thing," said Bela's father. "Let's make it a nice surprise, shall we?"

The manager, an older man and faithful guardian of the theatrical world, pondered for a moment whether he should warn Bela about the nasty surprise awaiting him. He was fond of the young man in spite of his brash arrogance and was certain he would want to run a mile in the opposite direction if he knew his family were lying in wait for him. They represented everything that was most humdrum and banal about the life he had left behind.

The father was clearly a thug, yet another of those harsh disciplinarians one found in isolated homesteads, one who believed himself to have virtually a divine right over his family. But there was something haunting about the young woman. She looked so very like Bela, with the same fine features and striking eyes, but she bore the marks of a woman whose own dreams had already been shattered. Bela had told the manager that he had run away from home at a very young age, and the man wondered how lonely life had been for the sister Bela left behind and how much she might have paid for his mad dash to freedom. She deserved to be reunited with her brother.

Many years later, Bela would weep in the arms of a woman he barely knew, recounting the scene that greeted him as he stepped through that door. He did not know it then—as he faced his father's anger, his mother's reproachful gaze, and of course his sister's tears—but it was to be the last opportunity he would ever be given to be reconciled with his parents. That was the true tragedy which the Bela of the future wept over: it was the last chance to feel *something* for them, to be drawn back into a world that was humdrum and tiresome and painful but at least was real. It was the world in which he had grown up, the world to which his flesh and blood belonged, but he stood before them like a princeling straddling the earth, and they were too insignificant to him to be indulged. The paternal rage that would have put the fear of God in him once now bounced off him like raindrops.

"You walked away from your mother's table without a word," roared his father, "without so much as a farewell note! Have you never thought how we searched and searched through the night for you? The whole village scoured the countryside searching for you."

"Well, you didn't search very well," Bela retorted. "I had gone only as far as the travelling circus. It shows how little you knew about your own son that it never occurred to you where I had gone."

Next came guilt. Bela felt his mother's thin arms around his neck, the moist face sobbing into the folds of his shirt. "You never so much as gave me a backward glance," she cried. "We had no idea whether you were alive or dead. Anything could have happened to you; you might have been kidnapped or killed. Did you care so little about us that you could not find time at least to write and tell us you were safe?"

Bela disengaged himself from her as gently as he could, wishing all the time that they would simply go. In his mind, he re-created the moment he noticed that his dressing room door was ajar and a light was burning within, imagined himself realising the implications and making a bolt for the exit. But it was too late. "I couldn't risk your finding out where I was," said Bela, not caring particularly how cold he sounded. "If you had known I had joined the travelling show, Father here would have dragged me all the way home to God knows what retribution. I couldn't let you interfere with the life I had chosen."

Bela's father gave an indignant growl and rose to his feet, but Vilma stepped between them as she had done many times before. He felt her tiny fingers curling around his hand as he remembered from childhood. "Sit down, brother," she begged him, motioning for their parents to leave the room. "Please sit with me."

For once, their father stepped out of character and had the humility to take his daughter seriously, pulling his wife with him out the door and into the silent corridor. He was prepared to leave them alone together if there was a chance Vilma could make him see sense.

They sat in silence, each behaving as though in the company of a complete stranger, whilst the door slammed shut behind their parents. Bela took advantage of Vilma's uncertainty to study her a little more closely. He was relieved in later life that it did not occur to him to share his thoughts with her: that she could have looked almost worthy to be his sister if she had made a little effort. Her face was still rounded like a child's—he suspected she still had dimples when she was smiling (which she most certainly was not)—whilst at the same time, she took so little care of herself that she might have been twenty years older. Bela tried to picture her with her face carefully made up and her tightly braided hair styled in the latest ladies' fashion. He wondered how she would carry herself in elegant shoes and a nicely tailored gown, rather than sitting hunched up in a chair, wearing an old frock that no longer fit her mother. It looked as though she had tried to take the dress in at the waist, but it still hung loosely about her person, refusing to flatter her figure in the least. He would curse himself one day to have had such shallow thoughts about her, but at least she never knew.

Bela noticed that Vilma was scrutinising him almost as critically. "How handsome you have grown!" she said. "I should hardly have recognised you."

"I'm a man, Vilma," answered Bela with the beginnings of impatience. "Did you expect to see a little boy sitting here? Is that whom you have come searching for today?"

"We came searching for you," said Vilma quietly, but the hurt tone clattered in his ear. "Do you want to know what happened when you ran away?"

"No, I don't."

"Perhaps you should know," she persisted, looking fixedly at him. She had waited years to confront him, and she would not allow him to blow her off course. "Father thought it was my fault. He thought I had helped you run away. He did everything he could to make me tell him where you'd gone, but I didn't know. I couldn't make him leave me alone, but I didn't have the answer. I cried myself to sleep every night for weeks, waiting for you to return. You never did. I prayed so hard for you."

"If Father was harsh with you, it's not my fault," was all Bela could find to say, but he was forced to look at the corner of the room to avoid noticing the tears his behaviour had provoked in Vilma. "Perhaps you understand now why I ran away?"

A second later and she was kneeling at his feet, clasping his hands so hard he would have cried out if he had not been so shocked. "Come back to me, brother!" she pleaded. "Something terrible is happening to you. I hardly know you; you're being dragged away. I can feel it!"

Bela stifled a shudder. "Don't be ridiculous, Vilma," he snapped, but she had driven an invisible blade into his heart. "You were always superstitious, all of you were. I'm an actor; that is all. If you are jealous of my success, then perhaps you had better leave."

Vilma brought a hand to her mouth to cover a gasp, which Bela merely thought childish. "Please!" she pleaded, "I want you to be happy more than anything, but this will not make you happy. There is something at work here; I don't understand it myself, but it's as though you belong to another world now."

Bela stood up, taking her hand to help her to her feet, as though she were a stranger who had taken a tumble and deserved his momentary courtesy. "I do belong to another world now, Vilma. It's a world in which I am loved and respected, where I have everything I could possibly want. None of you belong here. You should go home."

Vilma stood frozen to the spot, shaking her head in utter despair; then she made a dash to the door and flung it open. Before leaving, she turned back to look at him, her face unattractively pink and swollen with tears. "This world of yours, it is not just giving, it is sucking the life out of you like a vampire. It will take everything, everything you have ever loved, everything you have ever desired."

With that, she closed the door quietly behind her as though apologising for taking up his time. As he stood by himself in his dressing room, Bela knew once and for all that he was now alone. No member of his family would ever cross the threshold into his world again, and he would never stoop so low as to return to theirs.

Hugo leant back in his chair, listening intently as Evi finished reading aloud from the article. "You know what I am going to say," he said with a smile, reaching out to take the papers from her. "There is no way of knowing that encounter happened that way, but I suppose it is as likely that it happened that way as not. In any case, the parents are long dead and unlikely to sue. The father lived to a ripe old age, a widower of many years. I'm afraid the mother did not fare so well."

"It's horrible," Evi announced to the world in general. "Such a terrible way to deal with one's own family."

"Perhaps you have never known what it feels like to *have* to walk away," Hugo suggested. He then immediately regretted it. He had learnt an important rule during his military career, in living closely with men from such different walks of life: one never assumed anything about a person's background. It was like lawyers never asking a question in court to which they did not know the answer;

assumed knowledge about another person, however close, inevitably ended in embarrassment.

"For your information, Mr Radelle," replied Evi, with the sort of tone that made him instinctively brace himself, "I ran away from home myself and could claim to have had good reasons to do so. Any youth who runs away will have a compelling reason to do so, even if only in his own mind."

"Sorry." Too late.

"When my father went mad, he got it into his head that I was involved in some conspiracy against him. He began to persecute me, watching my every move for signs of disloyalty, turning my brothers against me. After months of isolation in my own home, he flew into a temper and told me that I disgusted him, that I had ruined his life, and that he could not think of a single good reason to tolerate a thing like me in his home. I couldn't think of a good reason either, so after they'd all gone to bed, I packed my bags and left. Fortunately for me, war had just been declared. There were plenty of places for an aspiring reporter to go, with all male competition conveniently marching off to war."

"I'm afraid I asked for that," conceded Hugo. He could think of no other way out of the hole into which he had dug himself and made an elaborate gesture of offering her a jam tart as though it were a libation to a pagan goddess. "I should have realised, of course. There's a lot of emotion in your writing—for a reporter, that is—especially one who cut her teeth as a war correspondent."

"I know his sister did not give up on him, however much good that did him," said Evi, putting them both out of their misery.

"Yes, indeed. Vilma kept writing to him for years, desperately trying to call him home."

"Like a distant bell," said Evi.

"That's very poetic."

Evi shrugged. "Not really. I always imagined that if anything could call me home, it would be the cathedral bells ringing out the end of the war. But there was no cathedral by the end of the war, and I was too far away from home to hear the bells anyway."

Hugo noticed that Evi had the habit when she was nervous or unsettled of stroking the ring finger of her left hand. "Since I have already put my foot in it with you once today," Hugo continued, "would it be impertinent to ask why you never wear your wedding band? You obviously miss it."

Evi looked for all the world like the proverbial camel broken by one final, flimsy straw. "It's quite simple, really," she answered, with forced coldness. "I'm not married anymore. The phrase goes 'till death do us part', as I recall. My husband is dead; therefore, I am a widow. Therefore, I have no need any longer to wear a symbol of marriage. I am not married."

"I wasn't being nosey, I promise. It's just that a lot of widows keep wearing it, just as they keep using their married names. I'm sorry if I spoke out of turn."

"It would feel fraudulent, pretending to be a married woman when I am no longer any such thing," she said, speaking with an increasingly brutal pragmatism that did not feel entirely sincere. "I cannot stand anything fake. Fake smiles, fake friends. I still have my wedding ring; I choose not to wear it for the sake of appearing as I am. I hope that makes sense."

If Evangeline had been any other woman, Hugo would have been tempted to show her some modest gesture of sympathy—a gentle pat on the arm, perhaps—but he found her so difficult to read that he could not be sure how she would react. "What ... what am I to expect next? Are we going to the Eastern Front?"

Evi smiled—another little deception to which she would never admit. She did not want Hugo to know he knew more about Bela Lugosi than she did. "You're getting ahead of yourself now." She began the ritual of putting on her hat and gloves. "Thank you for your hospitality. I had better dash if I'm to get this to my editor in time." She pulled a man's fob watch out of her pocket, an eccentricity Hugo had not noticed before.

"I hope I shall see you again next week?" he asked nonchalantly, getting up to help her with her jacket, but she was ready to go. He stepped ahead to open the door so that he would not be rendered entirely useless. "Same time?"

"Thank you, if it's not too much trouble," said Evi, looking over her shoulder. "I'm not sure I could last any longer without another taste of home."

Hugo followed her downstairs into the shop, which was depressingly empty. "I forgot to ask, whereabouts in England are you from?"

Evi paused at the door to let a solitary customer in. "Oh, didn't I tell you? Coventry."

5

Wars. The Great War. The real harbinger of darkness that stole the lives of millions and ensured that there could be no peace for decades to come—perhaps no peace ever again. Evi had known that Bela's own life must have been overshadowed by the outbreak of hostilities in 1914— every man of that generation had faced that same battle to survive—but she had dreaded the moment the conversation would inevitably turn to that summer in Vienna when young men lined the streets, pledging their blood and undying allegiance to crown, country, empire ... like the young men of Germany and France and Russia and Great Britain.

Evi's hand hovered over her husband's hip flask. She could see Christy in his uniform, hesitating to leave her. He showed none of the boyish enthusiasm to go and get killed that those Great War photographs of young volunteers betrayed; by then he was a battle-hardened old soldier who had lost his youthful sense of invincibility on the ravaged beaches of Normandy. "Aw, don't look so scared, Evi!" he had joked. "You're not afraid of Red China, are you?"

"Well, let me think about that," she answered, tilting her head onto one finger as though deep in thought. "Hmm. I think I might be, along with much of the English-speaking world." It was the banter of the stressed, but so much easier to indulge in than a soulful conversation that would inevitably sound like a deathbed farewell, however hopefully they tried to talk. They had already been through the difficult conversations: what Evi was to do if Christopher died, how much he hoped she would consider marrying again one day. They had said all that. It left them free to glance wryly across the room at one another, pretending it was just another day. Before Evi could duck out of the way, Christopher jumped at her, lifting her into his arms as easily as if she were a child, leaving her struggling and giggling against him.

Let her remember him that way, laughing and teasing her, enjoying her mock resistance and indignation. She had no way of knowing whether he had ever laughed again, she knew so little of what had happened to him after that day. He had fought bravely, apparently—but Evi suspected they always said that about the fallen. He had been captured, and then he had vanished into the night and fog of a network of prison camps. It had taken two long years to learn that he had died, and even then, she did not know how or where, which inclined her to imagine the worst.

"Come back to me, won't you?" Evi had begged him, allowing herself a discreet cliché as her husband left. It was a foolish expression, like telling someone to have a safe journey, as though the person had any control whatsoever over whether the train derailed or the ship sank. Yet she had said it, as much to fill the unnerving silence of those last few minutes as to remind him to stay alive. After he had gone, she had plenty of time to break down and cry; tearful farewells were not for them. She let him leave as though he meant to return by the next train.

And she let herself remember him the way he had looked when their eyes had first met across a noisy, smoke-filled room, not riddled with bullets in a snow-filled ditch or starved to death or crawling with maggots. It was the curse of an imaginative mind to fill in the unknown details in any situation, and because she had no idea how he had died, she inevitably found herself walking through darker and ever darker scenarios until out of sheer despair she reached for the only comfort she knew.

"Would you prefer to return another day?" asked Bela solicitously. He had been talking about the outbreak of war for nearly half an hour and had noticed that Evi was distracted. "You look like death this morning, my dear. Perhaps the afternoons suit you better?"

You don't look exactly like the life and soul either, thought Evi sulkily. For once, she was glad of the semidarkness; she had worked late into the night writing up Bela's war experience, only for her thoughts to become haunted by her husband's last war. She remembered very little of the hours that had followed, apart from being woken up in the early hours of the morning by her stomach churning. She had only just made it to the bathroom in time to throw up, and she sat in Bela's room now, her stomach still empty and her head screaming with pain.

"I'm perfectly well, thank you," she answered primly. "You told me last time about your war service as a junior officer."

"You know, you should get yourself some help; I've been dry for years," he persisted.

"You described your time in the army as the acting out of a role. Is that really the way you saw it?"

Bela sighed. "Very well, it is none of my business. Yes, of course it was a role. The uniform was a very smart costume, and the war itself—well, you might call it another play. We do not speak of a theatre of war for nothing; it is a form of unreality. A macabre pantomime acted out by thousands."

"Except that nobody actually dies performing a pantomime, and the actors don't usually use real guns with real bullets," Evi snapped, feeling her temper rising through the pain of her hangover. "And in your theatres, people pretend to cry, they pretend to be in pain."

"A turn of phrase, my dear, I assure you; I do not need to be reminded of how real the horrors were. Perhaps you would prefer me to say that a circle of Dante's Inferno opened at our feet, and we obligingly marched in. Thousands of us. The rest I daresay you know."

She thought she knew, even though she had not witnessed that particular war for herself. All wars must share the same macabre details: the infernal clatter of the guns and cannon, the cries of slaughter from morning to night, whilst all the time the wounded lie dying in makeshift hospitals. Disease and vermin everywhere, the sight and stench of death so overpowering it is a blessed relief for some to take a bullet in the head. Better a quick exit to the inevitable, a move from the dark trench passageways to the dark caverns that await all the dead, or so the soldiers must think as they face the constant, grinning companionship of Death.

"You talk as though you knew you would survive," said Evi softly, "but at the time, nobody knows whether he will live the next hour. I remember that feeling, listening to the doodlebug rockets overhead. One would pray that the bomb's engine would not cut out, knowing there would be no time to pray again if it did."

"So you do believe in prayer," Bela put in, almost mockingly.

"In the way a small child believes in screaming the place down, yes."

Bela laughed aloud; even when he was genuinely amused, he managed to sound like a ham horror villain, and Evi could not tell whether he was doing it on purpose. "You must understand, Evangeline, I truly believed that death could not touch me. I felt it stalking my every step, but I knew it could not touch me then. Trench bombardments, gas attacks, machine-gun fire—I took a perverse pleasure in living through it all."

Hell spat you out, thought Evi, restraining herself, but what came out of her mouth was almost more damning. "The best of men never return from wars." There, she had said it. "Forgive me, but you almost sound as though you are mocking the dead."

Bela indicated the folder Evi carried with her. "Dear Evangeline, you might be more tolerant of my love of horror stories if you had read the real ones I lived through."

"I have read your accounts of life in the trenches," said Evi. "Were you really buried alive, or was it meant to be a metaphor?"

"I was buried alive," said Bela matter-of-factly. "It was not an uncommon misfortune, but it felt a little like a metaphor, I suppose. The living buried with the dead, never quite destined to return to the land of light. In war, some might say that there are no survivors."

Evi stared down at her shorthand until her vision blurred. "You look like a survivor to me." Suddenly, Christopher was standing before her, his face thin and pinched like Hugo's, his manner world-weary but at the same time relieved. Alive. Alive and reaching out to her, ready to start the next chapter of their lives together. "Why don't you tell me what happened?"

"What did I write about it?" asked Bela, walking over and taking the folder from her. "I am sure I wrote it down more eloquently than I could say it now. All memories fade after a time." He leafed through the pages, pausing at a place where Evi had inadvertently left a bookmark. "You marked the place," he commented. "It must have made an impression."

"I wanted to ask you about it because it was such an extraordinary account; that was all."

Bela glanced down at the words. "You know, I think you had better read it out. My eyes cannot bear the strain."

"You could always open the curt—" Evi stopped herself, took back the folder, and began reading.

> I remember awakening from my sleep to an even more pronounced darkness. I experienced an uncomfortable sensation of a pressure weighing heavily upon me, and I found that I could not move. Needless to say, I panicked and began to struggle frantically, only to find a human body on top of me, a lifeless and dirty one, and then, to my horror, another such to my side, and then another, and another, and another.... I was buried beneath many corpses, too many to count. Somehow, for I have no recollection of how this event came about, I had wandered to a dugout which subsequently had been bombed and then loaded with corpses collected from various points along the Front. I climbed through this human rubble, struggling to stop myself from standing on dead men's faces; it seemed such an outrage to clamber over men who had been alive just hours and days before. Gasping for breath, I finally broke into the light and air, exhumed from that foul mess of rotting humanity.

Evi found it impossible to say anything else. Her mouth was parched right to the back of her throat, and she could feel the tingling of pins and needles creeping up from her hands. She could see Christopher again, his dead, wasted body stretched out at the top of a mass grave. His uniform was torn and bloodstained, hanging off a body shrunken with months of suffering. No dignity, no sense of peace around him, just the cold, perfunctory hand of battlefield death.

"You're trembling," said Bela, but Evi shrank away from him as though he truly had just emerged from a mass grave. "There's no need, you know. It sounds terrible, but I was not afraid, not even disturbed by it. I was a young man in the midst of a war; death held no mystery for me."

Evi closed her eyes, but the image of her dead husband—of the vision she imagined to be her dead husband—loomed before her like hell's last horror. And this man thought she was trembling on his account. "Easy enough to say that now," she said softly. "Everyone is a little afraid to die."

"Truly, I felt no fear," he persisted, not picking up on her tone at all. He was too absorbed in his own story or in the acting out of the ultimate role, and she was merely the audience. "It felt like some macabre burial and resurrection. It seemed to prove to me my sense of invulnerability and the power of the mysterious covenant that had been made for me, or by me, with the forces of Darkness."

The witching hour again—a long night awake after a hellish day, tangled up in the berserk reminiscences of a man who spoke of being buried alive, as though the entirety of the war had existed merely to give him a particularly gruesome film set on which to practice. The nerve of it! Millions of men dead, young men barely out of school who cried for their mothers, all those orphans, all those widows ...

It was no good; she couldn't help herself. Evi reached into the drawer for her comfort but found it empty. She reached her hand right to the back of the drawer, but there were no bottles, no hip flask, and she knew she had filled the drawer that morning. It was unseemly to panic, but Evi jumped out of her chair, scattering papers as she went. It was not just the absence of alcohol when she desperately needed it—she could not remember moving anything.

She made a dash for the kitchen cupboard, searching for a remedy, and found it, to her immediate relief. A large, unmarked bottle full of dark tawny liquid, what her American friends would call moonshine. Evi was not even sure if there was a name in England for the toxic homebrew she bought from a store around the corner when there were no other customers about and the proprietor could slip it to her from behind the counter.

Evi felt her eyes growing hot, before sitting at the desk and bursting into tears. There were so very many things she was glad Christy had never lived to see. She knew it was never meant to be this way, that *he* would never have imagined her falling apart. She had been raised to be stronger than this, the lucky recipient of an education so many girls were denied; she had survived as a wartime runaway, earning her own living, keeping herself alive whilst the bombs rained down on London.

She had once seen herself as a pioneer who let herself be carried away to the New World in the arms of a brave soldier with a wicked sense of humour and a temperament to match hers—Christy, carrying her across the sea to quieter shores, where there were no unhappy memories and no bombed-out towns. No death.

Evi took a long, desperate drink before sitting herself back at her typewriter. Death, she should always have known, could never be outrun, even by two young people with their own claims to invincibility. She had tried and failed, and it was failure that had brought her to this. But she had been running from a worse horror than even death, and that nightmare had caught up with her at the same time. She forced herself to read over her work; the night was slowly slipping away, and she had not finished her instalment. It was not far off now—perhaps another two hundred words, and then she could rest—but it had to be written. She had to step into Bela Lugosi's seductive world where death would not touch him because it had already laid claim to him ...

He was the only man on the Front who knew he would survive the war. As the bullets flew, he knew that none were meant for him. The Gypsy had already told him his fate; and however terrible she claimed it would be, he knew he at least had a future, and no one could dislodge that conviction from his mind—no one, even the czar of Russia himself with his mighty army, even when Bela found himself wounded in the Carpathian Mountains.

What a mercy it was to have a superficial injury, serious enough to take a man from the mire of the trenches to the tranquillity of a hospital but not bad enough to put him in any great danger. He luxuriated in the months of convalescence and attention, resting in a comfortable bed whilst his comrades huddled together in dugouts, until the role of the wounded soldier began to irk him and he longed to be released.

It had only been a flesh wound, but he cursed the czar nonetheless, both him and his Holy Russian Empire, allowing himself to feel personally aggrieved by Nicholas II, as though the doomed leader had personally shot him. He cursed him from the depth of his being, willing him to suffer and fall. Soon after, Bela was standing in front of a newspaper kiosk when he saw a headline bearing a revelation greater than he could have hoped for: CZAR ABDICATES. He stood stock-still, taking in the news that the empire had fallen, and wondered at the power of the curse. He had cursed a man, the czar of all Russia, and now he and his family were prisoners devoid of all the great power and wealth they had ever enjoyed. Bela was invincible whilst one of the world's most powerful men had been rendered as helpless as a child.

Hugo's shop was a hive of activity when Evi arrived, meaning that he was too busy to greet her at the door this time. "I'll be with you in just a moment," he called to her as she stepped inside, immediately overpowered by the presence of too many bodies in a small space. Evi was unnerved by crowds at the best of times, and Hugo's quiet little haven full of strangers felt like an invasion. And no ordinary strangers. It had taken Evi a minute for her eyes to adjust to the dim light inside the shop after the brightness of the street, and when they finally did, it was as much as her life was worth not to make a break for it.

Hugo's quaint little shop was filled with monsters. Really full of monsters: vampires with huge fangs and capes, faces white and menacing; Frankenstein monsters with bolts through their necks, and vast, square heads; wide-eyed zombies, hair wild, clothes blackened and torn. Evi turned to the door, just in time to see a small skeleton strut past her.

Hugo was at her side in an instant. "This way," he said calmly, taking her arm and guiding her fearlessly through the morass of villainy he seemed to have attracted. The monsters quite politely stepped aside to allow them to pass. "You'll be safe upstairs," he said to reassure her. "Up you go. There's tea in the pot."

Evi did not wait for an explanation and fled upstairs to the cool quiet of Hugo's flat. There was indeed tea in the pot. And Eccles cakes. She helped herself, trying very hard to dislodge from her mind the thought that the drink might have broken her mind, just as she had been warned it would. That, and the unedifying murmur of resentment she felt that Hugo's attention was being drawn away from her by an invasion of the Undead.

It was half an hour before Evi noticed the low rumble of activity simmering down beneath the floorboards, and Hugo emerged, none the worse for wear. "Interesting clientele you seem to be attracting," mused Evi as he sat down, exhausted. "I took the liberty of making a fresh pot. I hope you don't mind."

"Not at all," he answered gratefully, rather enjoying the thought of her making herself comfortable in his home.

"Not at all. Don't mind my customers; they're a good bunch."

"Grown men wearing fangs with red paint all over their shirt fronts?" demanded Evi. "What on earth was that in aid of?"

Hugo laughed softly. "Have you been living in a cave waiting for the apocalypse? There's been a gothic convention in town all week."

"A what?"

"You know, all the horror fans gathering together ..." He trailed off. "You know, you really do look like a young Queen Victoria when you look at me like that. I keep expecting you to say, 'We are not amused.'"

"I would not be so presumptuous as to use the royal we," answered Evi, wryly, "but I fail to see the point."

"It's just a bit of fun," promised Hugo. "They've fairly cleaned me out, thank heavens. Busiest week of the year."

Seeing Hugo in his overtired state made Evi aware for the first time of the thinness of his face. He always wore such a cheerful manner that it was only now, when he was off his guard, that she realised how pale and drawn he was for a man in his prime. There were grey smudges under his eyes that she recognised as the marks of many sleepless nights, though she doubted he had ever gone to her lengths to drug himself into rest. Evi could never quite have described it, even in an article, but there was something she noticed that haunted so many men who had been soldiers—they were not frightened or angry for the most part, just marked out somehow, like men who had been through a debilitating illness.

She put out a hand to stop Hugo from getting up, rose from her seat, and poured him some tea. "Now stands the clock at ten past three, and is there honey still for tea?"

"I'm afraid you've lost me again," said Hugo, throwing up his hands in mock surrender. "Which dead poet wrote that?"

"Rupert Brooke," she answered, taking out her folder, "a man who went to war to die for his country and was killed by a mosquito. Sorry. I always sound more bitter than I mean to."

"It's quite all right," said Hugo, taking the folder from her. They were well versed now in the afternoon's routine, and he knew there would be an article in draft form for him to read. "By the way, I'm awfully sorry about the other day. I should have realised, of course."

"What?"

"Well, I wondered why you had not returned to England after your husband's death. It would be the natural thing to return to your family. When you said you were from Coventry ... when I think about what that city suffered ..."

"You were hardly to know," she interrupted. "In any event, it wasn't the only English city bombed out of existence by the Luftwaffe."

After pausing long enough to let him read her draft, she asked, "Well, what do you think? Have I been led very badly down the garden path this time?"

Hugo smiled, not looking up from the paper. "No, no, there is a fair amount of veracity in all this. Lugosi enlisted in the Forty-Third Infantry, and he was commissioned as a second lieutenant. The geography is correct as well; he did fight Russian forces in Serbia and the Carpathian Mountains."

"Buried alive?"

"I'm afraid I can't vouch for that story, but it did happen sometimes. There were so many bodies, it wouldn't be too hard to assume that a deeply unconscious man was dead." Hugo heard the sound of a stifled whimper and looked up in alarm at Evi's bowed head. He could see her twisting her gloves in her hands and knew she was already at the end of her tether. "Look here, Evi, why not skip through this part? The war and the revolution—they don't matter much to the story. Bela Lugosi is famous for being Dracula, not a soldier."

Evi looked up at him, dry eyes blazing with rage. "He talked about surviving the war as though it were his God-given right! All those dead men, Hugo! Where are my parents? Where are my brothers? I notice my husband did not have the right to survive!"

"Evi, it's bravado; soldiers always talk like that. They're as scared as the next man when it comes to it. We were all scared. None of us had a clue who was going to live or die."

"Christy thought he would live," said Evi quietly. "At least that's what I always tell myself. I'm not sure I could bear it if I thought he had gone off to war believing he would never return."

"Evi ..." He trailed off at the sight of her drooping shoulders. It was futile to argue that no soldier in his right mind marches off to war with the expectation of getting himself killed; to a civilian, any decision to be a soldier must seem at least partly suicidal. "I'm sure he meant to come home to you."

"You never speak about Korea," she said, carefully screwing the lid of her fountain pen back on. It was her way of signalling that their work was done. "I can't help wondering about it."

"There's not much to tell," Hugo replied, getting up to open a window. He knew she was about to ask the question he had been anticipating since he had first heard her voice at the end of the phone, and he needed to put her off. "We all exaggerate our war stories a little, just like Bela Lugosi. The worst part of being a soldier is the boredom. All the waiting around and marching. The endless discipline."

"It's funny," mused Evi, undeterred by Hugo's turned back, "Christy was frightfully anarchic as a person. I always wondered what could have attracted him to army life. All those shouted commands, all that marching in step with everyone else. He said he was the naughtiest child at school, always being thrown out of class. Just like me."

Hugo turned back to her with a relieved smile, sensing a brief opportunity to put her off. "You don't strike me as the naughty type at all," he teased, "far too prim and proper."

Evi threw him a look of mock indignation. "When I was at school, my headmistress said that I was the most difficult child in the history of the universe—which, of course, I took as a compliment at the time." She looked down at her hands. "Now that I think about it, she was Irish like Christy. Well, not quite like him, I suppose. He was one of those Americans who are more Irish than the Irish. Miss Kelly was from Belfast. She was always saying I was being bold, and I'm afraid I thought she was praising me until she explained she meant naughty."

Hugo sat down again, a huge weight evaporating from his shoulders. "I thought it was just the English and the Yanks who were divided by a common language."

It was the first time he had seen her let her guard down, thought Hugo, watching her remember a time without pain or regret—not much pain, anyway, and nothing much worth regretting. He would have to find more of those places of silliness and innocence from her past before war and bombing raids and youthful widowhood. A thought struck him. "Come here when you've finished your work next week," he said. "I'll trust you to get the facts right without me."

Evi gave him a suspicious glance. "What are you up to?"

"It's a surprise."

6

The Austro-Hungarian army lost the war, and following the Armistice of 1918, Karl I, emperor of Austria and king of Hungary, withdrew from political leadership. For a young revolutionary like Bela, the collapse of the vast, decayed empire was as great a victory as the smashing down of the whole Russian edifice. Bela returned to Budapest with an imaginary triumph behind him, laughing with glee when he heard about Lenin and Trotsky. Crafty fellows, he thought, actors too with a strong dramatic persona, but with no sense of performance.

The winds of war had swept away the old aristocracies. Chaos followed soon after, as it always did, and Budapest, as in the other cities of old Europe, was alive with talk of revolution.

It was the battle for freedom for some—a march of progress, enlightenment, whatever other epithet an idealistic youth might have given to the carnage waiting to be let loose upon the world. But for Bela it was to be merely another script, another role. The more he mused upon the coming trouble, the more certain he was that a revolution needed an actor to play any lead part that might emerge, and as the finest actor in Budapest, who better to lead the way?

It was a truth universally acknowledged that revolutions were led by second-rate actors, so why, thought Bela, should this one not be led by a first-rate one? He sought out the many revolutionary parties, all sporting different political colours, all rising to the same battle cry: Revolutionary change now! Like the young Adonis he still imagined himself to be, he offered his services to a group whose identity was of such little consequence to him that Bela later forgot its name. His arrogance would one day come back to haunt him, but his offer was accepted, and he embraced his role with childish excitement. He had a new part: the dashing young officer, wounded and left for dead by the evil forces of czarist oppression, returned in triumph to fight for his motherland and her children. The role had endless possibilities.

But whilst Bela dreamed of storming barricades and blood on the streets, a small revolutionary army consisting of the mediocre, the mad, and the criminal converged on him, talented only in the art of talking incessantly. And how they did talk of the promised tomorrow, of love and equality, laced with the language of vitriol and vengeance. The nightly plots of revenge against adversaries which Bela knew would come to nothing became so suffocating that he longed for the fighting to start if only to turn his rifle on his own whining comrades. Hardly the attitude of a revolutionary leader, but the role would never be Bela's most convincing.

In the end, the planning of revolutions was all well and good, but it did not pay the bills; and it was not long before Bela was back on the boards again, resuming his role as a bourgeois actor entertaining the well-heeled inhabitants of Budapest.

"Aren't you interested in motion pictures?" asked Bela nonchalantly, returning Evi's supercilious look with one of his own. "I'm not sure why you are talking to me if you are not?"

Touché! thought Evi, but she was far too polite to tell an elderly movie star that she could not stand the cinema and was interviewing him only because she was strapped for cash and had been landed with a job nobody else wanted. "Perhaps I have never truly appreciated it."

"Spoken like a lady," said Bela. "It may come as a surprise to hear that I did not appreciate motion pictures when I first discovered them. A frivolous little fad, that's all it was, I thought."

Evi smiled. "It's funny the way that always happens with something new, isn't it?" she mused. "The invention of the lightbulb or the telephone or the motorcar. No one imagines it will ever come to anything, and suddenly the world can't live without it."

"They said that about the talkies, of course," added Bela, effecting an indignant voice. "Who on earth wants to hear an actor speak? I'm afraid I thought it was just more passing silliness."

"I can't say I can remember," said Evi apologetically. "I don't remember the early days of cinema, and my parents didn't like the pictures very much. Sitting in a dark room watching cops and robbers, and men pretending to be heroes. Sorry."

Bela gave a magnanimous shrug. "If it's any consolation, the early motion pictures were not to my taste either." Evi sat up sharply. "Yes, really. You have no idea how poor they were in the very early days, all jerky movements and exaggerated features. Fine for the stage, but projected onto the large screen without words, it looked simply grotesque."

"But you made films," said Evi, "right back in 1917. You made a picture."

"Indeed. I needed the money." Bela lolled back in his chair, carefully tilting his head to give Evi his best side. She suspected that he knew he still looked striking in profile. "But my dear," he went on, "making films was so tedious for a theatre actor, all that waiting about, acting out scenes in fragments. No appreciative audience admiring my every move. I was so ashamed of my entanglement with such a base art form that I even gave myself a stage name."

"Arisztid."

"Very good. Don't ask me why I called myself Aristocrat; I cannot remember now. I cannot even remember the dozen or so films I made, they were all made so fast. The only one I remember well was the one Curtiz directed."

Evi blushed at her own ignorance. "Who's he?"

Bela looked sadly in her direction. "So passes the glory of the world ... I am sure you asked the same question when you first heard my name, didn't you?" Evi bowed her head. It occurred to her, as she stoically avoided meeting his gaze, that virtually everyone dreams of being famous at some stage in his life, and perhaps it is better never to be known if, once known, you are forgotten. "Michael Curtiz became a great Hollywood director. We met again when we were both rich and famous. In a way, I suppose we were both revolutionaries of a kind, though we never knew it at the time."

Bela descended into morose silence that would have looked like sulkiness in a much younger person. He had not only lost his fame, thought Evi, he had lost his money too. They both knew what poverty felt like, but she had never known the sort of affluence Bela had experienced at the height of his success. She had been blessed with parents who had made sure she was as materially uncomfortable as possible even when they were flush with money. In the great British tradition of boarding school, Evi's parents had paid for her to spend much of her childhood cold, hungry, and bruised, enduring the sort of living conditions normally reserved for soldiers, prisoners, and orphans. The penury of widowhood was not such a fall from grace in the grand scheme of things.

"Why don't you tell me about your wife?" said Evi, forcing herself to get back to the case in hand. Bela's brooding was contagious. "You married then, didn't you?"

Bela gave a sheepish smile. "The first of many mistakes, I'm afraid. I suppose you had a right to bring up the lovely Ilona."

"Did you love her?"

Bela shrugged. "I wanted her. She was beautiful, young, and had lots and lots of money."

Evi felt her temper stirring again. "But did you love her?" He gave no answer. "Was she just another audience to you?"

"A most appreciative audience—to begin with, at least." Bela either did not care what Evi thought of him or had somehow failed to notice the accusation in her voice. "She ought to have been appreciative; it was my finest performance. The young lothario smitten by the loveliest of human creatures. You would have been as convinced by my performance as she was."

"It was all acting?"

"I'm an actor; I act," answered Bela matter-of-factly. "One of my first films was called *A Wedding Song*, and so the lines came easily to me when I courted her; in fact, they came directly from the script. Ilona was a middle-class Hungarian girl who had led a life of privilege. Naturally, she was attracted to a dashing young revolutionary leader and fancied herself a Communist. It was a whirlwind romance, overwhelming at one moment, vanished in another."

"She wasn't a woman to you at all, was she?" demanded Evi, her hands shaking with the effort of keeping her composure. "She was just an object you collected when it suited you, and shattered when she no longer satisfied."

"She was most definitely a woman," Bela insisted, issuing Evi a smirk that made her flesh crawl. "An exceedingly tiresome woman with an unbearable family breathing down my neck, accusing me of snatching from the cradle."

"They had a point. She was sixteen," said Evi. "I was still sitting on the school bench at that age."

"She knew what she wanted—a home, children. For all her absurd claims to a be a faithful daughter of Marx, her head was full of bourgeois plans I could never allow to constrain me."

"Silly girl," Evi put in, standing up to leave. "I think I had plans like that once. Home, husband, children. A nice, quiet, uneventful life. Don't tell the Reds; they'll be putting me against a wall." She stuffed the folder into her bag with unwarranted violence.

"Come here," said Bela looking steadily at her as she packed away her things, waiting until she straightened up before repeating the command. He said it very slowly this time, sternly and deliberately delivering each word. "Come here."

There was something unearthly about his tone that made Evi take a step back. "I shall do no such thing," she answered pertly. "I am not a servant; I do not answer to you."

Bela's face broke into a smile. "Forgive a rude old man who has forgotten his manners. Please, come closer. Is that better?"

Evi stepped warily towards his chair. It was hardly as though she seriously expected him to pounce on her bare neck, but the plot of the famous novel was clouding her judgement. She stood before him, awaiting an explanation, surrounded by half-remembered scenes of tragic females lying helplessly in the shadow of a blood-sucking monster.

"Please do not be angry," said Bela softly, reaching out to grasp her wrist. His grip was so weak, she wondered why she felt threatened by him. "I was a truly selfish boy, driven by greed and vanity. I did not deserve the happiness I might have known, married to a good woman. It may have been Ilona who had the lucky escape when the revolution came and we were parted forever. She had a right to a husband who was worthy of her."

"That's not how you saw it at the time, is it?" said Evi relentlessly, but the man seemed to have the power to touch every raw nerve in her body. "You abandoned her."

"Her family were desperate for me to leave; her father personally filed the divorce papers. A young man on the wrong side of a revolution was no husband for their daughter—or anybody's daughter."

Evi looked fixedly at him. "Did she want you to go?"

Bela stared back, not breaking her gaze for an instant, but his voice cracked with the effort of speaking. "No, she wept and pleaded with me not to leave her. My heart was flint. I felt nothing for her at all until it was too late for me to beg her forgiveness."

"What happened to her?"

"I have no idea, I'm afraid. So many lives have been lost in my homeland, and now it is sealed off from the world." He seemed to realise he had the upper hand and pressed his advantage. "There, you see, we are both exiles, but you have the freedom to return."

Evi prepared herself to leave, using the same sharp, precise movements she remembered her mother using when she was angry and trying to subdue it. She motioned for him not to trouble himself to get up as she left. "To whom would I return?" she asked.

There would be few consolations for Evi that night, other than the absence of her husband from her nightmares. There was no good way to dream about Christy. If she had a happy dream about him, remembered him in some delightful place during the early months of courtship, she would wake up to an empty bed, weeping with disappointment; if she dreamed that he was dead, she would awaken shaking and distraught, her worst horrors confirmed in both her waking and her sleeping.

But that night she dreamed of England again, the England of her childhood, to which Bela was so sure she could still return when she chose. She was back in Coventry, walking down a familiar street near the old mediaeval cathedral, swinging her arms with all the energy and carelessness of youth. The street was a busy one, and

Evi had some sense that she was out-of-doors to escape her mother, probably because she had done something silly and was trying to avoid the inevitable penance. Passers-by nodded to greet her, each one a familiar face, though it is said that there is no such thing as a stranger in dreams—our minds cannot create faces out of nothing, only from memory. She felt safe, part of a well-worn script that had been written for her and into which she fitted perfectly.

In an instant, darkness had fallen all around her. There was no twilight, no dreamy gloaming, just the sudden, smothering darkness of a nighttime city under war-time blackout. No streetlamps, no friendly, glowing window-panes to light her way. And from some undefined point within the ever-deepening gloom, Evi heard the roar of death coming to devour her city.

Time and space collapsed all around her; the world of nightmares and memories had no laws of physics, no lin-ear time span to maintain some sense of order; every hor-ror her family had suffered in her absence came upon her as though the whole burning city were crushing her to death. She began to run blindly in the direction of what she thought was her home, but she was running through fire, she was forcing herself through hell's darkest circle; smoke blinded and choked her, she felt her flesh burning as she fought her way through a forest of flames, burning debris falling all around her. She could hear the mad, demonic thunder of bombs falling in clusters for miles around, the screech of glass windows shattering in the heat, and the screams of men and women burning alive in their homes. Men and women like her own family, the ones who had had the presence of mind to run down to the cellar to shelter from the raid and found themselves trapped, surrounded by the poisonous gases of an inferno only man could have created.

Her childhood home lurched before her, flames six feet high tearing at the roof and upper walls. She hammered at the front door, knowing she had just minutes, perhaps seconds, to get her family out of there, whilst knowing all the time she never would. Evi could hear someone calling her name from the other side of the door. Not so much calling—screaming. She knew it was her mother, but her voice was like nothing she had ever heard before, that calm, cold tone abandoned for a piercing animal scream. Evi could no longer hear her own name being shouted; the earsplitting rage of the firebomb attack drowned out every other sound except that desperate, savage scream from a woman burning to death.

Evi began screaming. It was the only way she could drown out the horrors around her and the only way she could respond to it all. Some people screamed to alert others to their peril, others in the hope of rescue; an unfortunate few, like her and her dying mother, screamed in utter despair and panic, simply because there was nothing else left to be done. She was still screaming as the last dregs of the nightmare drained away, and she found herself in her bed drenched in sweat, her throat dry and raw.

A small part of her did not even want the pain to stop, because she was afraid it was all that was left that allowed her to feel human. If that perpetual ache died deep within her, she might die with it.

Evi buried her head under her pillow as tears came.

Evi wondered whether it was churlish of her to have thought the 1919 revolution boring when Bela had told her about it. No Winter Palace, no revolt of peasants and workers, no overthrow of centuries of serfdom. A parliamentary sleight of hand and little else. Foreign armies did come, he had told her, Czechs and Romanians, but that was later, and only after the Communists had shown their true colours: nothing more than fanaticism and brute force. Good heavens, violent Communists! Who would have thought it?

She could have told him the Communists' true colours, thought Evi, as she walked in the direction of Hugo's shop, but hindsight made everyone wise. Had he really been so surprised by the pitiful and sordid tales he had read in Vilma's accusing letters, of young armed Communists breaking up religious services, of priests murdered at the altar? Had any enthusiastic young revolutionary been so naive as to imagine that the Communists' heroic efforts would end in anything other than bloodshed?

Hugo would have an answer for her, no doubt. A calm, logical answer forged in the safety of his film emporium. Now, there was a test. Would a man who had been a prisoner of the Communists be his usual reasonable self when it came to it? She hesitated at the door, but it swung open before she could reach out to open it.

"Good afternoon," said Hugo, standing to attention in the doorway.

"Good afternoon." Evi waited for him to step aside and let her in, but he did not seem to want her to go inside. She noticed immediately that he was dressed to go out, and made space for him to step outside and lock the door, watching him slip the key into his pocket with what sounded like a sigh of relief. "What are you doing?" asked Evi. "Aren't you going to give me tea?"

"I told you I had a surprise for you," he said, moving around her so that he was standing nearer the road. He gestured in the direction he meant them to walk and waited as she fell into step beside him. "Come with me."

"Where are we going?" she asked, trying not to sound disconcerted. It was the wrong moment to declare that she hated surprises for disrupting the plans and routines upon which she relied to keep her sanity intact. A surprise meant that someone else was in control of the situation and might spring something on her without her consent. Surprises were not convenient or comfortable.

"No need to look so pained," promised Hugo, slowing down to stop her from lagging behind. He realised he still had the habit of marching along, and she could not keep up with him. "You'll love it."

"You're going to think me a frightful bore, but I wanted to ask you about the revolution."

Hugo chuckled. "I thought I told you not to bother with all that. It's not important. Well, it was important for quite a few people, I suppose, but the only thing about the revolution that mattered for Bela Lugosi in the end was that it forced him to make a run for it."

"So we have a revolution to thank for giving the world Dracula, then?" answered Evi breathlessly. Hugo slowed down a little further.

"In a manner of speaking, yes," said Hugo. They took a sharp right turn into a neighbourhood that immediately felt less welcoming to Evi, but only because it was unfamiliar. "Bela had to distance himself from his former comrades. Whatever else he was, he was no fool. He saw the country's ruling elite holding firm, he saw the writing on the wall—as they say—and he knew he had to get himself out of the country."

"He spoke of himself as an exile from a land sealed off from the rest of the world."

"I'm not sure he was so maudlin about it at the time," said Hugo, with a mildly dismissive tone that irked Evi. "He had always cast himself as the lonely wanderer upon the earth, one with no homeland. He was his own homeland. Pretentious nonsense, of course. He had no whimsical reasons for going into exile. He was caught between the banality of the bourgeoisie and the brutality of the Communists. Not to mention his name appearing on a few incriminating lists."

"An enemy of the state?"

"Something like that. He wouldn't have felt quite so invincible if the authorities had got hold of him. So he did the sensible thing and took a night train to Berlin." Hugo stopped short in front of an insalubrious building decorated with vast, tattered banners and posters. "And thank heavens he did."

"A picture house?" asked Evi, with the same tone she might have used if he had lured her into an opium den. "What has this to do with the revolution?"

"Everything," promised Hugo, escorting her through the door before she could make a break for it. "Bela Lugosi left Hungary and fled to the dark, twisted world of cinema."

"You've brought me to see a film?" she asked, but for all her efforts, she still managed to sound mortified. She stood stock-still, taking in the details of the hellhole to which Hugo had brought her, as he went up to the counter to buy tickets. They were obviously early—or so she thought—as there were mercifully few people milling about to trouble her. The last time she had visited a picture house to see a film had been with Christy, not long after they had started walking out together. She could not remember much about the main feature, just the taste of mint humbugs she had saved for weeks before and the old woman behind them complaining about the rustle of the paper bag. That had been a better visit than others she could think of.

"I'm not awfully keen on this sort of thing," Evi admitted, holding back from the theatre doors. "Sitting in the dark for hours."

"Not afraid of the dark, are you?" teased Hugo, removing his hat. "I promise the monsters won't swoop out of the screen and get you."

"I'm not afraid of the film, you numpty!" she hissed, but he had opened the door for her, and she was overwhelmed by the stench of humanity at leisure. A thick cloud of cheap-cigarette smoke rolled across the rows and rows of occupied seats—and there were a lot of occupied seats. They had not been early at all; most of the people in the room had clearly been sitting in their places for hours as the films had run over and over again. It appalled her to consider that some of them had probably watched the same two Bela Lugosi pictures two or three times by now. "I was first at the scene when the Regal took a direct hit," she said in a stage whisper as the usherette's torch guided them to two empty seats near the back. "Most of the charred bodies were still sitting in the leather seats. I am *not* sitting at the back!"

"Quiet!" hissed Hugo, helping her off with her coat. "Just try to relax. This is California. Who's going to drop a bomb on us?"

"The Russians?"

"If the Reds drop the Bomb in our vicinity, it won't much matter where we are!" He helped her to settle herself, deliberately taking the outside seat in case she was overwhelmed by the urge to escape again. "Just enjoy the picture."

"What is it?"

"We're just finishing *The Black Cat*. *Dracula* is next. It's okay; we can always stay on after *Dracula*. They are sure to repeat *The Black Cat* again."

A beefy man in front of them, who appeared to have no neck, turned around and glared at them. "Will you fellas shut up!"

"I'm not a fellow," Evi retorted, suddenly spoiling for a fight. "Why don't you learn some manners?"

Hugo raised a placatory hand like a policeman. "Please excuse her; she doesn't get out much."

The man shrugged and turned back to the screen. Evi sank into her chair, resolving to be absolutely quiet until they left. But as the finishing credits were rolling, something cold jabbed the back of her neck, causing her to shriek out loud and leap out of her chair. An embarrassed youth aged around thirteen was sitting behind her. "Beg your pardon, ma'am. Please, would you take off your hat? I can't see."

Evi thought she heard Hugo laugh softly beside her as she unpinned her hat and placed it on her lap. The man in front was not the only head that swivelled in their direction. "Has she got a screw loose?"

Hugo leant forward. "Awfully sorry, her husband died in Korea. She's a bit nervy, that's all."

The man nodded sympathetically and turned away again. Evi felt a black cloud descending on her as *Dracula* announced itself across the flickering screen to the wholly inappropriate sounds of *Swan Lake. Why didn't he tell him I was a raging alcoholic as well?* she thought, oozing resentment whilst a young Bela Lugosi wafted up and down the stairs of a decrepit castle, oozing dark sensuality. She had to concede that he was a fine figure of a man, even if the cape seemed to be doing most of the work, skilfully accentuating his height and his formal, poised manner of moving.

Hugo nudged her gently to alert her to the fact that she was groaning out loud at the sight of wide-eyed peasants crossing themselves frantically at the words "Count Dracula". She could not imagine Christy looking quite so clueless if he were stoned out of his mind, robotically making the sign of the cross in a drunken trance. "Catholics aren't like that," she hissed.

"I know."

"Shhhhhh!" swelled a chorus of protest around them.

"Sorry."

There was an obviously sketched picture of a spooky-looking castle, then a scene involving a driverless carriage, followed by bony fingers slipping out from under coffin lids to reveal heavily made-up women who looked every bit like pale-faced versions of 1930s fashion icons. Then there were bats—an awful lot of bats—and rats and cobwebs. The only time Evi actually jumped was when an enormous meaty spider crawled out. The wind howled relentlessly, doors creaked, candle flames wobbled; the camera seemed incapable of capturing Bela Lugosi's face unless it was in shadow. *Strange that shadows are supposed to be frightening*, thought Evi, stifling a yawn. *If there are shadows, there is at least still light somewhere near.*

There was some inordinately long scene playing out surrounding a mirror inside the lid of a cigarette box, revealing Dracula's lack of a reflection. Evi closed her eyes to alleviate the irritation the cigarette smoke was causing her. She suspected she would not miss a great deal if she put her head down for a minute or two. In the far distance, she could hear the crackly voice of an actor swearing to drive a stake through Dracula's heart, which somehow sounded ill-mannered to Evi. If Van Helsing needed to do that, it was hardly reasonable to rub the vampire's nose in it ...

Evi had that uncomfortable feeling of being in disgrace again, for the first time in many years. Hugo was striding along at his usual military pace and was making little effort to allow her to keep up. "You know, I'm not sure I understand why we were thrown out," she said lamely. "You've no idea how many times I wanted to burst out laughing. You were all taking it so seriously!"

"You were snoring your head off!" Hugo exclaimed, turning around to look at her. "You couldn't even fall fast asleep discreetly, could you? I can't believe that someone as small as you could possibly make that much noise! And when I tried to wake you up, you nearly jumped through the ceiling!"

"Oh, I'm frightfully sorry, but how was I supposed to know I was snoring?" she said, looking back at him blankly. "One can't control something like that."

"You could perhaps have controlled the urge to curl up on my shoulder and snooze," he said, quite reasonably, but there was something about her girlishness that he found disarming.

Evi answered, as she became suddenly very still, "Look, I'm sorry I've ruined the evening. Would you do me a favour and walk me home?"

Hugo put a hand on her shoulder, the first pangs of guilt making themselves felt. "It's quite all right, Evi. Don't feel bad about it; it was quite funny, really. I've never been thrown out of a public building before. Have you eaten anything today?"

Evi shook her head. "I've been busy."

"Well, I'm sure that won't be helping." He hesitated, hoping he did not sound too much as though he were asking her out. "Why don't we get a bite to eat somewhere? It's still quite early."

A minute later, Evi had taken Hugo's arm, and he was leading her in the direction of another surprise, with the warning that if she fell asleep again, he would pretend he had no idea who she was.

7

"I would have brought you to a German restaurant," said Hugo when the vast, bearded proprietor of the trattoria had shown them to a table, "but I wasn't sure you would appreciate it. I still find it hard to think of the Italians as the enemy somehow."

"I can hardly hold every German responsible for the deaths of my family," said Evi, "and plenty of them lost their own families. I'm sure grief is the same in any language."

"That's a generous attitude, Evi," said Hugo, nudging a menu in her direction, as she seemed unaware of what she was supposed to do. "The hatred will take years to heal. Luigi and his family suffered a lot on account of Mussolini, and they fled Italy years ago because of him."

"I've never seen the point in hatred," answered Evi, coolly. "It takes up so much of one's time. And hating the Nazis and the Communists would be awfully time-consuming."

Hugo could not tell whether her understated quirkiness was at all deliberate or simply the conclusion of years of bookish childhood loneliness, compounded by the disasters she had faced as a woman. He found himself drawn to her nonetheless. She was glancing nervously about her, taking in the red gingham tablecloths and curtains and the two men—one older, the other younger—walking easily among the customers, chatting about the food and pouring glasses of wine. "It's a family-run business," said Hugo. "That's Luigi's son over there. He'll take over one day. Are you all right?"

"You're going to think me awfully ignorant," said Evi in a small voice, "but I've no idea what to order. I'm not even sure how to say most of these things!"

Hugo smiled, taking the menu from her. "Is there anything you know you don't care for very much?"

"No, not really. I'm happy to try anything. Except perhaps horse."

"We'll skip the horse course, then." They exchanged a glance across the table; they both knew that, at one point or other during the war, neither of them would have refused a plate of horse stew. They belonged to a generation that had lost the ability to be fussy eaters back in '39 or thereabouts. "Why don't we skip the wine as well? I'm not much in the mood tonight."

Evi let out the smallest possible sigh of relief at another social nightmare painlessly avoided. "Thank you."

When Luigi appeared at Hugo's side, Hugo began conversing easily in Italian with him and told himself he was not deliberately trying to impress his dinner guest. "We'll both have the lasagne," he began, calculating that it would be the easiest dish for Evi to eat, "and some garlic bread. No wine."

Luigi looked down at Hugo as though he had just cursed. "Are you ill?"

"Not me, Luigi. My lady friend—she can't drink, so I won't. Could you find us something else?"

Luigi gave Evi the warm paternal smile he reserved for the more fragile members of the human race. "No problem, my friend. Leave it with me."

"I didn't know you spoke Italian," said Evi when Luigi had disappeared into the raging interior of the kitchen.

"I spent six months guarding Italian POWs after I was wounded," Hugo explained. "They were bored; I was bored. I asked them to teach me the language." He hesitated. "They were good souls, most of them. None of them wanted to be soldiers."

"Well, they seem to have done a good job."

"I'm not sure about that. Luigi says that some of the expressions I come out with are disgraceful."

Evi giggled. "I had a French pen pal who did that to me. I always knew she'd taught me a dirty word when I tried it out in class and the French mistress hurled something at me." The relaxed atmosphere was having the desired effect. "Why did you want to take me to a German restaurant anyway? This is perfectly pleasant."

"I wanted to re-create the world of the Weimar Republic for you, for research purposes."

Evi raised an eyebrow. "No food on the plates, everyone in rags, and an angry mob outside smashing the windows?"

"It wasn't all like that, you know. Berlin in 1919 would also have felt very dynamic and new, avant-garde even, to a man like Bela Lugosi. He must have felt pretty stifled in Budapest by that time, living with his in-laws in some boring third-floor flat."

"I think that's why I should have made a very poor historian," admitted Evi. "I have never been able to get over the problem of hindsight. Tell me about those bustling Berlin streets, and all I can see is millions of people sleep-walking into the abyss."

Hugo was relieved by the momentary distraction of Luigi appearing with two steaming plates of food and a tray of thick slices of garlic bread. Luigi set down the food, glanced at the table, and noticed his mistake. He vanished into the kitchen and came back within minutes, carrying a tray with a large pitcher of what looked like lemonade and two glasses. "*Grazie,*" said Hugo, wishing the blunder had not drawn quite so much attention to the absence of the obvious. He cringed as Luigi filled two glasses, half expecting to be asked if he wished to sample the bouquet.

"Are you sure you don't want some wine?" asked Evi, looking at him quizzically.

"I don't dare at this hour," Hugo lied. "I'm so exhausted, I'm afraid I'll fall fast asleep after the first glass. I hope you don't mind?"

"Not at all."

Hugo watched as Evi attempted to eat a slice of garlic bread with a knife and fork. He picked up a slice in one hand so as to give her permission to do the same, and she copied him, picking it up gingerly with her fingertips. "It's interesting, your choice of words, of course. 'Sleepwalking into the abyss'. You know that some people believe that the nation was falling under some kind of possession at the time, don't you?"

Evi swallowed, her eyes reddening with the effect of the garlic touching the back of her throat. "Hindsight again. It's easy enough to say that now."

"No, even at the time, there were rumours in some quarters that something was being unleashed upon the land, and motion pictures, unwittingly, were conducting it into every secret place. As a figure associated with darkness, Bela arrived on the scene just in time."

"Horror films. They're just films, silly entertainment. It was a struggle not to burst out laughing in there, you know."

"I know, but you see, you have an unusual innocence about you."

"I can't think of the last time I was told that."

"The devil is afraid of laughter. The devil hates to be mocked. Just be careful, when you laugh in the face of darkness, that you truly understand what you are facing."

Evi felt her fingers growing numb; she quietly dropped her food and brought her hands into her lap to warm them. She felt inexplicably cold. A moment ago, they had been laughing at some passing silliness; now she was afraid so much as to look at him. "I'm really not sure I understand you. He was a horror actor; there were men in costume, spooky sound effects, nothing more."

Hugo looked steadily at an undefined space a little to the left of Evi's head to avoid intimidating her by looking at her too intently. "Think of how dark those early horror films were, all those visions of madness and despair, and darkness. Always darkness. Now, I don't imagine that everyone knew quite what he was doing, in the way a child playing with a Ouija board may not know what he is playing with, but somehow I suspect Bela knew the dangers." Hugo watched Evi's face growing more and more alarmed. "You knew all this already, didn't you?"

"I was rather relying on your pouring a bit of cold English common sense over it all," answered Evi, stabbing her fork into the lasagne with an unpleasant level of aggression. Tomato sauce bubbled upwards through the hole she had made. "This is exactly what Bela wrote in his account. I took it to be the ravings of a madman, frankly."

"What was his account?"

"That a once-dormant spirit was being summoned that would cause suffering and disaster for the whole German nation and the world. The only way I could make it make any sense was to assume he was writing in riddles: 'A great European civilisation slowly drawn into an inexorable darkness whilst its citizens looked away, too distracted by their wild parties and the promise of a greater tomorrow to notice the cold dank grave into which they were all marching.' If one reads it as merely metaphor—"

"But you are not sure it was meant to be metaphor."

"I'm not sure I want anything more to do with this," said Evi, looking down abruptly, but Hugo noticed her eyes closing tightly shut with the effort of keeping her composure in public. "On the one hand, it all feels so ludicrous, the obsession of silly boys who think it funny to dress up in capes and stupid makeup. But the more I delve into Bela's life, the more I feel as though I'm slipping into some sort of horror story myself. I can't describe it without sounding insane."

"Don't worry, I'm listening," said Hugo. "Try to act as normally as you can; we can be seen."

"I know." She took several long, deep breaths before trying to speak again. "I wish I could have something to drink."

"Not tonight, Evi. I think it's better if you keep a clear head."

"I can't describe it. I can't describe what is wrong with him. He comes across as having been so self-contained, so completely unconcerned about any other member of the human race—his parents, his sister, this young first wife. Even the fact that millions of people would be facing danger hardly seems to have made an impact. He spoke of Germany as being a temporary abode. If someone were going to have to pay for the evil about to be unleashed, it would not be him. But the evil was borne by so many others, including my family and possibly even his. Women, children. If he truly foresaw what would happen to Germany, how could he say it was none of his business?"

Hugo watched Evi's sad face staring back at him and felt a powerful urge to touch her, just to place a hand over hers, to give her some kind of signal that he understood what she meant. "If it helps at all," he said—and he suspected it would not—"Bela Lugosi was hardly alone in behaving like that. Most people do not regard the safety of others as their concern. If more people had cared about the dark spell being woven over Germany, it could have been broken. Hitler need not have come to power; the country would not have provoked a bloody war; there would have been no Final Solution. These horrors happen because of the silence of the majority."

Evi was touching her ring finger again; Hugo knew she must be seriously struggling to gather her thoughts. "I suppose that's what I find most sickening. These films are the opposite of laughing at the devil; they make us laugh at a childish effigy of the devil whilst the real demonic power does its work without hindrance. The whole horror industry—it's so ridiculous, so infantile. I was more frightened in the dentist's chair than watching Bela Lugosi pretend to bite an actress' neck. But there's something so ugly underneath it all." She trailed off, adding almost angrily, "I don't know what I'm trying to say!"

Hugo took a risk and rested his hand on hers. She did not brush him off or even appear to notice. "You don't have to say anything; I know what you're feeling. Now, will you take some friendly advice?" She nodded. "Try to avoid working alone. Don't do any more writing tonight when you get home. Tomorrow, bring your notes to my place and work there. I have a typewriter, and I won't interfere. I'll be downstairs dealing with customers and sorting through stock whilst you write."

An obvious obstacle came to mind. "I wouldn't want to intrude."

"Evi, you know you won't intrude. But you should go where you won't be tempted. And loneliness carries too many temptations."

How much does he know? Evi wondered, when Hugo had walked her to her door and bade her good night. She told herself it did not matter; if he knew she drank, he was trying to help her, not running away from her, so it could hardly disgust him too much.

Evi stood in her empty room in front of the cracked, mottled mirror and unpinned her hair. There was no grey yet, not a single strand, when by rights she ought to be white and shrunken by now with all the torment and neglect she had inflicted upon herself. She felt stifled by the silence across the flat; it was unnatural, ominous. It made her hear every creak and rumble of noise from the other inhabitants of the block of flats or from the street below. Hugo was right: if she had to live alone, it was better not to work alone.

Bela Lugosi had no sense of foreboding whatsoever as he immersed himself in the excitement of a new country—and such a country for an actor on the make! Bela felt the same exhilaration he had experienced when he had first run away with the travelling show, but now he was thrown into the most advanced film industry in Europe.

Filmmaking was developing at a dizzying pace, and work was available in plenty, starting with the wickedest of wicked roles in a film whose title left nothing to the imagination: *Slave of a Foreign Will*. Among a people sleepwalking their way to ruin, Bela Lugosi played a hypnotist who used his skills of manipulation to prey upon women.

"Be careful not to see Adolf Hitler everywhere," warned Bela, anticipating Evi's next question with an accuracy she found disarming every time. Evi had to assume either she was boringly transparent or he had a touch of the mind-bending hypnotist lingering somewhere in his psyche. "There have always been plenty of villains in the world. He was just a villain in the right place at the right time."

Evi stifled the urge to get into an argument with him. She knew he goaded her with every intention of getting a reaction, and she was far too good at obliging him. "Tell me about the pictures you made," she said instead. "You enjoyed working in Germany."

"It was the most exciting time in my whole career, Evangeline."

"More exciting than wars and revolutions?" She was goading now, but he was too caught up in his own story to notice.

"You cannot imagine how exciting it was to see cinema emerging into the world like that. The idea of cinema, I mean. The making of a dream factory for the masses."

"Nightmare factory might be more appropriate, given the films you made."

Bela took the hint and cackled with laughter.

"European films were about much more than scaring people at the time. Have you heard of the Expressionist movement?" Evi shook her head. "A strange philosophical mix of the abstract and reality. Compared with today, these films were intellectual, full of ideas. And yes, I suppose there were nightmares there too. We were all fascinated with the occult at the time."

Evi sat up sharply. Had she heard him correctly? "The occult?"

Bela looked at her, or rather, he seemed to be looking through her. "I called it the Darkness. It felt more like a being than an idea, an entity haunting the screen worlds of that country from the very outset." He shifted position in his chair, but he was still looking through her. "When I visited the movie theatres myself, I would sit and watch as all sorts of weird phantoms drifted across the screen, bizarre creatures unleashed into the chaos of that nation. Somehow, the silver screen reflected everything that nation was going through, still punch-drunk from its recent humiliation—the self-loathing, the confusion, the seething rage and despair."

Evi tried to shrug, but she felt as though the despair in the room were clinging to her, and she shrank back close to the curtained window, from where between drapes a sliver of daylight crept across her notepad. "Art always imitates real life, I suppose," she said awkwardly.

"We should have been healing a wounded nation, but we trapped people in their own worst nightmares. All that wallowing in darkness and horror. There was no escape from the chaos anywhere."

"Didn't you feel a little culpable?"

"No," answered Bela brightly, sitting up in his chair, "all I cared about was getting plenty of work and learning as much as I could about the new craft of film acting."

Evi groaned inwardly. He had changed roles so quickly and naturally that she wondered whether she would ever see the real man during the many invisible costume changes he seemed to go through—one minute the brooding prophet of doom, the next minute a heartless careerist. "You arrived at the right time, it would seem, and perhaps left at the right time too."

"I didn't leave at the first sniff of trouble," Bela said to assure her, as though afraid she would think him a coward. "I had a good nose for revolution by then—I could smell the stench of it on the streets of Berlin—but I chose to stay out of politics. I preferred to enjoy the party while it lasted."

"I hope it was a good party," Evi retorted. Bitterness again. It was never far away.

"It was not my country; it was not for me to go around telling the Germans I thought they were doomed, even if they were." He folded his arms. "It's no good looking at me like that. I would hardly have been taken seriously if I *had* said anything."

"Who was Karl Freund?"

Bela looked positively pained. "Who? Oh, that really hurts. He was the master of cinema's inner sanctum. A master cinematographer."

Evi nodded sagely, though she had absolutely no idea what a cinematographer even was, other than a very big cheese in an exciting, dynamic, and—as far as she was concerned—utterly pointless movie industry. All she had thought when she had read his name in Mr Goldberg's notes was that he sounded like a Viennese psychiatrist with whom she was familiar.

"He was a great man, cold at first to my displays of enthusiasm, but I persisted, and eventually he let me into one of his film sets. He was making a film called *Satan*."

"How subtle."

"Too subtle for me, I fear. I had no warning I was to become possessed."

Evi waited for Bela to explain himself. She was accustomed now to his theatrical turns of phrase, and the pronouncement did not shock her in the least. The long silence that followed was more startling. She waited for him to break the silence and continue with his story, but he stared into a corner, keeping so still that if his eyes had not been wide open, Evi might have thought that he was asleep.

If Evi had not known better, she would have thought that the temperature in the room was dropping, but the silent man with his gaze firmly away from her did not seem to have noticed that she was shivering. The clock over the fireplace began to chime the hour, causing her to jump out of her skin. Evi snatched up her things and fled the room with the ominous clanging of the clock echoing all around her.

It was a prize greater than Bela could have hoped for: entrance into a film set ruled by the great Freund and his director, Murnau. It was unlike any another film set Bela had haunted during his short career, down to the faintly surreal atmosphere that pervaded the whole studio and the air of dedication in all who worked on that production. It was more akin to some religious act of devotion than a group of men working together on a commercial venture.

Bela sensed that Freund was studying him as closely as he was studying the set, and he tried to distract himself by taking an inordinate interest in the men painstakingly trying to get the lighting right. The strangest feeling was taking him over—something close to what he had experienced in those early, heady days as a stage actor in Budapest, but stronger and darker than anything he had known back then. He might have been back in the fortune-teller's room again, entranced by feelings he knew instinctively he should fight but which consumed him so utterly, he wanted only to succumb.

"May I return, Mr Freund?" asked Bela as he was shown out of the studio, the strange aura of the set dissipating as soon as he stepped out into the street. "I shan't be any trouble to anyone, I swear. I'll just sit in a corner and watch."

The older man hesitated, perhaps wondering whether an overly enthusiastic jobbing actor was worth the trouble on a busy film set. "There are many excitable young men out there who dream of a life in film. I receive begging letters all the time. What sets you apart?"

Bela remembered the response he had received the last time he had given an honest answer to a similar question, but he did not care. "It is my destiny. Something is calling me to this."

It may have been Bela's imagination, but he was sure he noticed Freund's face whitening almost imperceptibly. He had the demeanour of a man used to hiding everything. "Is it indeed?" he said quietly, and any other young man might have felt a little threatened. "Then you had better give into it, hadn't you? You come as often as you can, and you make no trouble."

"I wouldn't dream—"

"You watch, and you learn the art of filmmaking. Bring no silly notions with you; you have learnt nothing of any use until now."

Bela could hardly believe his luck. If Karl Freund had insisted upon dragging him into a satanic cult as the price for a life in film, Bela would have accepted the demand without reservation. "Oh, thank you, I really am most—"

Freund gestured for him to stop. "You have nothing to thank me for; I never do anyone a favour. There are the useful and the useless. Consider this an initiation."

Should that uncanny choice of words have served as a warning? Bela had time to consider the possibility much later in life, when the prospect of a reckoning felt rather more plausible than it did in his youth, but on that day Bela felt only the intoxicating excitement of a man seeking his own glory in the tortured twilight of Germany's nightmare factories.

This thing of Darkness, I acknowledge mine!

The Darkness can only ever possess, never be possessed by any mortal man, but Bela was young enough to believe that he was not mortal at all, and he fed on the dark, delicious aura of the nightmare factory. Freund kept his many promises to Bela and introduced him to Murnau, a man who was already well known as the director of bizarre, haunted films almost as strange as the man himself.

Bela extended a hand in greeting and felt Murnau's limp, cold hand momentarily touching his. He tried to convince himself later that it was only an overactive imagination that made him shiver, but the moment they greeted one another, Bela knew he imagined nothing. Whatever Darkness was slowly stealing him had taken Murnau before. They were both enthralled with it, subtly, quietly without anyone else knowing it.

Evi stood in the doorway of Bela's room, too embarrassed to step inside without permission. Her breathing was still a little heavy. She had run three blocks like a bat out of hell before the hot, taunting light of day had brought her to her senses and she had staggered to a halt near a shop window. A quick glance around her told her that she had got herself into a state for no good reason, as usual. There was nothing to be afraid of in the middle of a busy street: cars and buses roared past her; happy men and women strolled along the pavement, going about their lawful business; a paper boy called out the day's headlines.

The only fear was inside her head, as it always was. She had run away from a morose old man in a chair because he had not answered her question quickly enough. She could almost hear Christy laughing at her. Or wished she could. He would have had a field day, watching her running as though she had the devil at her heels. It would have been Dracula impressions and ghostly noises from him for months afterwards.

Somehow or other, Evi forced herself to retrace her steps, back to Bela Lugosi's home. She knew she could never face Mr Goldberg with an unfinished project, and all because her subject gave her the creeps. That was how she found herself standing back in Bela's presence, making her apologies. "I'm frightfully sorry. I'm afraid I had rather a turn," she said. "I'm not sure quite what came over me."

Bela had not moved from the position in which she had so recently abandoned him, and he did not move as he answered her. "You were more sensible than I was. I should have run. I should have been afraid." He glanced up at her slowly; she squeezed a gloved hand behind her back to stop herself from backing away. "Will you sit down?"

Evi shuffled past him to her chair and settled herself down before asking the obvious question. "Why weren't you afraid? Were you too young?"

"Not at all. I was older than you by the time I arrived in Berlin." He lowered his voice, forcing her to move closer to him to hear. "You see, I wanted to be possessed. I wanted to serve the Darkness."

Evi tried to swallow, but her mouth was dry. "You were an actor, that's all. An actor making films."

Bela looked across at her, the semblance of a smile touching the corners of his mouth. "And do actors not have souls to be lost? I faced the same questions any man must ask. Who was to be my master? Whom would I serve?"

Evi shuffled in her seat. She almost regretted coming back for more of this. "I see," she said.

"No, you do not. You have no notion of the struggle that commenced in me. The question that would not leave me alone. I seemed to hear a soft, ancient voice interrogating me, a voice I already knew. It was urgent, unnervingly so. But when I did run, it was not fear that made me flee the studio."

"So you did run?"

Bela was avoiding her gaze again, almost as though he thought he had lost control of the interview somewhere along the line. "You remember when I spoke about walking through the streets of Budapest by night?" She nodded. "It was not unlike that time. I walked for hours—through busy streets this time—knowing that I had to resolve this existential crisis that had come upon me. The question posed remained even when I was lost in the crowds. A decision had to be made."

Bela's head rested in his hands. Evi sensed that it would not be long before he was too exhausted to continue. "What choice? What decision?"

He hardly seemed to notice the interruption. "I sat upon a park bench and tried to collect my thoughts. There were children playing nearby, and all I felt was envy for the innocence they enjoyed without knowing it. My paranoia was so great that when I saw clouds gathering overhead, I felt that they were gathering for me, and for me alone. I rose and walked on through this gathering gloom to my rooms."

"I thought you wanted to be possessed?" This was madness, a crazy old man rambling about dark voices calling out to him, and creepy clouds in the sky like something from one of his lousy films. "Never mind, it's not important. You chose."

"I chose."

There was a finality about the statement that echoed around the room like a death knell. "It was all too intoxicating. Somehow I knew that submission would bring with it everything I had always dreamed of; I have no idea how, but I just knew. I flung myself headlong onto my bed and cried out for sleep, for any respite at all from the turmoil I was in."

"I know that feeling," remarked Evi. "My grandmother used to say that more sins are committed by night than by day. The darkness hides so much."

"The darkness is more than that—it is a tempter and a tormentor," Bela replied, "and yes, a hiding place for unwelcome visitors."

Evi felt a shiver run down her spine. "Someone's walking on my grave," she said absently.

"I beg your pardon?"

"Nothing, I'm sorry. Please continue."

Bela looked steadily at her until she was forced to look away. "Would you believe me if I said I had a visitor that night? A familiar presence, perhaps one that had accompanied me from the dark and lonely forests in my far-off homeland. It was as if an icy claw were scratching outside the window, demanding entry, demanding possession. I seemed to be watching it all from afar, watching myself rise as if in a trance and walk toward the window. In a trancelike state, my will obedient to the summons, I allowed It entry."

"It was a nightmare," Evi burst out, unable to listen to any more of these ramblings. She felt the pain creeping across her neck as her every muscle tightened with the effort of sitting still. "Perhaps you had a fever. Your description fits well with the symptoms of delirium."

"You may call it that if it pleases you," said Bela without emotion. "It is of no consequence. In any case, I cannot remember much of what happened afterwards, only the feeling of strangeness when I woke up."

"There, a dream," she said, but she knew without looking at him that she should not pursue the argument. He clearly did not want an innocent explanation.

"Some dream it would have had to be," Bela continued. "When I glanced at the clock, I had been unconscious for nearly twenty-four hours. If I had suffered some feverish attack, it had passed. The agitation was gone; my mind felt inexplicably at rest. My body felt stronger than before the war. And that was the truly strange thing. I looked in the mirror at my reflection, and my face looked different to how I remembered it. My eyes were brighter and redder, my skin paler. I thought that perhaps I had been ill after all, but when I peered closer into the mirror, I saw the evidence …"

8

Evi's hands rested against the locked door. In spite of the blistering heat, the hard, unyielding metal felt icy cold beneath her fingers, as though the life locked away behind it had already been taken. She had some sense that she had been standing at that door for a long time, waiting patiently for it to open, but now she clenched her fists and began to hammer at the barrier before her; she would force it open. Somehow or other, she would find a way into the chamber if it took every ounce of her strength; she knew Christy was trapped in there, separated from her by just a few inches of steel. She hammered and hammered at the door until her wrists seared with pain; then, almost in a frenzy of desperation, she began hurling herself bodily at the door. She heard the thud of her own body hitting metal over and over again, as though she were listening to the actions of another person. She could not remember how she came to be in this accursed place; she knew only that she had to open the door ...

Evi opened her eyes to the familiar sight of the long, jagged crack across the ceiling directly above her head. She was in her own bed, her temples throbbing, whilst very near to her she could hear the repeated thud of someone knocking on a door. Her door. She staggered out of bed, the room lurching as though she had just fallen off a carousel. The knocking was getting louder and more urgent. Somehow or other, she pulled down her dressing gown from the hook at the back of her bedroom door and threw it on, tying the cord untidily around her waist as she made her way out of the room.

Evi heard Hugo's voice calling her name as she heaved open the front door, narrowly avoiding his fist in the process. He took a step back at the sight of her dishevelled figure still in her nightclothes. "Dear God, Evi," he exclaimed without a thought, "you look awful. Are you ill?"

Evi felt her face growing hot and suspected she would have blushed if she had had enough blood in her veins. "It's nothing, I must have overslept. What time is it?"

"It's half past ten."

Not too bad, then, thought Evi, hardly reason for him to come hammering on her door like that. "There was no need to fuss; I must have slept through my alarm. I was . . . I think I was up very late writing last night."

Hugo looked anxiously at her. "Evi, what day of the week is it?"

"Is that a trick question?"

"Could you tell me?"

Evi narrowed her eyes. "It's Wednesday."

"Evi, it's Thursday. You didn't return to the shop on Monday afternoon after your appointment. I thought something must have come up, but then you did not appear all day yesterday. You've been out for the count for twenty-four hours."

Evi's knees buckled under her; she clutched at the door frame, but there was nothing for her to hold on to, and the room was still lurching. She was aware of Hugo's abandoning propriety to pick her up off the floor and carry her inside, away from the prying eyes of her neighbours. She noted him hesitating for a moment, getting his bearings in a strange home; then he strode into the sitting room and laid her down gently on the tattered sofa. "It's nothing," she protested. "It's a touch of fever, that's all. I'm all right now."

"You are most certainly not all right; you're shaking like a jelly," said Hugo. "The last time I saw anybody in a state like that, I was in Korea."

Evi covered her eyes, willing the room to stop spinning so she would not throw up with the turmoil. "I can't remember a thing since I arrived home on Monday afternoon. I wasn't feeling well, so I put myself to bed."

Hugo was comfortingly businesslike. "If you've been sweating out a fever all this time, you'll be hungry and dehydrated," he said. "Are you still running a temperature?"

Evi shook her head mechanically. "I don't think so. I suppose a raging temperature would explain the bizarre dreams I was having. I must have been delirious."

"Let me get you a glass of water."

Evi lay very still whilst Hugo blundered about in the kitchen. Shades of her nighttime adventures were starting to come back to her: a locked door that would never be opened, the door that would lead her to Christy. Other images had slipped out of her mind as she woke up: the lonely road to a prison camp, or what she must have imagined a prison camp would look like; an endless tangle of barbed wire spirals; men in uniform ... a body not quite dead, not fully alive; a face she would have recognised if she lost her memory of everyone else. A face disfigured so horribly she wanted to believe it did not belong to the man for whom she was searching.

Hugo helped her to sit up and placed a glass of water in her hand. "Drink it," he said, waiting a second to see whether she held on to the glass firmly enough before he let go. "All of it. You'll notice the difference immediately." He drew up a nearby chair and sat down. "I'm afraid I couldn't find much to eat in your kitchen, and the tea caddy is empty."

"No tea?" enquired Evi between gulps; she was indeed feeling a great deal better already. "I must be letting myself go."

"Do you feel strong enough to take some gentle exercise?"

Evi gulped down the rest of the water. "I feel perfectly well," she said, "much better than I really ought, I suspect. Just a little drained, but I suppose that's perfectly normal."

"Well, I shouldn't overdo it today if I were you," Hugo cautioned, standing up to take the glass from her. "Why don't I call back for you in half an hour, and we can get a cup of coffee somewhere? I daresay you still have a deadline to meet this afternoon."

Evi groaned. "It's on the desk; I think it's finished." She sat up, planting her feet purposefully on the floor. "That's a point; I can't have put myself straight to bed. I remember typing for hours before the fever took over. It was like writing in a trance or something."

Hugo smiled. There on the desk were several typed pages. A half-filled page was still in the teeth of the typewriter. He noticed that two of the keys had locked together; it was probably the hassle of unjamming them for the hundredth time that had caused Evi to admit defeat. "Well, it should make for interesting reading, then."

"Hugo, you never talk about Korea."

Hugo busied himself unjamming the keys of the typewriter as carefully as possible. "That's because there's nothing to say. It happened, I came home."

Evi knew, with the sensitivity of an army wife, that she was on dangerous ground. "I'm just saying, if you knew anything about my husband, you would have said so, wouldn't you?"

It was a rather good typewriter, Hugo thought, as he gently pulled out the page; Christopher must have bought it for her before he went away. It was one of the few objects in the room that she had looked after. The rest of the desk was a chaotic mess of papers never filed away, rubbish that somehow had not made its way down to the wastepaper basket located a few feet away, and a blotting paper sheet splattered in ink that desperately needed changing. "Are you left-handed?" asked Hugo, noting the position of pens and ink.

Evi stood up. The room had stopped spinning, and she was aware only of Hugo's turned back. "I'm not supposed to be," she answered tersely, "but there's no one standing over me here to stop me from writing the way I find most comfortable." She paused, waiting for him to get the hint that she had noticed the clumsy change of subject.

He did get the hint but replied, "I'll take the article with me, to read before we meet for coffee." Then he folded her article and put it away in his bag.

For some reason, his heavy leather satchel reminded Evi of a doctor's bag. "I hope my untidiness does not offend your military sensibilities too much," she added.

Hugo turned to her with an awkward attempt at cheeriness. "Well, I'm a civilian now, thank heavens. I should let you get on." He walked to the door. "You know, there were thousands of men in Korea."

"I know. See you in half an hour."

"Well, you've had a field day, by the looks of things," said Hugo, helping Evi off with her jacket. In the end, he had thought it easier to bring her to his shop for breakfast, partly because he could not get into the habit of closing the shop during business hours, and partly because he thought she would be more relaxed in a familiar setting. Without blowing his own trumpet, Hugo also knew that the tea he made would be infinitely more to Evi's liking than anything they purchased at a coffee bar. "Why don't you make yourself at home? There's some reading matter for you on the coffee table."

Evi walked over to the table, smiling at the orderly fashion with which Hugo had presented his material. There were several piles of newspaper cuttings and foolscap pages, neatly stacked so that the top right corners of all the papers were perfectly aligned. The large, faded poster—too large to fit comfortably with everything else—formed the centrepiece of the whole display, with the bundles of paper on either side in perfect symmetry. "I thought you said you were a civilian now?" Evi demanded, hardly daring to touch anything in case she spoiled the effect. "Even your paperwork looks as though it's standing to attention."

"Would you like some toast?" he called. "You need to eat something."

"That would be lovely." Evi flinched at the sight of the black-and-white poster. A man's head was sketched in profile, his features grotesquely out of proportion, leering in the direction of the spindly figure of a young woman drawn from behind. The two characters—that bloated male face and the tiny, fragile female—were set against an unnerving background of harsh lines and distorted angles, suggestive of a dark, narrow street into which a victim might be lured and quickly trapped. Evi had felt so much better since Hugo had come to wake her. In fact, she felt so much back to normal that she had hoped against all hope that her latest instalment was as thin on detail as she remembered. But the poster dragged her back to Germany's horror film industry and Bela Lugosi's nightmare descriptions of being seduced by dark forces. "What ... what does the title mean?" she asked weakly.

Hugo was at her side. "*The Head of Janus*," he said, "a 1920 film based on the story of Jekyll and Hyde. Are you familiar with the story?"

"Naturally," answered Evi. "Dr Jekyll is a respectable doctor by day and a hideous murderer by night. The Victorian obsession with monsters again. Was this a Bela Lugosi picture?"

"I'd hardly call it that, but he did get to play Jekyll's butler. Veidt was the star. Bela remained close to Freund and Murnau for the rest of his time in Germany, and they were useful friends to have." Hugo touched her hand. "You know, you're still a bit trembly. Why don't you sit down and eat?"

Evi sat down on the lumpy sofa as Hugo placed the tea tray on the coffee table in front of her. The tea was very sugary, almost unbearably so to a palate used to wartime rations of thick, boiled, unsweetened tea, but she drank gratefully. She noticed a plateful of thick buttered toast. "You're very kind to me, you know," she said awkwardly. "I do appreciate it."

"Not at all," said Hugo, perching himself on the arm of the sofa. "Tuck in. You're ever so pale."

"I feel much better. Have you watched all these films?"

"Not *The Head of Janus*, unfortunately. It was made more or less by the same team that made *The Cabinet of Dr Caligari*."

Evi used the fact that her mouth was full of toast to avoid the humiliating admission that she had never heard of a film that was clearly very famous. She nodded in acknowledgement.

"Some say those films were a terrifyingly prophetic vision of where Germany was going. Others say that the films influenced the way things went. Films can be highly influential, of course. Look at the way they were used during the war by both sides."

"Was it popular? *Janus*, I mean."

"Oh yes, very much so."

Evi put down her plate and picked up a newspaper film review. She could not read German, but she recognised one word in the title: *Todes*. Death. She picked it up and noted a signed photograph underneath, one of those typical photographs of the time of a young actress pouting into the camera. She had a sweet, doll-like face that looked a little incongruous with the pose of a worldly inhabitant of horror films. "Ought I to know who she is too?" asked Evi sheepishly, lifting the photograph with her other hand. "Was she a friend of Bela's?"

"That's Dora Gerson," said Hugo. "She was a cabaret singer and actress. Made a couple of pictures with Bela Lugosi: *On the Brink of Paradise* and *Caravan of Death*."

"I thought I recognised that word," said Evi, nodding at the headline. "A pity it is almost the only word I know in German: *Tod*. That, and *Führer* and *Luftwaffe*. If Goethe wrote in it, it must be quite a beautiful language at heart."

"I'm afraid the title *Caravan of Death* turned out to be rather tragic. Dora was Jewish, married to Veit Harlan, a man who made Nazi films for Goebbels. The irony's almost unbearable."

"What happened to her?"

Hugo took the photograph from Evi, looking at it with the affection he might have shown a relative. "The inevitable, I'm afraid. She was deported to Auschwitz and died there with what remained of her family."

"With her husband making films for her killers?"

"Ex-husband. They divorced."

"So?" Evi sunk into the back of the sofa, clutching her head with the effort of holding all the facts together. "It's all so twisted! The man might as well have dragged his own wife into the gas chambers himself!" Evi looked up at Hugo; she was almost pleading. "It's not my imagination, is it? There is something so sordid about all this."

Hugo sat down beside Evi, aware that leaning over her was troubling her. "You know something, Evi, I can't help feeling that this is becoming a little too much for you. Your last piece of writing felt a little ..." He searched for a sensitive word. "Overwrought. Why don't you take a break from all this for a while? I'm not sure it's good for you."

Evi gave him a withering look that made Hugo immediately regret opening his mouth. It was hard to imagine that she was the same wan, frail little waif he had picked up off the floor such a short time before. "I don't have a choice, Hugo. I have a job to do." She held out a hand to him, and he helped her sit up. "I don't suppose you could write down the name of that actress for me, could you?" she asked as she rose to her feet.

"What are you up to?" asked Hugo.

"I have a plan."

"I was not sure whether you would return," said Bela, showing Evi into the room. "You surprise me every time."

"I wanted to ask you about somebody," said Evi, settling herself mechanically. "What do you remember of Dora Gerson?"

If Bela was surprised by the question, he did not show it. "I never thought to hear that name again," he murmured. "Poor little Dora. Poor Jewish child."

"You do remember her, then."

"Always. The sweetest, happiest of creatures, happy in her private life, happy in her work. There were few of us who were happy in both."

"Do you know what happened to her?"

The muscles of Bela's face tightened a little, but he showed no emotion. "I can only guess, I'm afraid."

Evi made the pronouncement with deliberate coldness. "She was killed at Auschwitz concentration camp in 1943." *Show some human feeling. I dare you!*

Bela did not move. His chin rested on his hands as though he were contemplating the mysteries of the universe. "Poor little one," he said without conviction. "It was her destiny to be claimed by the Darkness." He looked across at Evi, who had positioned herself so that he could not see the disgust on her face. "You know I did some wonderful films with Dora? *Caravan of Death* was the best, of course, but the film industry in Germany was the finest in the world."

There it was, thought Evi, just as she had imagined. Even the knowledge that a former friend and colleague had been murdered in a Nazi concentration camp for the crime of being Jewish was not enough to cause this man to stop and think about something other than his own film career. That woman whose face had stared out at her from an old photograph, beautifully groomed with feathers in her hair and a look of expectation that all would be well with the world, a woman betrayed by her own husband's malice or foolishness ... Dora need not be mourned or remembered as the person she truly was by her own colleagues because it was her "destiny" to be exterminated. "There's no such thing as destiny," said Evi. "That's superstitious nonsense. No one is destined to be a victim any more than a man is destined to be a murderer."

"I have always thought it strange how the public appetite for horror comes and goes," mused Bela, ignoring her completely. Evi had noticed that if she said anything that did not fit with his expectations, Bela would simply behave as though he had not heard. "As if there hadn't been enough horror in the war, the public needed to have more, and that is precisely what they got. *Golem* and *Janus* were both a great success; but there was greater to come."

"*Nosferatu*," answered Evi blandly. "*A Symphony of Horror*."

Bela looked more put out than he had when Evi had told him about Dora. "You know, you spoil a good story by giving away the punchline," Bela complained. "But you are learning, I see."

"I have an excellent teacher."

"As did I—Murnau and Freund were as great as they come for a pupil studying the art of horror and its uses." Bela looked quizzically at Evi. "Do you know the story?"

"I can guess," Evi replied. "Monsters, vampires, ghosties, and ghoulies wandering Transylvania in search of blood—preferably human blood, with children's blood being the vintage port of the vampiric wine list."

Bela flashed her a smile. "Very good, but I thought it was ridiculous too when I first heard about it. You forget that I grew up surrounded by legends of the Undead. As children, we would scare each other with tales of Vlad the Impaler and his legions of Undead who roamed at night in search of victims. It was a good story for tourists and for frightening children, but nothing more."

"What was your part?" It was pointless to try to hold a conversation with him about something as apparently inconsequential as a murdered friend—what was another of the war's many innocent victims compared with the making of a celebrated horror film? She might as well indulge the man's Hollywood ego. "I assume you were in it?"

Bela shook his head. "Your teacher has been remiss if he told you that."

"He didn't."

"It was my part to witness this great work being wrought in secret. Film shoots by night—unheard of in the business—and the crew spirited away to Transylvania. This was to be a film that would cause shock waves throughout Germany and beyond. Its very production was the source of rumour and myth."

Evi studied the hunched, withered figure sitting in that shadowy corner of the room and wondered how much frustration lay beneath the hubris. No actor could be content to be a mere witness to a cinematic event, no matter how well Bela's new colleagues had sold the idea to him. She imagined him tormented by curiosity about this mysterious project being put together in such secrecy, like a child excluded from a school play being rehearsed all around him. Nobody likes to be excluded from the party.

Nobody likes to be excluded from the party, and Bela—as he liked to remind himself from time to time—was not a nobody. He nursed his hurt pride with the thought of those serious faces staring at him, requesting his absolute silence and discretion on the matter. It was an initiation of sorts, two stars of the film industry drawing him into their plans and trusting him with them.

It was cold comfort on an even colder, rainswept January morning as Bela waved off his friends at the station. They were off to Transylvania without him, the one among them who had once belonged there. "Cheer up, Bela!" the other men joked as they boarded the train. "If you go, you will get yourself on the wrong side of a revolution!"

"I suppose you had a right to remind me of that little detail," answered Bela, with a poor attempt at good humour; he was livid and needed every ounce of acting skill to hide it. "Give my blessing to the Carpathian Mountains."

Freund and Murnau flinched, but even after they had boarded the train and given Bela a friendly wave, Bela was still not sure whether his choice of words had been intended to unsettle them. Could any of them now give a blessing to anything? Men like them who were doing little more than bowing down and worshipping all that was darkest and most twisted in the world? Bela watched the train as it disappeared along the tracks to the land of his childhood and suppressed a shudder. The official story was that they were scouting locations for the film, but Bela's every instinct told him they were entering that wilderness in search of far more than a suitable castle to use as a film set.

And Bela was left alone, bored, and isolated as he awaited the return of his comrades. Perhaps it was simply boredom that made him feel so adrift, but during the solitary days that followed, Bela felt himself being swept away by the strange music that came to him from beyond those far-distant mountains. At night, when the moon was high, he could hear the seductive hum heard only by those with ears attuned to its mournful calling. The symphony of horrors, with all its sweet strains, moved like some strange fog from a land beyond the forests, over the Carpathian Mountains before sweeping down into Germany.

In the feverish nightmares that followed, Bela saw his friends in a desolate wilderness, tiny figures against the vast, starless cavern of the night. They walked in silence in the direction of an outcrop of rocks as though in a trance. Partially concealed from the path on which they had walked, there was a wooden door, locked and barred, as though it had been that way for a thousand years. It looked so impenetrable that Bela thought in his dream-like state that his companions could never hope to break it down, even if they had come armed with pickaxes and a battering ram—but they were empty-handed and quite bedraggled after a long, punishing journey through that inhospitable land. They walked up to the door and pressed their hands quite gently against it, pushing it open with no effort whatsoever.

Bela was suddenly filled with terror. The door should not have opened. He knew where he was now; he was back in the land of his childhood with its dark myths of ancient creatures slumbering in the deep, waiting to be summoned by men foolish enough and corrupt enough to desire such wickedness to roam the world. Bela knew he should rush to close it before it was too late, but instead he found himself drawing slowly closer to the void left by the open door, irresistibly drawn to witness the appearance of this wonder, to look it in the face . . .

"You missed us, then?" asked Freund, when Bela burst in on them in the studio. In spite of his impatience and excitement at the news of their return, Bela could not resist adding a touch of melodrama to the occasion and timed his arrival to coincide with the midnight hour. "Come in, my friend; just do not distract us. We are busy."

It may have been an effect of his bizarre nighttime adventures, but Bela could have sworn that Freund looked a little sickly. The man had never had a hearty Teutonic complexion, but he had lost weight during his travels and allowed his beard to grow without careful grooming, though the pressure of editing the film might be draining his energies. "Why the secrecy?" asked Bela, seating himself in a corner like a sullen child. "You slunk back to Berlin without a word; you are editing a film entirely by night, and rather in haste by the look of it. What are you up to?"

"You will see soon enough."

"There are rumours," Bela persisted, shifting impatiently in his chair. "Nighttime-only shoots in Transylvania, an unknown lead actor playing Count Orlok?"

Freund turned round to look at Bela, who flinched in spite of himself. There was an intensity and exultation emanating from the man that Bela had never noticed before. "We know what we are doing, Bela," said Freund. "Remember that your job is to watch and learn."

Bela was learning. He was learning that the deeper he immersed himself in this nocturnal world of undead monsters and ever-more-secretive creators, the more adrift he felt. But his feelings could not matter. *Nosferatu* was coming to Germany, and Bela would shiver in its long shadow.

9

Bela clung to the railings, praying for the storm to end. Beneath his feet, the ship lurched and listed on an angry ocean apparently intent on consuming him before the dawn arrived. They were somewhere in the lonely midst of the Atlantic, as far from any friendly shore as Bela had ever been in his life, and he was overwhelmed by his first experience of seasickness. The metal railings felt reassuringly cool beneath his shaking hands, and from where he stood, the spray of the waves tearing at the ship baptised him with hope that the ordeal might soon be over.

So, this was what a journey to the land of opportunity felt like. Dear God, he might have been better off staying in Germany, whatever his friends had told him about the promise of Hollywood and the prospects that would open up thanks to the success of *Nosferatu* and other German horror films in the United States. The journey felt like an ominous manifestation of the turmoil he was feeling. He was not a man heading towards a land of opportunity; he was a fugitive escaping a country that was being invisibly conquered by fear and paranoia. Something terrible was happening to Germany, and in his clearer moments he did not doubt that he was one of the lucky ones. Whatever was coming, he could escape, leaving Germany with even less than he had taken with him from Hungary.

Or could he escape? Could a mere change of location part him from this death-worshipping cult into which he had been drawn? Like any addict who was both compelled and repelled by his vice, Bela felt the comfort and the horror of it all. It would have been childish and undignified to admit to any of his friends that he feared the coming of night, never knowing if he would awake engulfed by the dregs of blood-fuelled nightmares. It would have been impossible to describe how it felt to be trapped when to all the world he looked free.

And he was not alone. The ship's crew were a bunch of drunks and pimps, all of them on the run from the police or their wives, or both. And among the wealthy passengers, there was the one they never saw. He had a cabin with a name on it, but he was even more reclusive than Bela, always alone and never to be disturbed—under any circumstances.

Bela was spending too long alone out on the deck—especially at night, when the mind could play tricks on him—but the sense of isolation made him feel close to his childhood self in a way that the bustle of Budapest and Berlin had rendered impossible. Standing alone engulfed by the crushing emptiness of sky and sea, he could believe in eternity, but only the eternal punishment of solitude without end. It was the lonely call of his rustic boyhood, hiding out in a barn from the angry spectre of his father striding about close by, ready to drag him out by the scruff of the neck.

He was unsettled by the memory; that was the only reason Bela's heart raced as he stood facing the empty sea, his hands squeezing the bar so tightly he could see the white bony knuckles pressing through his skin with the effort of keeping himself calm. There was someone near him, a figure moving around the rigging as though seeking out a wicked soul on the run. From where he was standing, Bela could make out a tall, angular figure—more like a ghost than a man, his frame was so insubstantial—and he knew he was watching the mysterious passenger no one else claimed to have seen. The figure raised a claw-like hand as though saluting the full moon.

Bela felt his chest tightening. He longed for someone else to emerge from his cabin, for someone else to witness this bizarre apparition he knew he would never otherwise be able to describe. He had seen so many horrors, not least on the Eastern Front, but nothing compared with the feeling of being in the presence of this creature so near to him and in a place where there was no escape other than to jump into the freezing darkness. Bela did not need to hold his breath; he simply could not draw breath during the long seconds he was forced to watch the black silhouette of that creature reaching out to the moon. He knew he would not rest again, knowing that the ship contained such a traveller.

"The Darkness followed me across the Atlantic," said Bela simply, "just as it had followed Jonathan Harker back to England in the old novel. His mark was upon me, sealing my fate."

Evi found herself struggling to write down what Bela was saying. It was not just the profound creepiness of the story; her hand simply did not want to form the shorthand characters anymore. Her body was going into open rebellion against her. "You think you saw a ghost?" she asked, trying to sound as nonchalant as possible. She already knew that the version she would show Hugo and submit to Mr Goldberg would be so severely edited, it would be as though this berserk conversation had never occurred.

"You can call it that. I might call it the shadow of the Dark Lord falling upon me." Bela's eyes were closed, which hardly seemed necessary since it was already so dark in the room, but he was noticeably weaker than in past weeks, and Evi wondered whether it was simply exhaustion that was making him rave like this. "The slow approach of the Dark Lord was like hearing the steps of a stranger following too closely on a dark night—only this creature's hollow footstep was never to leave me. It haunts me still."

"You were on your way to America," Evi put in. "New starts and all that. Perhaps you were just very distressed at leaving Europe behind forever, and it confused your thinking a bit."

Bela's eyes half opened. "I never left Europe, not really. The ancient world of forests and castles and deserted graveyards clung to me. I longed for a new beginning, away from the bloodshed and superstition of old Europe. You must understand that; you left the Old World behind yourself."

"If you'll forgive me, Mr Lugosi," said Evi with an ill-suppressed sigh, "I come from an ancient land like yours, but our castles and forests are not frequented by the Undead, as far as I am aware." Evi heard her own rudeness and searched for a diversion tactic. "It must have been exciting coming to America in the twenties and quite a daring-enough crossing without imaginary passengers. Is it true you got yourself on board without a passport or any money?"

There it was—a nice, normal human-interest story. Penniless European migrant blags his way aboard an Italian ship as a member of the crew, gets into a few nasty scuffles with his crewmates, and jumps ship upon arrival. Readers liked that sort of thing. She would frame the story that way, whether he liked it or not. It was a story so many of her readers would relate to: arrival in a country full of hope and excitement, near penniless, quite alone in the world, but ready to embrace all that promise and be worthy of it. The poor immigrant made good.

Bela the poor immigrant could hardly have believed he had once been the toast of Budapest's elite as he walked, hungry and dazed, through the streets of New Orleans. The European-flavoured architecture offered a sense of familiarity, but the riot of colours—on the walls of the buildings and the faces of the people—was something entirely new. He assured himself there were possibilities in this country if he only knew where to look. There had to be a place for a homeless Hungarian with the devil at his heels.

Bela made his way to the railway station and boarded the first train heading to New York City. Looking out the train window, he said good-bye to New Orleans before settling into his seat, ready to watch the passing of the countryside as the train slowly journeyed north. He was so disoriented that no emotions came to him as he sat with his forehead pressing against the window. He felt numb as the train pulled away from the station, when by rights he ought to have been desperately excited.

The regular motion of the train picking up speed had a predictably soporific effect on Bela, and he drifted off to sleep, finding himself back in Hungary again, in the forest, far from home, with the darkness of night falling all around. He had the terrifying sense that he was being pursued through the gloom. He ran wildly, weaving through the menacing trees with their exposed roots ready to trip him and their sweeping branches cutting him as he went. Bela did not know what it was that pursued him, only that it would catch him. There was an inevitability to the chase, as though he had tried to escape before and been captured, only to escape again with this invisible horror back at his heels.

Bela slipped in and out of his nightmare several times during the many hours the train took to arrive in New York. He had not realized how vast America was. Even if he had known before purchasing his ticket, he could not have afforded a sleeper car; he did not even have enough money to buy a decent meal in the diner car.

When he staggered out of the massive Pennsylvania Station a day and a half later, exhausted and famished, New Orleans seemed like a quaint village compared to this metropolis with its streets teeming with humanity hemmed in by towering buildings.

Bela stood still, looking upwards, dwarfed by the magnificent skyscrapers. He felt his heart sinking with humiliation. He wondered whether everything about the way New York was constructed was intended to make its inhabitants constantly aware of their own insignificance, although any city would have felt overwhelming to a man with no resting place awaiting him. As he gazed up at the dizzying spectacle of a building that could pierce the heavens, the cold realisation hit him: he had been granted his wish of a fresh start, with nothing to his name—no friends, no contacts, no work, and nowhere to lay his head that night or perhaps ever. He was back at the beginning again, a runaway in search of a travelling circus to carry him off.

"I wish it would rain," mused Evi, glancing out the window at the street below. She was sitting on the broad stone windowsill of Hugo's flat, hunched up in a manner that looked charmingly girlish to Hugo. He had suggested that she sit near the window when she had taken a nasty turn and needed the fresh air, but even with her head directly in the draught, she felt stifled. "I would love to feel the patter of raindrops on my face."

Hugo came and stood facing her. "Are you feeling a little homesick, by any chance?" Evi nodded. "Do you often get homesick?"

Evi looked back at the urban wasteland stretched out beneath her feet. She longed for rain—but not just rain. She longed for those long sweeping fields of green grass she remembered from her school days; the steamy classroom windows in winter on which she could trace swirling patterns with her fingers whilst the teacher droned on; the smell of bread baking early in the morning when sleep deserted her too soon, as it always did. "Always," she finally answered. "At least, always since Christy disappeared. It's harder to make sense of living here without him, since he was the one to bring me here."

"I can imagine," said Hugo, "but you've not gone back."

Evi continued to stare out the window. She could always sense danger around her when a conversation took a personal turn. "I'd have nothing to go home to. Everyone's dead." Her hand traced figures across the glass pane, but there were no condensation clouds here to bring them to life. "I suppose I feel closer to him here, even if he died somewhere else."

Hugo reached up to help Evi down. "Come down now; you're getting sad." She took his hand and slipped from the windowsill, landing elegantly on her toes. "Are you feeling better?"

"Yes, thank you," she said, straightening up and walking back to her chair. The mound of paper next to the typewriter made her heart sink. "I suppose I should be grateful, really. I have never been homeless like our mutual friend, and there were thousands back home who found themselves without a roof over their heads when the bombers came."

"You really do have to look on the bright side," promised Hugo. "A home can be found."

Evi ignored him. "And I have never lived in a country where I was unfamiliar with the language. Well, unless one considers American English a different language." The joke fell flat; they were both staring at the floorboards.

"It's all right, Evi."

"Was it as bad as I have described it?" she asked, sitting down daintily at the typewriter. "A poor immigrant sleeping rough, taken overnight from the finest hotels of Budapest and Berlin to the park benches and doss houses of the Lower East Side. Tired and destitute."

"You have captured it quite well, yes," said Hugo, crossing his arms. "It must have been the most miserable period of his entire life, his later misfortunes notwithstanding. I'm not sure it occurs to most people how many sacrifices immigrants make when they leave their country. Any man who has tasted success must struggle to start again from nothing."

The paper in the typewriter was already almost full, the many rows of heavy print mapping out the final phase of Bela Lugosi's penury before he was whisked back into the bosom of the theatre. She turned the dial to release it. "I suppose you started from nothing, didn't you?" she asked, remembering a previous conversation. "You came here to be an actor."

"Well, by definition I had nothing," said Hugo with a wry smile. "But I can't pretend I spent my nights sleeping under the stars. I could always make a few bob doing something useful, even if there was so much poverty everywhere. I even managed to get a few parts as an extra."

"Oh, but that's exciting!" exclaimed Evi. "Your face is captured on celluloid somewhere. I think that's splendid!"

Hugo chuckled. "You wouldn't recognise it if you saw it, my dear. I played a Mexican both times, with a ghastly floppy moustache glued to my upper lip."

Evi burst out laughing. "Oh Hugo, but that's priceless! You simply have to show me the pictures now!"

"Fortunately, there is no evidence of my idiotic escapades," said Hugo, with evident relief, "or I doubt I should ever have heard the last of it." He looked at the page Evi was holding. "Are you going to read it to me?"

Evi looked long and hard at the page, as though discerning whether or not she could bring herself to read her own words aloud. There was something so exposing about such an activity. "Why did you return to England when war broke out?" she asked quietly. "You could have stayed safe and sound in Hollywood, hiding behind your giant moustache, and no one would have been any the wiser. Why did you do it?"

Hugo did not miss a beat. "Because it was my duty, Evi. Our country stood alone, and I knew it was my duty to defend her. Perhaps no one would have known, but I would have known. No man wants to be a coward."

"It was good of you to do that."

"Not really," he answered quickly. "As I've said, the army life rather suited me. Made me the man I am, for what it's worth." Evi was looking fixedly at him. "I know what you're thinking, Evi, but I would not go back on any of it."

"Even Korea?"

"Even Korea," he answered emphatically. "Even the prison camp. It was a privilege to fight and live among such great men. That's what I choose to remember." Hugo sat down, indicating the end of that particular conversation. "Now, why don't you read to me?"

Evi took the hint to change the topic and picked up her paper. "You'll hate it. I'm afraid I may have become a little carried away."

"Surely not!"

Bela's lonely nighttime walks took him to the Hudson River. The swirling water reminded him of the Danube and those feverish wanderings on the crest of success. One night, when he was at his lowest point, he stood watching the Hudson making its progress before him, and he thought of Budapest, of Ilona, of the Gypsy fortune-teller with her black arts, cursing it all as an infernal joke played out at his expense. He closed his eyes with the face of the old Gypsy fresh in his mind, as though he were seeing it across the table for the first time.

He opened his eyes, only to see a very different face regarding his, one he also remembered from his theatre days in Budapest. "Bela?" enquired the man. "I am not mistaken, it is Bela, is it not?"

"Adam." Adam, the first man, a link with the past, brought into Bela's presence by some strange alchemy, or so Bela believed at the time. A friend working in the theatres of New York.

"That's right," said Adam. "You look a little down on your luck, my friend."

"I'll admit I am in want of work," said Bela awkwardly, aware of how shabby he must look in the presence of an acquaintance who was clearly doing well for himself. "I am learning the language."

"Why don't you come with me, Bela? There is plenty of theatre work if you know where to look."

Before he knew it, Bela was sitting in a nearby café, a hot coffee in hand, with Adam talking through the possible stage work available in the city. Ever the man to grab an opportunity, Bela had found all he needed to tread the boards once more. Within a week, Adam had secured him a part in a theatre company among the Hungarian exiles touring throughout the United States. It was a new start, and Bela was once more practising the craft he loved.

10

Bela was in a brighter mood when Evi next paid him a visit, more so than she had ever seen him. He greeted her with a smile and ushered her into his darkened room. Bela's improved mood had done nothing to make the room less claustrophobic, and Evi longed to pull back the curtains and throw open the windows, flooding the room with fresh air and light. She spied a magazine on Bela's coffee table, the pages open to her last feature. "You liked the last instalment, then?" she asked, settling herself down in her usual chair without being prompted.

"Yes," he replied, picking up the magazine. "I thought you described my poverty perfectly, even though you have never known it."

"Not poverty like that, I suppose," she conceded. "I have never slept rough, even when I was homeless." He looked quizzically at her. "Well, when I ran away from home, I made sure I had somewhere to go, even if it was only the sofa at a friend's house."

"Ah, a runaway! Just like me. Are your parents still living?"

"No, they died during the war. My city was destroyed."

Bela nodded slowly. "Of course. I'm afraid an old man forgets. An orphan and a widow. That's why you describe loneliness so well."

Evi's pen was poised at the top of a blank page. "You were happy with the touring theatre, weren't you? Living among your own people again after so long."

Bela rose to the bait, always happy to start talking about himself again. "Oh yes, they were happy years of touring the new country, especially during the Roaring Twenties. Food, shelter, and the company of happy, intelligent people—I could not have asked for more."

"I'm sure you could," said Evi, not intending to sound as sharp as she evidently did. "I mean, we all have our ambitions."

Bela shrugged. "You are quite right, of course; we all crave more than we have. I should have liked to feel a little safer, a little less afraid that it all might end. I could still see the poor, hungry people huddled near the theatres each night as I left through the stage door, and I was terribly afraid I might return to that."

"Was that when you met Ilona?"

Bela smiled in silence. Evi knew that this Ilona, like the last Ilona, was just one of the wives he managed to pick up and discard during his life, but the name appeared to stir no negative emotions in the old man. She was just another individual to cross his path, give herself to him, and find herself left behind when she was no longer needed. "I always found it amusing that she was also called Ilona. It felt like an omen at the time. And she was of good Hungarian stock too, even if her parents had emigrated many years before."

"And she was rich."

"Oh yes, or so I was led to believe," he agreed. "How could it fail to be love at first sight?"

I'm not sure I can cope with much more of this, thought Evi, trying hard not to grimace. She thought of her own wedding day, dressed in a sweet white dress borrowed from a friend who had married before the days when fabric could be obtained only with vast numbers of hoarded coupons. Evi's friend had been rather taller and broader than she, so they took up the hem, and still she managed to stumble on her way into the church, saved only because someone caught her on the way down: Mr Roger Nesbitt, her first and finest editor, dressed in his old naval uniform to lead her down the aisle in place of her dead father.

Evi could wallow in the inverted snobbery of knowing that her wedding had been a simple affair in which every detail had at least been real. Love in time of war, a sacrament bestowed across national borders giving her a suitably absurd married name to demonstrate the coming together of different worlds: Evangeline Kilhooley. Her friends had joked afterwards that she had married a GI only because of the lipstick and nylon stockings he was able to find for her, and the oranges and doughnuts they had enjoyed at the informal reception. It had been real, and it would have lasted. It should have been allowed to last.

"It was not a happy union," said Bela, blissfully unaware that Evi's mind had been on a quite different marriage. "How could it be when she was so possessive. And of course, I could never be possessed. A free spirit always."

I wanted him to possess me, thought Evi wildly. *That's the whole point of marriage, you foolish man! You were supposed to be one flesh! I wanted that mutual surrender; all true lovers do.* Instead, she said, "Really?"

"Love turns to hate so quickly, and a marriage ends more quickly still when jealousy creeps in. One night, after yet another fearful row, I found myself alone, staring out across the city. In my heart, I knew that my time there was drawing to a close and that I would soon have to flee and leave behind this jealous, embittered woman."

"You left her?"

"Not immediately. Broadway was calling me, and I needed to keep up the charade that I cared for her for a while longer."

Evi felt small explosions of rage like miniature grenades going off inside her. "Which role did you find more of a challenge, Mr Lugosi?" she asked, as coldly as she could manage. "The faithful husband or the hero of *The Tragedy of Man*?"

"Most certainly the faithful husband," Bela replied without hesitation. "Tragedy is easier to act than farce. I had lived through tragedy already, and I saw it everywhere. On the opening night, I walked past a crowd of labourers and saw one of my own companions from those recent days of poverty. I stopped and stared at him in evening dress whilst he stared at me in his dirty, worn clothing. It had not been so long since we had stood side by side in the gutter."

Evi felt the glimmer of a story coming. "What did you say to him?"

"Nothing, of course," Bela replied. "I turned and continued walking, leaving him to his shock."

"Of course you did."

Evi closed her eyes and let him talk. She could see the advantage of this shadowy room in such a moment. She could slant her face away from him so that he could not make out her expression—not that he was even looking at her as he drew her onto the stage of New York City, surrounded by a rapturous audience with the glow of happiness all around him. She could almost hear the applause ringing in her ears as she walked with him out of the theatre and into the night, lost in his happy thoughts and ambitions.

More nighttime wanderings, as though he had always belonged to the darkness—a trancelike walk to the Hudson River and the very spot where his fortunes had so lately turned, but this time he was bathed in moonlight, certain that the Gypsy's curse had been a fraud. He was a man destined for greatness; tragedy was for the past and for other men. The bright lights of Broadway guided his steps back to adoring audiences and success after theatrical success. He could congratulate himself that he was in the ascendency, his name circulating beyond the confines of the expatriate theatres and—perhaps inexorably—towards the studios where motion pictures were taking America by storm.

It was time to travel again, but not as an aimless wanderer any longer. Bela Lugosi was destined for Hollywood.

Hugo was busy wrapping a parcel behind the counter when Evi stormed into his shop, causing the bell over the door to clang maddeningly as she slammed the door shut behind her. "How many wives can a man collect in a lifetime?" she demanded, throwing her bag down at her feet. "How many of these insufferable liaisons must I commit to print?"

Hugo looked up from his work. "You know, from this angle you look like the avenging angel from a Victorian melodrama who has burst on stage to the wrong cue."

Evi tried hard not to smile. "How flattering!"

"I didn't say avenging angels were not attractive," Hugo put in immediately, coming out from behind the counter to greet her properly. "You simply appear to be delivering your lines in the wrong place." He took her hand. "Here, why don't you give me a hand with this parcel, and we can have some tea?"

Evi followed him behind the counter to a pile of old magazines Hugo was packaging up with inordinate care. "Who are they for?"

"My favourite kind of customer," Hugo replied, getting on his knees, "a wealthy enthusiast. If you would just hold those two ends of paper together for me ..."

Evi did as she was told, losing herself to the mundanity of balls of string and sealing wax. "Are they valuable?"

"Well, all I'll say is that it won't matter much if no one comes to the shop for a fortnight," answered Hugo, slipping string around the bundle. "The six issues of America's first film magazine. One of them is signed by Rudolph Valentino, no less. Here." He slipped back the wrappings to reveal the brooding monochrome features of a young man in quasi-Arab headgear. "Appeals, does he?"

"Not at all," answered Evi curtly. "All film stars look the same to me."

"Fake?" suggested Hugo.

"Quite." She replaced the paper. "There was only ever one man for me. Marriage is for life."

Hugo picked up a stick of sealing wax he had left on the counter and took a box of matches out of his pocket. "Quite right," he said. He lit the wax stick and set about methodically sealing over all the knots of string. "But it does say 'till death do us part'."

"Bela was never widowed."

"No," said Hugo. He turned the parcel over very carefully and finished his work before snuffing out the flame between his fingers. "You know what I'm saying, Evi. He wouldn't have wanted you to remain alone on his account."

Evi rose to her feet. "Everyone says that, and how on earth can anyone know?"

Hugo placed the parcel on the counter as carefully as though it were a newborn baby. "No man wants to think of the woman he loves being alone. Memories make poor companions."

Evi looked intently at him. "What did you say?"

"I think it's an old proverb," said Hugo, realising his mistake. "It's the sort of thing my grandmother would have said."

"It's not," she said. "Not a proverb, I mean. And it was Christy's grandmother who used to say that. He was always quoting her."

Hugo turned his back on her and moved in the direction of the back stairs. "Why don't we talk about this somewhere else?" he ventured. "It's three o'clock."

But Evi had grabbed hold of his arm and refused to let go. "It was one of the last things he ever wrote to me. I can show you the letter if you like. His last letter. Would you like to read it?"

Hugo ushered her out of sight of those glaring shop windows where passing strangers could peer in and watch a couple having an argument as though they were watching a movie. In the private world of upstairs, any argument could be resolved. "Evi, please don't jump to conclusions. It's not such a striking choice of words."

"Striking enough." She paused, awaiting an answer. "Look at me!"

But Hugo could not raise his head. "Evi, don't."

"Don't what? Ask the same question I've been asking you since we first met?"

Hugo took a chance and placed his hands on her arms; he felt her trembling with anger or nerves, but he had noticed before that she had a mild tremor, which he had assumed was caused by the drink. "Evi, there is a reason I never speak about Korea, even though I know you are desperate to talk about it, and that is because it is *too late*. I cannot change the past, so what purpose does it serve in dwelling on it?"

Evi shrugged him off and stomped up the stairs. "Well said from a man who runs a film mausoleum! Well said from a man helping me write about a man who ceased to be of any significance to anybody twenty years ago!"

Hugo followed her, half hoping she would stumble so that he could catch her, but she did not oblige. "That's a little harsh, if I may say so," he said. "There's a difference between having a healthy interest in the past and being trapped in it. You, if you'll forgive me, are trapped in the past."

Evi turned to face him, glowering at Hugo with such rage, he actually took a step back. He had seen her angry but never so deeply enraged as to unsettle him. "I don't see why I should forgive you for that, as a matter of fact," she spat out. "And I will trap myself in the past if it is the only way I can find out what happened to my husband. Christy is buried in the past, and I'm not leaving him alone there."

"Evi, you're still young; you have a future."

"Don't bother."

Hugo pulled up a chair and sat down, hoping it would encourage Evi to do the same, but she refused to budge. "He died, Evi. You know that. There are many women out there who may never know what became of their husbands, but you do know the truth. Isn't that enough?"

"I do not know how, and I do not know why," she said coldly. "That is enough to keep me where I am."

"It may never be possible to know," Hugo said. "Most widows never know precisely what happened. All sorts of details get lost in the heat of the battle."

Evi inclined her head to one side as though she were seriously considering what he had said. "You're a liar," she said, so pleasantly that it took a moment for Hugo to realise he was being insulted. "But you're such a charming liar, I didn't want to notice."

"Evi!" But the indignant tone carried no conviction.

"Don't pretend to be shocked," she said. "You know precisely what I mean. All of this is fake, every single detail of it. I'm working on an assignment about a man who was fake all the way through, who made his living pretending to be what he was not until he had no identity of his own left at all. This is all a pretence. All of it."

Hugo stood up, desperate to regain some authority over the situation. "So I'm fake too, am I? Because I deal in film memorabilia? Come now, how is that fair?"

Evi stepped towards him, much closer than was truly proper, but she wanted to break down his reserve. "Had we ever met before my editor sent me to see you?"

Hugo shook his head nervously. "No, of course we hadn't. You know we had never met before."

"Quite. But the strange thing is that you have behaved from the start as though you knew me very well. Without even noticing it, you have anticipated my needs and wants every step of the way." She took another step in Hugo's direction, forcing him to back away or let her collide with him. "Those quaint English afternoon teas of yours. They weren't an expatriate's kindly gesture to a fellow country-man at all; you knew it was what I would want."

"It was intended as a kindly gesture," Hugo put in. "I somehow knew you'd like it."

"You knew perfectly well I would," Evi retorted. "I used to tell Christy about afternoon tea at my grand-mother's house, the names of all the different cakes and treats. The wartime diet made one rather obsessed with food, and I could list them all for him: Victoria sponges, Eccles cakes, scones oozing with jam and cream. You even poured my tea exactly the way I liked it without having to ask. You've been so kind, but it's the kindness of a man under an obligation."

Hugo raised a hand like a traffic cop, but Evi misread the gesture and jumped back like a scalded cat. Hugo's face flushed with mortification. "You didn't really think I was going to hit you, did you? You ought to know me a little better than that!"

It would have been better to stop at calling him a liar, thought Evi as she made her way to the foot of the stairs, but now she really had insulted him. "I'm not sure I know you at all," she said, picking up her bag. "I know you knew my husband. It's the only way any of this makes sense, but you haven't the decency to tell me the truth. I'm not sure we have anything left to say to one another."

Hollywood, the epitome of everything Evi most despised—the false, the pretentious, the shallow, the mercenary; men and women in makeup and silly costumes posing before cameras; a privileged few made fabulously wealthy on the gullibility of the populace. The perfect place for the newly divorced Bela Lugosi, she thought, a playground for him to craft the dreams and nightmares that would guide America through the misery of the Depression.

Evi had been unable to settle herself to work when she had arrived home, and in the gathering twilight, even reading and rereading her other manuscripts in progress did nothing to steady the surge of emotions crashing through her. It was only when she was nearly halfway through her second bottle that she felt numb enough to set about the task of bringing Bela Lugosi's new film career to life. She was not above a little escapism herself, for all her posturing, and Hollywood was perhaps less dangerous to her survival than a series of empty bottles like the ranks of a death squad lined up across her desk.

An actor drawn once again into the realms of darkness: *The Silent Command, Daughters Who Pay, The Midnight Girl, The Rejected Woman* . . . The Darkness seemed to have found him all the way across the ocean in America and was feasting on his innermost thoughts, nudging him firmly, carefully into the production of horror and fear.

His bitter, rejected wife whispered her tales of woe to a judge who believed her. Her marriage to Bela had been a nightmare, a horror that had sapped the life from her as though he had sucked her own lifeblood. He had become a phantom to her, holding her in a trancelike vice until a court broke the spell between them and she fled into the night.

Bela would never see or hear from his second wife again, and she would become a memory to be recalled with a mixture of regret and shame and fear—the one wholesome response to that nagging sense he could not shake off that he was being moulded by a force beyond his control. Somehow or other, he had found himself trapped once again, but this time between the films full of adultery and violence from the West Coast and the plays of the East Coast, macabre, satiated in madness and despair and the inexorable draw of the occult.

Then came the visitor—just as Bela felt at his most alive, goaded onwards by his dreams of becoming a truly great movie star. His bags were packed to leave New York once and for all, the tickets bought. Bela sat in his dressing room removing the last traces of his makeup when he heard the door opening softly, causing him to stand up sharply to greet the intruder.

The visitor stood before him, dressed in black. "Good evening, Mr Lugosi," said the stranger, with a nod. Bela was startled to realise that the man was speaking Hungarian, albeit with an accent he could not place. "I have a play to produce. I require a star."

More Hungarian theatre, thought Bela. "Forgive me, sir, but I am a little beyond ..."

"The play will be in English, performed on Broadway," said the stranger immediately, sensing Bela's concern. "The play has a wealthy backer from our country who wishes the lead role to be performed by a Hungarian. You, to be precise."

"I see." What actor alive did not thrill at the sound of a man requesting his presence in a play—and a lead role, no less, on Broadway? Nevertheless, it all sounded so odd, fantastic even. "Would you care to sit down?" asked Bela, buying himself some time.

The stranger shook his head, lifting his bag onto Bela's dressing table instead as if to demonstrate the veracity of his offer. He opened the bag and brought out several large pieces of gold, which he placed carefully on the table in front of Bela. "You may take this as a deposit," said the stranger.

Bela swallowed hard. He was so intrigued that the gold was scarcely necessary. "May I know the name of the play?"

The stranger nodded. "*Dracula*."

Minutes later, with terms quickly agreed upon, the stranger left, leaving Bela alone in his room with an unnerving sense that a presence had been left behind to watch him. He changed and left the theatre, feeling that a deal of sorts had been struck and that it was about more than a stage play called *Dracula*.

The night air was warm as Bela strolled down the neon-lit streets of the metropolis. Far in the future, he would look back and feel as though he walked through those streets directly onto the stage—he remembered little of the weeks of learning lines and rehearsing. He passed effortlessly from the thrill of an offer to the applauding audiences and glowing reviews, hailing him once again as the star of the moment, an overnight sensation, the latest discovery upon the Broadway stage. Fame, glory, wealth—it was all his, and yet Bela was not overwhelmed or overjoyed. It was his right, his entitlement, a day that had always been meant for him.

The other actors quickly learnt to accept Bela's aloofness, putting his detachment from them down to an odd character quirk or a skill learnt in adversity, little knowing that Bela believed himself to inhabit a different realm from theirs altogether. Each night, on stage, he escaped from the noise and heat of the city to the cool calm of Transylvania; he returned home. In the fantasy world of the theatre, he could walk again through those ruined castles, deep within those sprawling dark forests where the children of the night serenaded his every step.

He was a man in a trance, never quite sure where fantasy ended and reality began. Both cast and audience were suitably awestruck by the power of his performances, but

Bela was aware of nothing other than himself and his role as he strode onto the stage every night as a newborn master of the unreal, the embodiment of the Lord of the Undead. The newspaper reports talked of a strange magnetism that emanated from the stage. Bela would have expected no different as he was conscious of a strange power that went forth from him in that role, enfolding him so that he could have gone on forever in that one role, the undead Count Dracula, haunting the world.

But the inner darkness called him on to new opportunities and new excitement. It was time to heed the call of Hollywood.

11

Evi was falling. If she could have found words to describe despair or even thought to describe it to anyone, she would have said that it was simply like falling—falling somewhere without an exit, without any means of escape, like down one of those deep, narrow canyons Christy said could be found in the remote places of this country, deep enough to swallow the Empire State Building, full of the creatures of the night living undisturbed by human trespassers or the harsh rays of the sun. The pattern was always the same. She would hover at the edge of that precipice for hours or even days, staving off the inevitable in the only way she knew; then something would happen to throw her off, and she would fall. She would fall, she would keep falling, and all the moonshine in the world would not drag her back.

She was still falling as she wrote. Surrounded by empty bottles and crumpled, discarded pages, her subject became muddled with her own nightmares, and even her dream journeys no longer made any sense. She imagined she was back in her family home in Coventry, standing before the maternal judge because of something a gossiping neighbour had said she had done. Then she was standing with Christy in the prison camp, holding his hand as though he were a little boy, telling him it was all going to be okay. Through the portal of dreams, her identity slipped from helpless victim to guardian angel, and neither felt real; she was sure the most awful beating ever had never prompted her to plead like that—it would have been beneath her dignity to cry out if someone had been removing her fingernails—and even in her drunken slumbers, Evi knew she was not in Korea either. She knew she had never saved him.

There it all was before her eyes—the cold kitchen floor with its black-and-white tiles; the aromas of dinner cooking on the stove, meals she would not be invited to join; the round, squat table leg with its spiral engraving, the white paint scratched away from the many times she had dug her fingernails into the wood and squeezed and squeezed ... and stifling heat, a world she ought not to have known at all, but it was there all the same. The prison camp as her imagination had created it: coils of barbed wire everywhere; the maddening murmur of insects; the rows and rows of weary men trying to stand to attention, all looking the same, the generic faces of a newspaper photograph. But Christy was real. He stood away from the others. Evi knew he was in terrible trouble—that was why he was standing in isolation—but she stood beside him and squeezed his hand in hers. Yes, he was real. She could feel the warmth of his skin against hers, his grip a little too tight because he was afraid and trying not to show it.

"You shouldn't be here," he said quietly, but he did not let go of her.

"This is exactly where I should be," she said. "I won't let anything happen." It was absurd. Even in the confusion of her dream, Evi was the same size she had always been, and Christy towered over her. "I'm here."

"Evi, you should go." His voice had a tone of urgency now; his fingers uncurled from around hers, leaving a space between them. "Some things can't be shared."

Evi was having none of it. "I shan't go anywhere!" She stepped towards him to close that tiny gap between them, but something or someone was holding her back, and she could not move. She could not reach him. Evi began to struggle ... in an instant she was back in her family kitchen, being thrown bodily onto the floor ... then she was fighting this invisible assailant, who was keeping her from her husband at the moment he needed her the most ... she flailed and shouted only because there was nothing else she could do. She did not know where she was any longer. One moment she was battling to stop a person from hurting her; the next moment she was employing her every scrap of energy to stop herself from being rescued. She knew she was being taken away from Christy because he was going to suffer; she was being taken out of the firing line. But she would not let them do it; she did not want to escape ...

She was adrift and, hardly for the first time, trapped in the cavern of her own mind. Evi was falling into that state of despair in which she lost any sense of night or day. The hours and days slipped away in a blur of grief-induced nightmares and empty bottles and pages and pages of notes she had taken during her interviews with Bela.

Writing was the only constant. It had been the same way for her father during the last year before she left the house. Battling the misery of falling sales and financial hardship, combined with the misery of an ever more foul-tempered wife and distant daughter, Evi's father had retreated into his work until his characters and plots seemed more real than the world around him. That is what madness is—the seeking of refuge in a place that exists only in the mind. It was his place of refuge, and it was Evi's now, that endless sojourn into the life of a man whose star had set many years before.

In the stifling heat of her room, Evi journeyed to Hollywood; she watched an actor in his prime on film sets playing bit parts, then minor characters, then lead roles. Films and films, and another wife collected and discarded between pictures. Bela's world, so ludicrously superficial, so fake, so wholly irrelevant to her own solitary life, compelled her to sit at her desk and work. It forced her to wash and dress and leave her place of refuge for the noise and clamour of the outside world, where Mr Goldberg briskly took her work from her and handed her the means to survive for another week.

Writing forced her back to Bela's abode, which looked much more familiar now that her own habitation was beginning to resemble it so closely. Evi no longer felt the need to sit near the window, craving the little shaft of light that broke through. The darkness suited her well enough after all.

"You are very pale today, my dear," commented Bela, escorting her to her seat. "I trust you are not unwell?"

You should talk, she thought, her own sense of irony returning like an old friend. "I have been working long hours," she said, which was not a lie.

"You could be the heroine of one of my pictures," he said with a charming smile, "a pale, sad innocent threatened by a monster."

"Would I be dead or alive?"

"Does it matter?" he chuckled, enjoying the banter. "The audience would fall in love with you and want to protect you from the wicked Lord of the Undead." He stood up so abruptly that Evi jumped, her nerves still unsettled by her days of isolation. "But I had almost forgotten! I had intended to surprise you when you arrived." He swept to the door. "Wait here."

Evi put down her bag and stood up as she waited for Bela to reappear, which he quickly did, wafting into her presence wrapped in a vast cape. He drew the cape up over his mouth in a ham horror gesture Evi recognised from the film *Dracula*. It was no good; she felt her shoulders shaking, and the giggle had escaped her mouth before she could swallow it.

Bela dropped his hands to his sides and looked at her, a wounded vampire repelled from his intended victim by the shrill sound of ridicule. "Audiences were scared half to death by my performance in my films, you know."

Evi shrugged, startled by the effect her reaction was having. She wished now that she had pretended to be terrified. "Oh, I shouldn't like to meet you on a dark night, I assure you." She floundered for something else to say. "Is that the actual cape?"

"Yes, indeed. The cape that made me Dracula." He raised his head again, his pride restored by her feigned curiosity. "Come closer."

Evi struggled with nervous laughter again. She was sure Bela had taken on his old role again as soon as he had donned the cape. His voice sounded more gravelly, and her mad imagination made his face seem paler and more sunken, the teeth—aided by prosthetics of some kind—a little sharper and more pointed at the front. She reached out to touch the edge of the cape, more in mockery than anything else, and he backed away from her immediately. "I'm sorry," she said, slipping her hand behind her back. "Have I offended you?"

"You have never worn that before," he said quietly, pointing in the direction of her neck.

Evi's fingers went to the discreet Miraculous Medal she had put on that morning. It had been buried at the bottom of her jewellery box, along with her engagement ring and wedding band, since she had received the news of Christy's death, but something had compelled her to put it on that day as she battled an irrational fear of going outside. "My husband gave it to me when we were married," she said. "It was his mother's. She put it around his neck when he went away to war because she wanted to protect him. He gave it to me."

Bela's face was flint; Evi could not quite tell whether he was angry or simply displeased. The object was unmistakably Catholic, and putting up with anti-Catholic abuse had felt like a rite of initiation when she had converted to marry Christy. "You should not put your faith in such trinkets," he said coldly. "It's a piece of metal."

"Yes," answered Evi, feeling her temper stirring. Christy would have been halfway to giving him a punch on the nose by now. "But there's so much more to it than that. It has a mother's love in it, and a husband's. It is hard for a man to go away to fight and leave his wife behind, and this was especially true at a time when my work took me into dangerous places, when so many civilians were being killed in air raids ..." Evi trailed off and sat down in her chair. She could not bring herself to cover the medallion—it would have felt like an admission of defeat—but she shifted her position so that he could no longer see it. "So you became Dracula," she said brightly, but she felt sickened by him.

Bela relaxed immediately, but he did not sit down; the gravity of the part he was reenacting demanded that he remain on his feet. "Before I even had the role, I knew it was mine. Why, they even gave me a home that looked like a Gothic castle! I could stand on the battlements to survey the City of Angels below."

"Los Angeles."

"City of fallen angels. I seemed to be the only one who saw them." Evi glanced at him in confusion. "Of course, you think I speak in metaphor," he continued, "but would that it were so. There were legions of them, walking the streets, guarding the boundaries of the city, controlling all who entered as well as those who tried to leave. I had been summoned to the city by the Darkness."

Evi could feel a migraine coming on. "You were not initially cast as Dracula, were you? I read in your own account that the first choice was Chaney."

Bela directed a smile at the corner of the room. "Indeed, Chaney, the star of *London after Midnight*. The biggest horror star in Hollywood, and the lead in no fewer than ten of Browning's films. But I knew he would never play it; it was my destiny to play that role, and Chaney was in the way." Bela looked sideways at Evi. "You have no idea who Chaney was, have you?"

"I'm afraid not."

"He was the greatest of the great, Evi, a formidable rival if he had not tried to flee the forces of Darkness. I know you think me mad, but if you only saw his films, his every bit part was a mad flight from the dark forces that ensnared us all. He chose to run. He failed."

"What happened to him?"

"He was cast in the role, there was much pre-production publicity, and I sat back and laughed," said Bela. Evi soundlessly moved her chair as far away from him as possible, until her shoulder touched the opposite wall. "Chaney as Dracula was a ridiculous proposition. He was a man who could pull faces and wear makeup to make himself look sinister, but he was no Lord of the Undead—merely a man living in fear of the shadow he had created."

Evi felt herself fidgeting. She knew what must have happened, but Bela's slow, lingering descriptions were too distasteful, and she struggled to keep scribbling her shorthand symbols. "How did you get the role?" she asked curtly.

Bela raised a hand in mild annoyance, as though she were heckling him from the stalls. "The way was opened. The chosen director, Leni, died suddenly from"—he paused—"blood poisoning ... opening the way for Browning to step into the dead man's shoes. Then what do you suppose happened next?"

"Chaney died too?" answered Evi coldly. She could not remember what she had read, but it was so obviously the way the narrative was moving; and she was determined not to give Bela the luxury of enjoying the moment.

"All in good time, my dear," answered Bela, looking alarmingly like Dracula descending the stairs to murder Renfield. "I had to bide my time like you. I worked on a few pictures here and there. *Wild Company*, as the title states, was an interesting diversion. The aptly named *Such Men Are Dangerous* was next. They will never know how right they were to cast me in that one. *Renegades* was a chore, but it passed the time. *Viennese Nights* was a musical, cheerful and bright, my first appearance in the new Technicolor light."

"What happened to Chaney?"

Bela closed his eyes. "You know, you would not be so impatient if you had seen what a great rival this man was. He was such a very great actor. He was a man like me, haunted by his childhood years spent in circuses and freak shows, and by something far darker than that." He turned abruptly to Evi. "You know I went to watch him on set shortly before the disaster struck him? I had to see for myself what he was like, and I was not at all disappointed. He was playing a ventriloquist at a fairground, so movingly I might have shed a tear if I still could. And all the time, the stagehands were whispering their concerns. Chaney was not at all well, they said. And he was so soon to embark upon the role of Dracula."

"You must have been delighted," Evi chimed in, like the voice of conscience.

"My feelings had nothing to do with it; I was destined for that role, remember? And so it happened. I woke up one morning, after weeks of agonising, to the news that Chaney had died. A 'throat cancer'—something lodged in his throat, anyway. It hardly mattered how it had happened. The telegram arrived, and that morning I was in discussions with Browning about the role."

Evi stopped writing and put away her pens and papers, closing the bag with an aggressive click. She was not going to sit and listen to this self-indulgence; she already knew about Bela's meeting with Browning from a book Hugo had lent her before they had argued. She could picture it all without the help of an elderly man trapped in the dreams of his cinematic successes. She knew he had played the part well, waiting on the upstairs landing until the doorbell rang and his servant ushered Browning in.

Bela had counted to three before appearing at the top of the stairs to greet him, striking a suitably dramatic pose. But Bela had been Dracula before and knew the plots and individual scenes better than the director. Browning looked up at the shadowy figure slowly descending the stairs and relaxed visibly, quietly measuring up the man before him for the role that so badly needed to be filled.

Both men knew that this was a screen test in all but name, and Bela played to his audience with every ounce of strength he possessed. "Good morning, my friend," Bela greeted him, standing before Browning in precisely the place in the hall where the late morning light threw the most shadow. "Welcome to my home," he said gravely, extending a hand of friendship to the anxious Browning, who was still reeling with the shock of losing Chaney so soon after the death of Leni. "I hope this will be a fruitful meeting for us both."

In Browning's state of near panic, Bela's calm, dignified presence was all the director needed to see to be convinced that this little-known Hungarian exile could rescue the picture. "You know why I am here, no doubt," said Browning, when the two men had sat down and Bela's servant had poured coffee and withdrawn. "I would like to offer you the role of Dracula. You will be aware of the desperate predicament we are in, and if filming is to commence at all ..."

Bela leant forward with the smile of a physician reassuring a nervous patient. "It is the very least I can do to help an old friend," he said gently, "and indeed, my beloved Universal Studios. My friend, you look terrible."

Browning nodded. "I must admit, my nerves are in pieces," he answered, reaching into his jacket pocket. Bela took out a beautiful silver cigarette case from his own pocket and opened it in front of Browning. He took a cigarette gratefully and let Bela strike a light for him. "There are wild rumours everywhere," he said, taking short, shallow puffs. "Hardly surprising, I suppose, with two men dead like that so suddenly, but there are people claiming a curse on the production."

Bela gave a good-natured laugh, cursing himself for managing to sound villainous when he had meant to keep the tone light. "My dear man, people say all kinds of crazy things. You must pay no heed."

Browning played with the cigarette between his fingers. "You don't believe there could be any truth to it, then?"

Count Dracula, as he was so soon to become, leant forward and touched Browning's trembling wrist. "There now, my dear Browning, you must think nothing of it. A mere coincidence, that is all. A terrible coincidence, but the picture will be a great success, and no one else will get hurt."

The two men drank coffee, the servant appearing just once to take away the empty pot and bring back a fresh one. The coffee was mixed with all Bela's sympathy and reassurance, so convincingly so, that before long they were talking through the prosaic reality of pre-production. They talked amid the swirls of tobacco smoke and Bela's barely supressed excitement.

Through the kaleidoscope lens of many years, Bela once again mislaid the weeks of rehearsals and preparations, those tedious hours of waiting. In his memory, he stepped directly from that room and walked alone down the narrow corridor that led to the set.

The lovely Helen was Mina, with Manners as Harker, and then there was Frye as Dracula's little friend Renfield. Bela stood before them, the Lord of the Undead, savouring the audible hush from the assembled cast and crew.

Bela stared ahead, in character every second, whilst inside he laughed at the thought that they all looked as though they had seen a ghost, not the nobleman from Transylvania in all his grandeur. Even Browning, sitting as director and therefore lord of all he surveyed, was lost for words—Bela took this as a silent genuflection to the real power behind this production. The force that in due course would touch them all, changing them all forever.

An old acquaintance from Bela's Berlin days was the cinematographer—Freund, an inevitable choice, connected to Bela by the horrors of German cinema, who could bring the fear of Bram Stoker's story into every shot, every camera angle, every exposure, every set design. Both men knew why they had been thrown together. They had both learnt their trade in Berlin; they both knew their place in the grander scheme of things. As Freund had helped unleash the Expressionist beasts across Germany, Bela was helping unleash a new beast across America and beyond. As the production moved inexorably towards release and the adulation of the critics, Bela and Freund became the closest of confederates, locked into a pact with Darkness.

Evi would not allow herself to become mesmerised by this tale of posturing actors. "It was a film," she said, the cut-glass vowels shattering the momentary silence. "Were you all in a pact with the devil? The extras too? Did someone make you all sign a contract in your own blood before you started?"

Bela turned to look at her. He so rarely looked at her directly that Evi found herself shuddering involuntarily at the sight of those cold, dark eyes trying so hard to pierce her. "You are a brave woman to mock the powers of Darkness," he said quietly. "Brave ... or foolish."

"Deride and conquer, as my husband used to say," she answered. "What greater insult is there to the powerful than a healthy dose of ridicule?"

Bela continued to stare at her. "You are quite right, of course, though it is hard to see the purpose of insulting the powerful if one wishes to survive. In answer to your question," he added, "if a question indeed it was, we did no such thing. Those of us who had been drawn that way needed to sign no such bond, and the others would not have done so. There was a division, one might say, between those who were doing a job and those who were responding to something more elemental. The cast were a mixture of those who were acting and those who knew this was more than just acting. Helen was the beautiful Mina. She was a woman reluctant to play the part. I sensed that even back then. She had some inkling of the evil she was embracing, I am quite sure."

"But it was just a—"

"If you think it all so preposterous, take the time to look at our scenes together. There was a certain tension between us that was more than theatrical. Then there was Manners, who played the part of Jonathan Harker with such seriousness that, like his character, he fought the Darkness at every turn. Rarely did we speak to each other. I'm fairly sure he thought me the personification of evil by the end of it."

"Artist rivalries are scarcely new ..."

"Evangeline, he *loathed* us all, me and Freund and Browning. No sooner was the shoot completed when he left Hollywood altogether, denouncing it as a false place."

Brilliant man, thought Evi. "I see," she said.

"He was perceptive beyond his understanding," continued Bela, "but also helpless. He may have understood what we were all playing with but could do nothing about it. And then there was Frye, the pathetic little Renfield. He was drawn to the Darkness, just like his character. The spell the film cast had repercussions for all of us, but at the time, all Hollywood seemed to lie at our feet."

"What happened to Browning?"

That question silenced him, if only for a moment. Evi was aware of her own pulsing headache and the yawning quiet from her subject. Bela never found it very easy to talk about other people, but her journalist's instinct told her it was more than self-obsession that made him struggle to find the words. "Oh, Browning. Poor man."

"What happened to him?"

"It was all going so well, you see," said Bela, as though that answered the question. "So effortlessly, as though some unknown force was at work behind the façade of the movie set. But Mephistopheles must have his wages, you see. That hidden force at work is never without a cost, and in the end"—he paused slightly—"someone must pay."

"Bela, what happened to Browning?"

"He fell into a deep depression. He became more and more depressed with each passing day. Whilst I became more and more exultant, he slipped into misery. Perhaps he felt almost redundant, the acting all unfolded so perfectly. It was as if his place had been usurped in a mysterious way, something he could not fully comprehend."

Evi tried to come up with a retort, but no words emerged.

"It must have felt all too strangely perfect for him. His own professional insecurities rose to the surface; Freund and I found ourselves reassuring him daily of his importance to the making of the film." Bela looked back at Evi. "Stop writing, please. Just for a moment, I want you to stop writing and merely listen."

"Why?"

"Please just do as I ask." Evi found it impossible to refuse and put down her pen very deliberately so that he would notice. "Thank you. You see, looking back, I realise that it was at this point that he began to suspect that something was not right, something unusual. He began to drink too much; he missed his old friend, the poor Chaney. He raved about a curse, but no one wanted to listen."

"He was grieving," Evi began. "I know the feeling. He was grieving for his friend, and everything became too much to bear."

"He could just let the cameras roll, Evangeline. As the shoot progressed, Browning would simply sit, transfixed, oblivious at times to what was happening before him. As we moved through the movie's dark passages, he would rip the pages from the script like a man caught up in something beyond his powers of comprehension. *London after Midnight* may have been his first foray into the vampire genre, but it was clear that *this* picture was something different."

"Why won't you let me write this down?" demanded Evi. "I'm a writer! I'm here to take down your story, but if I can't write about it, I may as well not hear it."

"Write the story if you wish," said Bela coldly, "but you will suffer for it if you do."

Evi rose to her feet. Her head no longer throbbed; she was far too taken aback to feel anything other than her own racing pulse. "Are you threatening me?" She had to get out of this room; she should never have sat here meekly listening to the ravings of a madman about curses and darkness. "I have been listening to you and writing about you for weeks. You needn't have allowed me to come in the first place."

Bela stood in front of her, blocking her exit. He was tall, an imposing presence even in the withered state of old age, and Evi was forced to step back to avoid colliding with him. "I am not threatening you; I am warning you."

"That's what a gangster says before breaking a man's arm." She stepped to the side, but his countenance seemed to fill the room. "Will you please let me pass?"

"I mean it, Evangeline. I am not threatening you," he said, placing a hand on her shoulder. "Please sit down. I assure you, I would not dream of hurting you."

"Why did you say I would suffer?" she demanded, unwilling to yield. "That's a dreadful thing to say."

"Please."

Evi relented at the sound of his pleading voice and let him propel her gently back into her chair. "Who are you to say I *will* suffer? You know nothing."

Bela stood before her, and she was certain he was using his imposing figure to force her attention. "Forgive me; I know you have suffered. I know you are suffering," he said haltingly, "but you must understand how serious this is. These are not the ravings of an old man—I know that's what you are thinking. If you expose the Darkness, it will come for you."

"I am not afraid of ghosts," said Evi, tonelessly. "I've been living with them for years. Tell me what I came here to learn about, and I will choose what I commit to paper."

Bela sighed wearily, stepping back from her and sitting down without once turning his back on her. "Brave or foolish," he said, clasping his bony hands in front of him. "What if I were to tell you that poor Browning suffered from nerves? That was the story put around the set, but

Freund and I knew better. What Freund had heard was that Browning was scared that something—in his words—inhuman was being created, something more than just a motion picture, something so macabre that he did not want to be part of it. We went to see him, and do you know what we found?"

"I've a feeling you're going to tell me," Evi retorted, but confusion was making her even more acerbic than usual.

"We found a man possessed, like some lunatic awaiting a ship from the Balkans to arrive and unload its hidden cargo. A man ready to bare his soul."

Evi did her level best to be riveted. "I see."

"He admitted to us that he had started to have nightmares, not just periodically but all night, and almost every night just after the production had started. I tried to joke that it was his own silly fault for being buried alive as part of a circus act when he was younger, but Freund and I had to work very hard to persuade him to accelerate the pace of the shoot. We could not risk our masterpiece being abandoned by a nervous director. Perhaps, we suggested to him, we could shoot it at night. Such a restful time to make a film ..."

"At *night*?"

"Oh, Browning quickly warmed to the idea, since he was not sleeping anyway. A time of quiet, we reassured him, nothing and no one to disturb us in our work, and then, finally, he could rest, we all could rest." Bela laughed as though Browning's breakdown were a private joke he still savoured. "I practically had to hypnotise him: 'Look into my eyes, Browning ... you are going to rest, and stop your fretting about this production, all this needless anxiety, so unnecessary ... Remember the time you were driving that car, such a terrible accident, such a tragedy for those two actors and their families ... Now desist from this needless worry. We don't want any more tragedy in our lives, do we? We are here to help you, Freund and I, so helpful, yes, so very helpful ...'"

Evi sat up straight. "Accident? Just a minute, what accident?"

Bela gave her a dismissive wave. "Everyone in Hollywood knew about it. Browning was tormented by the memory, and it helped. The filming continued. I could stay in that studio, in the realm of the Undead, and walk into my native land. I hardly needed to act; the Darkness simply flowed out of me, captured by the camera to be let loose on an unsuspecting world."

Evi stared down at her hands in silence until she was sure Bela had finished. "It was a film," she said, but even she had to admit it sounded lame. "It was just a silly, spooky film with shadows and pretend castles and pretend monsters. A splendid success, of course, but you must have known it would be."

"Actually, Evangeline, it was quite a gamble," said Bela, "but you know so little of the industry that perhaps you would not understand. In America, it was the first time a horror film had been made that was not funny or laughing at itself in some way. We could not be sure what audiences would make of it. But they screamed and fainted, transfixed by Jonathan Harker making his way from London fog to the eternal darkness of the Carpathians. They came to watch it in the thousands upon thousands. People do enjoy being frightened."

"And you became a star. Universal Studios offered you a contract."

"Naturally. I was what they call a 'hot talent' then." Bela fidgeted in his chair. It ought to have been his proudest moment, but he looked surprisingly desolate. "Everything was quite perfect," he said. "I was a star, the movie a sensation; and my old friend Murnau from Berlin days appeared on the scene. Freund, Murnau, and I could begin plotting again, just like old times."

Evi waited for Bela to continue, but he sank into the old wearisome silence she so remembered. She could hear an insect of some kind whining in a corner of the window, trapped between the glass and the curtain as though wondering what evil trick had been played that it appeared both free and caught perpetually by some invisible force. "Mr Lugosi?" she asked finally. "Would you like me to leave?"

Bela did not stir. Evi took the hint and began packing her things away, knowing that it would be easier when he was in a mood like this to slip away quietly. "You will come back, won't you?" he said quietly. "Promise you will return again next week."

"Do you want me to?" asked Evi, standing before him, bag slung over one shoulder. "I could end it here if you prefer. The rise of Bela Lugosi. I'm sure Mr Goldberg will be satisfied with that, and he can move me on to the next job."

"I do not wish that."

"You do not wish to talk about your own decline; I can sense it. You don't have to."

Bela reached up and took her hand. His increasingly poor circulation rendered his grip so cold, she wanted nothing more than to pull away from him, but there was something pathetic about him. Evi was aware of his frailty and age, though age was almost a euphemism. He looked to her like a man who had seen centuries unfolding before his eyes and been weighed down by the horror of the world's many tragedies. "Please come back," he said. "Do not wait a week. I fear that I do not have long before I must pay my dues, as my American friends say."

Evi felt her hand begin to tremble. "Mr Lugosi, I have not been well."

Bela nodded. "I know you have been unwell," he said. "You are surrounded by a shadow of sadness. You have been since I first met you, but it deepens."

Evi pulled herself away as sharply as she could, but she was visibly shaking now. "My sadness is my own. I do not want to cause you any."

"You could not cause me any such thing," he said warmly, reaching out for her again. She hesitated before placing her hand in his again. She could not bear to upset the man, for all her misgivings about him. "And I must have your company again. There is something I have to tell you, whether you choose to write about it or not."

"An exclusive?" she tried to jest, but she simply sounded as nervous as she felt.

"A secret. Please promise you'll come."

12

Is there anyone on this earth who is not encouraged by a tale of happiness and success? Here was Bela Lugosi at the height of his fame, the talk of Hollywood, a man his adopted homeland would have called a *movie star*. It was time to glory in it all—the exclusive restaurants that always had a table available for him when he stepped through the door; the excitable fans who approached him in the street, begging him to sign autograph books and to have photographs taken with them; the mail bags bulging with fan letters from audiences all over the world. Not that Bela had to trouble himself with these; the studio publicity department had the pleasure of sifting through the prose and poetry of the besotted, the sycophantic, and the politely adoring. The City of Angels was now at his feet. He could walk its streets knowing that it was his in all but name—the possession of the possessed?

This new prince of Hollywood sat at his bureau, staring fixedly at one of the letters the studio had sent on to him. The light of day was slowly dying all around him, but he could not find the energy to get up and switch on the light. It hardly mattered; he felt safer in the company of his own shadow. The studio must have realised that the letter was of a personal nature just from the stamp, but Bela had recognised the neat, prim handwriting immediately.

Vilma. A letter from the neverland of Bela's past meant to pierce his heart with remorse. For an age, Bela had held the unopened envelope in his hands, turning it over and over, afraid of what might be lurking in wait for him when his paper knife sliced it open and released the message inside. He thought of Vilma sitting at the kitchen table, the suffocating silence of that place disturbed only by the slow scratch of the pen defiling the thin, cheap notepaper with news of the family's troubles. *I have heard that you are famous now, brother. I hope now that you have the glory you have always craved.* Oh, the reproach! A rebuke to a conceited brother who abandoned his poor family in pursuit of glory! *Mother is dead. She called for you until her last breath, dreaming that you would return to her side before it was too late.*

Why the paralysis? Bela wondered. Was it really guilt for walking out of that very same kitchen all those years ago without kissing his mother good-bye and treating her—as he had treated his entire family—as a tiresome irrelevance to be quietly forgotten? Or worse, thought Bela, was he feeling overwhelmed with guilt because he did not care in the slightest that his mother was dead? Bela was an actor, after all, and he understood the importance of plot and character to the success of a story. The remorseful son made for a good character; his memory of a faraway childhood and the pivotal moment when the naughty little boy walked away from his home without a backward glance— now *that* made for a beautiful plot device. And this was the moment the rich, famous man is brought to his senses, when the whole, stunning edifice of the material world he had created for himself comes crashing down around him, and he understands the harm he has done to those who had loved and nurtured him. The next stage in the unfolding of the plot would be the return home, the tearful reunion, and the wistful scene at the humble family hearth.

Father still asks for you. I beg of you, dear brother, please write. It cannot be too much trouble for you to write a letter. Father grows so old and frail, I cannot say that he has much time left in this sad world. It would mean so much to him. If nothing else, he could die in peace. Do not deny him that comfort, I beg you.

Bela laughed softly to himself, curling the flimsy letter into a thin roll. He was the Prince of Horror; he would be thoroughly miscast as a remorseful son drawn back to his peasant roots, and Vilma's letter was not so much a plot device as a momentarily unsettlingly digression. He used the roll of paper to light his next cigar and walked out into the welcoming night.

Evi always felt shades of the prison house beginning to close about her as she stepped into Goldberg's office. As editors went, he was not really the worst of the bunch, hardly a jailor by personality. If anything, he reminded Evi rather more of a self-important headmaster, whose only contribution to the smooth running of his school is always to be pointlessly unpleasant to anyone smaller or weaker than he. Today, however, Evi could sense that he was in a good mood, and, as she sat down, she felt herself relax, as far as she was ever capable of relaxing.

"Not bad," he said, his swollen head bowed over her work. "The letter story adds a nice touch. And the ladies'll love the romance with Lillian." He spread out Evi's type-written pages on the desk in front of him and began to read, an act that immediately caused Evi to tense up. Goldberg had the inexcusable habit of putting on what he imagined to be a posh English accent when he was reading her work aloud, and he was at his worst that afternoon.

The very next day a young woman by the name of Lillian appeared. She had come to be interviewed for the post of Bela Lugosi's secretary. Young and beautiful, the minute she walked into the drawing room of the great man, she became a wonderful distraction from the dark clouds that were already threatening Bela Lugosi's promising career. As the days and weeks flew by with her, Bela Lugosi felt the first stirrings of love he had ever felt for a woman.

Lillian had no money and no connections, and to begin with, she responded to her employer's overtures with prim politeness. Her youth may have made her wary of him, but Bela Lugosi's love for Lillian grew stronger day by day. With the box office failure of *Murders in the Rue Morgue* and the subsequent loss of his contract with Universal, who blamed him for the failure of the picture, it was clear Lillian was becoming Bela's only light in the darkness that was already threatening to engulf him. She comforted him as his career began to suffer, and they celebrated their wedding as the drapes were being prepared for Bela Lugosi's premature exit from Hollywood. His marriage to a woman thirty years his junior was to be Bela Lugosi's happiest and most enduring union.

"Not bad at all," concluded Mr Goldberg, reverting to his own drawling tone. "Everyone loves a lover, true love never dies ... well, it did in this case. You're only one instalment away from the end."

Evi cleared her throat awkwardly, which immediately caused the smile to disappear from Goldberg's face; he could sense resistance coming. "I wonder whether I might stop there? It's such a nice way to end the story. A happy marriage, happily ever after—you know the type of thing. Every good story ends so."

"Except that it didn't, did it?" said Goldberg, looking quizzically in Evi's direction. "The story didn't end there! Anyway, I thought you'd be pleased by the prospect of another fee. Look, the man's life fell apart. He passed up a dream role as Frankenstein and opened the door to Karloff. Play it as if Karloff were the rival who made the world forget old Bela."

Evi glanced down at her hands, searching for a response. It was always difficult to construct an argument that involved making irrelevant points to ignore the real problem. "I suppose I just thought readers would prefer it that way. After all, Dracula is what everyone remembers Lugosi for. It would make a perfect conclusion—Bela in his black cape, marrying a beautiful young woman."

Goldberg narrowed his eyes. "I want the final decline, Evi. I want that. I want every last, sordid, lousy detail. Readers may like a love story, but they like a fall from grace even more; nothing beats that. Give me the drink, the drugs, the poverty; I want it all. Let me see him out of work, making a fool of himself doing bit parts in movies he was ashamed of and that no one watched. Let me read about the lovely Lillian leaving him after years of putting up with the bitter old man. Give me loneliness, his broken dreams. You get the gist?"

Evi stood up slowly. "I had better get to work, then," she said blandly. "I'm sure I can find enough misery in Lugosi's later life to please even you."

"Wednesday at two. Not a minute later."

How hard would it have been to say no to him? raged Evi, stamping her way along the pavement as though every slab of concrete was her editor's smug, sneering, fat face. The only person she was truly angry with was herself, as always. It was easy to blame other people for her own mistakes, and it was a reflex she fell into all the time. She could blame Goldberg for being the most heartless editor on the planet, manipulating a woman weakened by poverty and the problem he had managed to find out about; she could blame her mother for being a vicious bully who broke her will to resist anything and anyone who came after her; she could even blame Christy in her darkest hours, blame him for being a soldier, blame him for getting captured, for getting killed. If he had not been a soldier, if he had not gone to Korea, if he had not fallen into enemy hands ... But it was impossible to avoid the biggest culprit of all. If she had not let herself down, if she had picked herself up off the floor and gotten on with life just as so many war widows had been forced to do, she would never have found herself a jobbing writer, forced to consult with creatures of darkness who sapped all her remaining energies and will to live.

Evi decided to go straight to Lugosi's house, knowing that if she went home first, she would find some reason not to go today. It was better to get it over with, to hear this secret he seemed so desperate to tell her. If she worked quickly enough, she might even get the instalment written tomorrow, and then she could forget about it all. She might even scavenge a harmless couple of features to give Goldberg along with the final instalment. Yes, she would go to Lugosi now. *I'll get the damned article finished*, she cursed silently.

Approaching the front door, she wondered what about the house was unsettling her so much. It was a perfectly ordinary home, superficially at least. It may not have been as grand and luxurious as the places Bela had called home at the height of his fame, and like many homes inhabited by very elderly people who cannot afford to pay for outside assistance, the house was rather tumbledown and untidy. Standing at the front gate, Evi for the first time noticed the telltale signs of decay all around her: the peeled black paint on a gate that squeaked maddeningly for want of a little oil; the front yard overgrown with weeds; the accumulated rubbish that had blown in from the street over a period of time. Had it really been so bad on the last occasion she had visited? She was sure she could not remember it that way, but Evi had felt so strange recently that she mistrusted her powers of observation. Yes, it had always been a mess: the front walk had always been cracked, with strands of green fur breaking through like the signs of a hideous disease; the front entryway had always looked grimy and unwelcoming.

The moment Evi put her hand on the door, it began to open. Lugosi's wife must have failed to close it properly the last time she left. She was pretty sure Lugosi never ventured from the place. Instead of walking in without being welcomed, she thought, she should turn around and leave, find Hugo and patch things up with him, and ask him to come back with her. That was the crazy thing about horror stories: the heroes and heroines would find themselves stepping into terrifying situations, and rather than doing the normal thing—leaving, then coming back with company—they always went ahead and came to some horrendous end, set upon by a gang of demented skeletons.

Pull yourself together, Evi commanded herself, giving the door a shove and stepping inside, standing still in the hallway to let her eyes grow accustomed to the darkness. That was why the hero never turned back to get company, she thought; even in the fantasy world of film, he would have that prosaic sense that he jolly well ought to get on with things and stop letting his imagination run away with him. And curiosity was a more powerful force than she had imagined. "Mr Lugosi?" she called from the foot of the stairs. "It's Evangeline. May I come up?"

Evi felt her imagination start to play tricks. What if the man has died whilst his wife is out? He did seem so old and frail, rather sickly. Perhaps she should not further disturb his peace. But he had been so definite about wanting to see her again. *Go back, and don't come back alone,* said the voice of reason. Evi climbed the stairs, occasionally stumbling over the narrow, uneven steps.

By the time she had entered the upper corridor, Evi was almost convinced that she would throw open the door to Bela's room and find a dead body. This world of horror was playing havoc with her mind. She tried to imagine Hugo laughing at her, but she was still so angry with him that the very thought of him made Evi's pulse race, and for entirely the wrong reasons.

She tried to compose herself. "Mr Lugosi?" she called quietly from outside his door. There was no light streaming out from under the door, but of course, she did not expect there to be. She dismissed the gnawing sense of anxiety creeping over her before placing her hand on the doorknob. She nudged it open.

Breathing deeply, Evi looked into the room. It was exactly as it always was when Evi went to visit—dark, dour, and wholly unwelcoming—but, to her relief, there was Bela sitting in his usual place. The chair was turned away from the door, and his head was slumped forward in sleep. *Please don't be dead*, she thought, walking round on tiptoe to face him as though she might wake him from his eternal slumbers.

Bela looked almost like a child. His head lay upon his folded arms, which rested on the softly upholstered arm of the chair, with his legs curled up on the seat. He looked as if he were huddled up to shelter himself from the cold, not so much like a child but almost like an infant, limbs not yet unfolded, eyes still waiting to open and view the world. Evi swallowed hard and reached forward, placing a hand on his shoulder. "Wake up," she said softly, giving him a gentle nudge. He did not stir. "Mr Lugosi, it's Evi."

When the huddled body before her still refused to move, Evi braced herself and slipped her fingers under his collar, pressing them against his neck to check for a pulse. But for the coldness of his skin, there was nothing to feel, no reassuring rhythm of life under her fingertips. She felt her own heart thumping, and moved her hand a little, suspecting that she had the position wrong.

A split second later, she was staggering back, a scream frozen in her throat. Bela had moved so quickly and with such violence that Evi was not immediately sure what had happened; she simply found herself falling back onto the floor, her head roaring with pain, as though she had been electrocuted. Her hand went to the side of her face, but in her confusion she still could not register what had happened, just that she was lying on the floor of a familiar, dark room, staring directly into the piercing glare of a face that had struck terror into the hearts of cinema audiences all over the world. Here was Dracula standing over her, very much alive and perhaps as frightened as she was, having woken up to find that a person had crept into his house and was holding him by the throat.

"I'm sorry!" Evi stammered, but she could not lift herself off the floor. "It's me; it's Evangeline. I thought ... I thought you were dead."

Bela continued to glare at her, but Evi sensed that he was looking straight through her. There was no recognition in his face at all. "Who are you?" demanded a voice so enraged that Evi stopped trying to get up out of sheer panic. "What do you think you're doing?"

"Please," whispered Evi, "it's me; it's Evangeline. You wanted me to come and see you." It was no good; the words were being strangled out of her. He had reached forward and taken hold of her hand, quite possibly to help her to her feet, but Evi felt her knuckles being squeezed together. "Please, I was trying to help you."

"Why did you touch me?" asked the hate-filled face looking fixedly at her. It was one of those sights that would keep her awake at night, assuming she got out of the room alive. Evi felt her eyes becoming hot with tears. She saw the room blurring and rippling around her; she could no longer feel the effects of her fall or the sensation of a human hand crushing hers; the intense pressure he was exerting felt more as though icy-cold metal were being tightened around her fingers. She had blundered into a trap laid for her by this monster she had awakened, and she opened her mouth to scream; but she made not a sound.

Bela was no longer holding her, but Evi could not move. The blow to her face must have been worse than she thought, or perhaps she had struck her head against the floor as she tumbled backwards; in any case, Evi was losing all sense of where she was. There was a man standing over her, and in her dazed state, it was as if the demon of a horror film had walked directly out of the screen and dragged her into that monochrome world of shadows and cobwebs and winding staircases. She knew it was only her fear that was holding her down, but Evi felt as though death had crept over her. Her blood seemed to have frozen in her veins. In spite of the hot weather, she started shivering with the cold.

"I knew you would come," said Bela, but even his voice did not sound entirely like his own. "Women are so inquisitive. You knew it would be a mistake to return. Yet you could not help yourself. Yes, I knew you would come back."

She closed her eyes like a little girl struggling to free herself from a nightmare. "I had to finish the story," she said desperately. "My editor, Mr Goldberg, you know ... He wanted me to find ... to get ... the story of your ... after *Dracula* ... you know ... what happened ... what went wrong ... I'm sorry ... I'm so sorry ... I do want to end it ..."

She could hear a horrible, rasping noise like metal grating against metal, and she knew he was laughing at her, but she still could not open her eyes. "You were afraid, were you not? You should not be afraid to write about a man's broken dreams. Every single life that has ever run its course has been a life of broken dreams. None of us ever gains what he wishes from this world. Look at you. Your little dreams, those of a girl: a husband, beautiful children, the happy family with a garden and a picket fence. Well, you, too, failed."

"Don't," she said, but tears forced her to open her eyes. "I don't care anymore—about the story, I mean. I need to leave." Evi placed the damp palms of her hands on the filthy floor and attempted to push herself up. Her body felt weak and heavy, as though she were drunk. *I'm sober*, she thought. *Yes, I'm stone-cold sober.*

"You do not move until I tell you to," said Bela tonelessly. "Are you still frightened?"

Evi nodded. The effort of looking directly at Bela was squeezing the remaining energy out of her. "Yes."

"Good. You are a clever woman; you should be frightened. Perhaps for the first time you understand something of what is happening."

It was going to sound pathetic, but she could not help saying it: "Please don't hurt me. I was only doing my job. I'm a reporter, you know; I write for ..."

Bela took a step closer to her, which started her shivering again. "You will not believe what I tell you now; but before you leave—and you will leave—I will tell you something, yes, *something* that will make you believe. Now, Listen!"

Bela worried that for all eternity he would be haunted by the events of that night. It should have been an entertaining evening, enjoying a late supper at Brown Derby whilst discussing the role of the monster in the movie *Frankenstein*. He felt worse than ambivalent about the role—all those nuts and bolts and shots of electricity, the horror so obvious, so vulgar compared with Mary Shelley's heartbreaking novel of the man who played God. It did not help Bela's attitude to the project that he detested Whale, the man down to direct—an odd Englishman, a dabbler in things he clearly knew nothing of, just another film-making fool. Whale did not know what he was getting into, though that might have been just as well for him.

As soon as he arrived home, Bela dismissed the servants, who had awaited his return, and retired to his drawing room to sit by the fire and collect his thoughts over one final cigar. He knew he needed a little solitude before bed or he would never sleep, his head full of the evening's discussions. Except that he was not alone. Someone was seated in his favourite armchair, awaiting his company.

The room was poorly lit, but there was no mistaking who it was. Worse, Bela was aware of a certain lack of surprise on his own part, as though he had known all day that this encounter would happen before the clock chimed midnight. The visitor noted his entry into the room without moving or looking round, gesturing to the actor to sit. It had a voice, slow, halting, and strangely familiar, like the voice of a childhood invisible friend who all of a sudden had come to life. It was the voice he had imagined he would hear all those years ago when his father had broken up his nighttime séance.

"You know who I am, then?" said the voice as Bela pulled up a chair and sat opposite his visitor, positioning himself at a slight angle to avoid looking directly at it. "There is really no cause for alarm. I am very happy with our success. Really I am. I knew it would be a success, of course, but it is pleasing nonetheless." Bela intended to answer but found it impossible to respond. "It is hoped that what *Nosferatu* has done for Germany may now be repeated throughout this New World with *Dracula*. And then there must be others, of course—similar, shall we say, 'projects'. In fact, there must be many more."

It was giving words to the long-held disquieting thought that had haunted Bela ever since his days in the German horror industry. There was some dark force behind him, behind his work. It had been shadowing his every move.

"What is your name?" Bela asked, staring into the fire, which felt so sinister now in the presence of this companion without a name, without a face to speak of.

"There will be more films, a celluloid empire. So much so, we shall fill the world with darkness. I know you. And I know also you can do this for me. Remember, I chose you; you did not choose me."

Bela stared ever more fixedly into the fire, letting the savage orange flames hypnotise him as they tore at a helpless log and sent it plunging down into the inferno. He could feel a strange thrill juddering through his body, a sense of excitement and power mingled with a hint of threat. He could feel it looking at him, this thing so horrible. Bela could never have described it if his life—if his soul—had depended on it. "In the end, every bargain has to be honoured," it said softly. "I'm sure you'll agree. And, in any event, your gifts are not freely given."

Bela rose to his feet, shaking, but he was alone already. The only sound was the spluttering of the fire slowly burning out. He had been visited by the only director he had ever truly had in his long career, a director who had given him parts, given him lines to speak and acts to perform, but who was already preparing the curtain to fall on this personal production of *Faustus*. He had risen, and he might rise still further; but now he knew he would fall. He would be destroyed. The devil always claimed his own. There could be no other outcome.

Ah, Faustus,
Now hast thou but one bare hour to live,
And then thou must be damn'd perpetually!
Stand still, you ever-moving spheres of heaven,
That time may cease, and midnight never come ...

Bela thought he heard laughter somewhere in the room—a pitiless, mocking echo of a laugh that would hiss through his head again and again for the rest of his days. This was a prison of his own making. How had he come to this? He knew he was trapped. He sat through the long, still watches of the night. It was the worst sense of desolation he had ever known. Perhaps this was what hell felt like? Eternal emptiness. Nothing was any different, and the world went on its merry way, unaware of his imprisonment; but things had changed—or rather, the darkness was now visible, the path ahead was clear. Bela felt his eyes growing heavy as he stared at the cold, empty grate, and then, somehow, his eyes closed and he slept.

There are some nightmares that drift away to nothing in the welcoming light of the morning, but this was to be of a different order. Bela's nightmare would never leave him. He awoke, feeling stiff and sickly after a few hours' fitful sleep in a chair. There was the same sense of emptiness hanging over him. When he made it to the breakfast table, he sat alone. The servants sensed his mood and said nothing, too fearful to ask. He looked miserable, sat brooding over his coffee. Then one of the servants anxiously brought him the morning paper. Bela did not have the energy to look at it, but continued to stare into his still-full cup.

The debt must be paid. Those words …

Then, out of the corner of his eye, Bela saw it. A headline emblazoned across the front of the newspaper in vast, black, heavy print like the etching on a tombstone: MURNAU DEAD. He could not move. He looked away and then back, all the time trying not to turn his head. He did not need to read any more. Bela picked up and then set down his coffee cup before it fell from his hands. He fought the sensation of panic slowly creeping over him—that tight, gripping fear in his stomach, the cold sweat now breaking out all over his back. With stiff, cold hands, he grabbed the corner of the newspaper. With desperation he drew it towards him, forcing himself to look down at the words upon the page. A car crash, then; Murnau's hired Rolls Royce had crashed into an electricity pole. So that was the method, the method used to pay the debt. In Bela's confusion, his mind raced back to his first meeting with Murnau in Berlin, to the making of *Nosferatu* twelve years before. So now Murnau had paid for it with his own flesh and blood. With his soul. Bela's nocturnal visitor was a man of his word. Yes, that much was true, whatever else he was … And Bela? Nothing more than a condemned man, if one granted a long, scenic walk to the scaffold.

"I had to escape the Darkness!" shouted Bela. "I knew that creature would make me pay. My next picture was a signal to anyone who knew that I was already the walking dead: *White Zombie.* That was what I had become, a zombie, a tool in demonic hands!"

Evi did not flinch when Bela raised his voice, rather like a defeated boxer who is too punch-drunk to notice yet another blow when it is coming. At some point during these rantings and ravings, she had found—or been granted—the strength to lift herself up just a little before sitting on the floor. Her back resting now against the wall, she let him tell his bizarre tale of nighttime visitors and Faustian pacts. What? The sad career decline that followed had been caused by a desperate desire to escape the Darkness?

"I had to escape, do you understand? I had to flee this death trap I had built for myself, even if it meant the end of my career!"

Evi said nothing. She was sure she had read that Bela Lugosi's career had declined for other reasons, like booze and pills. According to Karloff, as Hugo had pointed out, it was Bela's unwillingness to master the English language sufficiently that hampered his career. He was typecast with a mid-European accent. Hugo had said that critics put it down to his being a "one-film star"; there have been plenty of those here in Hollywood. Or, she had snapped to Hugo, was it that audience tastes change—away from the absurdity of hammy horror movies? Oh, let Bela say whatever he wanted, she thought. So this was the secret he had been waiting to tell her, that he had not succumbed to the miserable fate of every other Hollywood has-been. No, he had fought a disastrous battle to save his soul from the forces that had given him that fame in the first place. It scarcely mattered now what a sad, sick old man believed—if she could only get out of this infernal room.

"I wanted to escape," said Bela, and now he sounded almost pleading. Evi risked making eye contact with him and immediately regretted it. Just looking at him seemed to cause her blood pressure to rise. She clutched her head, willing herself not to faint. "I sabotaged my own career, my art, my being, simply to escape. The critics said I became a parody—me! It was the devil; it was he I mocked. You know, the devil hates to be mocked! And it is also said you come to hate that which you fear ... I thought, let me turn Dracula into a joke, let me make the world laugh at the count, and his fellow monsters creeping about in the shadows."

"Is that your secret?" Evi answered, but her voice did not seem to be hers any longer. "Is that what I am to write?"

Bela got down on his knees at Evi's side, causing her to start shaking again. She closed her eyes involuntarily but felt his glacial touch upon her skin. His skeletal fingers wrapped themselves around her wrist in what was supposed to be reassurance, but the shudder of a scream lodged itself in her throat.

A split second later and he was on his feet again, backing away from her as though she had spat at him. Evi's hands went instinctively to her throat, and she touched once more the Miraculous Medal hung around her neck. "My secret stares at you, and yet you will not *see it!*" roared Bela. "You will not see it, but *you will!* You *will* understand what I am! Up! Get to your feet!"

Evi pressed her hands against the wall behind her to force herself up, terrified that Bela would attempt to help her up. "I have to leave," she said as firmly as she could. "I shall be missed ... Mr Goldberg says ..."

"You think I am a madman," said Bela, as though she had not spoken. "And why should you not think that? When you leave this room, believe me, you will question your very sanity."

Evi watched with a certain relief as Bela seated himself back in his chair, a gesture that seemed to take them both back to the way things had been between them when she had been just a writer and he another faded movie star with a story to tell. He gestured for her to sit down, and she sat near the curtained window, reaching out instinctively for her bag. She realised it was some feet away, where she had dropped it as she fell. She knew, though, that he did not intend her to write anything down. "I'm listening," she said.

"You will not forget anything I tell you," Bela answered. "I know you do not believe a word. But I have told you. I need prove nothing to you. There is a man vying for your attention, and he will come to claim you."

"Hugo's not—"

"I tell you, he comes for you. He knows, he knows more than he tells. Your husband, your dear husband died in battle."

Evi winced. "No, you're wrong. He was a prisoner; he died in captivity. I do not know how he died, but I know he was a prisoner."

"Battles are fought everywhere, even in the prison camp. Remember, I, too, was a soldier. I know better than you. Your husband was a warrior for the Truth, just as I became a foot soldier for the Darkness."

"Look, he died in a prison camp!" Evi would have shouted if she had dared, but she could feel tears rising in her throat. She had to put a stop to this nonsensical talk. "However it was, he died. It was all pointless. The war was already over for him; he had done his fighting. Perhaps he died of some disease—starvation, maybe. I will never know for certain, but he died a prisoner."

"Your husband was martyred," said Bela slowly. "He died a terrible, and a glorious, death."

"He was—"

"He died like his master, exactly like him. He would not submit to the Darkness. Your husband and I are opposites. Yes, in almost every way, we fight on different sides of an invisible war. That is why I know how he died. That is why you were sent to me. Your husband still protects you, even from beyond the grave. I cannot harm you."

"Do you want to?"

"A poor question. I have no will left—no will of my own, that is." Bela looked steadily at Evi, and she found it impossible to look away from that wan, cadaverous face. She studied his face more closely than ever before. He looked so desperately thin; his cheeks bore the sunken look of a man in his death throes; every bone, every sharp line of his skull seemed to be visible; he was like some mediaeval memento mori. "You may go now," he said simply, as though dismissing a servant. "Go!"

Evi needed no further instruction. She crossed the room, picked up her bag without stopping, and went towards the door. Only when she stood in the doorway did she turn around. She looked back at her companion, but Bela's chair faced away from the door. She could no longer see his face. "Good-bye, Mr Lugosi," she said, trying to be as formal as she could. "I will not forget ... I mean, I shall remember everything you told me."

She hurried from the premises, almost running. Just a few minutes to cross the landing, then down the dark, uneven staircase, back across the final stretch of corridor, and then to daylight, blessed daylight. That claustrophobic little house, unloved, untended for so many years, was now some sort of prison to her. She knew she could never return there. If she had to make up the final instalment of the wretched assignment, she would fabricate a final meeting. No, she was not going back there. *No, not going back, not ever*, she spoke to herself over and over. But as she paused for breath in the street outside and looked back at the house to prove to herself that she had really escaped, suddenly it struck Evi: Bela had never intended for her to return.

13

It was all Bela's fault that Evi could not work or sleep. Ridiculous man that he was, he had scared the life out of her, practically knocked her out, and then insulted her intelligence with that ludicrous tale.

Evi lay in bed, her heart racing every time she heard the slightest sound: the creak of a warped floorboard, the tick of the clock, the usually reassuring rumble of the water pipes. She had felt so frightened when darkness had fallen that she had been unable to switch off her bedside lamp, but the light seemed only to draw her eyes to every innocuous shadow in the room. She felt sweat gathering at her temples. Once more, she was a little girl afraid of the dark, afraid of the monster under the bed, afraid of the bogeyman. Her mother had warned her: it was coming to get her for being so disobedient. Let it stop, she thought. She was behaving like an imbecile, and it was all Bela's fault.

Evi's fingers strayed to the tender area at the side of her face. Now that the bruising was coming out, it hurt abominably, offering a grim reminder that the events of the day had actually happened. Everything else was such nonsense. If Christy had been protecting her from beyond the grave as Bela claimed, Evi liked to think he might have prevented her from getting thumped by a panic-stricken old man who had thought she was trying to kill him.

I need something to drink, she thought, *or I'm going to go mad*. The urge for alcohol was feeding Evi's panic almost as much as the horror of what had happened, but she felt too overwhelmed by events to move from her bed. What on earth had been wrong with her all day? It must have been a fanciful imagination, but she still could not make any sense of the paralysis that had overtaken her in that room. There were so many possible explanations: she had been so shocked by the prospect that Bela was dead, coupled by his sudden attack on her, that it had put her in a catatonic state (she had heard that a severe shock sometimes does this); the force of the blow—which had been considerable—had left her mildly concussed; or she had genuinely been forced into some kind of enchantment, trapped in the web Bela had spun so skilfully for her, from which her only escape was with his permission.

She wanted Christy to laugh at her; she needed his presence to turn this nightmare into a joke, because the *real* horror story remained the world she was living in without him. Perhaps that was all this was about in the end, this absurd wallowing in the macabre. This was why audiences had flocked to watch *Dracula*: the shadowy corridors and vampire brides of *Dracula* provided such a perfect escape from the horror story of the Depression, with its hunger and its cardboard cities and its dirty barefoot children. No clatter of chains and coffin lids could strike terror into the heart of a grown man like the sound of the bailiffs' hammering on the door.

Your husband was martyred. He died a terrible, and a glorious, death ... Evi was beginning to wonder whether that exchange had been the work of her tortured imagination, just like everything else.

Bela Lugosi. If she had not imagined it all, perhaps he was the dreamer? It might have been easier for Bela to weave such a story around himself: the great actor possessed by the Darkness, visited by ghostly creatures, part of some vast, devilish conspiracy to drag the world into the hell of war, mechanised slaughter, and the worship of death. Anything had to be better than imprisonment in the dungeon of B movies and budget serials, the humiliation of being forced to accept any useless bit part in order to support his young family. Was there any death more excruciating for an actor than the slow suffocation by Hollywood's very own Poverty Row, those soulless film factories where actors and producers came to die professionally: the endless slide down the casting list, from mad doctor to mad doctor's mad assistant, to mad gardener; the final death throes of obscurity; and finally, self-parody, dressed in false teeth and gorilla costumes? And all of this lived out in the shadow of Bela's English rival, the ubiquitous Boris Karloff, who could do no wrong in Hollywood and never would. Death by failure, death by broken dreams. Death … death … death …

She wanted to scream.

She let the swooning, dizzying unconsciousness claim her, clutching the damp bedclothes as the room lurched and spun.

This time, Evi sensed that she had arrived too late. She stood in what looked like a parade ground, but instead of walking among rows and rows of weary prisoners, she watched in confusion at a scrum of men as they rushed forwards, kicking up a cloud of dust in their wake. They shouted savagely at the tops of their voices as they were beaten back by the guards; they were men halfway to open revolt, and only a sudden volley of gunfire forced them to scatter. With the invincibility of a dreamer, Evi stood and watched as the angry mob were broken up and subdued. She saw men marched out of sight, their hands tied behind their backs, and she looked desperately for Christy. If there was trouble here, Evi knew from experience that Christy must be somewhere close, but she could not see him among the men being taken away.

Christy was the cause of this, she was certain. If a group of men had gone into mutiny against their captors, he would be among the ringleaders, and he would be the first against the wall. "Christy!" she called, but no head turned to face her, and that nagging sense of being too late returned. "Christopher!" Perhaps he had already been taken away, and these men were the remnant of a bigger battle she had missed. But in her other dreams, Evi was sure she remembered him standing in this place, set a little apart but very definitely in the company of others.

That was when she saw him. A few yards from where Evi was standing, a figure lay on his back in the dust, his arms outstretched in death like a macabre baroque crucifix. In her confusion, Evi could not recall how he had come to be so close to her or how she even knew he was her husband. He was barely recognisable as a man, let alone a man who had been her lover and adored companion in some other life they had shared together. Christy's face was so bruised and bloodied, it took the greatest possible effort to look at him; but when she did, Evi was too overwhelmed to feel any emotion at all. A scream in her head came out as a whimper.

It looked as though Christy had been so badly beaten that the front of his skull had split with the pressure. Boots had done that, not fists, Evi thought; he had been kicked over and over again. His whole body was a twisted, mangled wreck, his clothing torn with the violence of the assault he had suffered. With great difficulty, Evi knelt beside him. She was afraid to touch him in case she might hurt him, even though she knew perfectly well that he was beyond harm now. She had seen death before, seen it many times at its most violent—crushed bodies dragged from the ruins of bombed buildings, charred remains recovered after an incendiary attack, that worst of human horrors, the scattered fragments of human life, a severed arm, a foot blown away from the rest of its body but still snugly covered in a sock and a shoe.

But this was not the ugly human cost of an indiscriminate bombing campaign. Her husband lay dead, murdered just as Bela had said, and by people who must have looked him in the eye as they killed him. It was only as she got closer to him that she saw that his clothing was frayed and torn as though he had been mauled by a wild animal, revealing small, deep holes all over his body.

How was this a glorious death? Terrible, yes, the worst, the unbearable ending she had begged and pleaded God to have spared her husband. During those long, long months when Evi had not known whether her husband was dead or alive but had to live with the growing realisation that he would never come back to her, she had prayed just two things over and over again: Let me find out the truth; let it have been quick and painless. Death can be grieved, widowhood could be borne somehow, but she could not bear to think he might have suffered. If he had been killed, if he was never coming home, then let it have been sudden: a catastrophic heart attack, a bullet to the back of the head. There had been so much loss, there had been so much suffering that a quick and easy passport out of this life hardly seemed a great deal to ask of a God who had made mountains and oceans, a God Christy had taught her to believe was greater than death itself.

This was a death more terrible than anything she could have conceived during her darkest journeys of the imagination, a slow, pitiless death that might have taken several minutes to execute. How was it glorious? How could anyone, even a man as close to the eternal Darkness as Bela Lugosi, see glory in this act of pointless savagery? This was her worst nightmare, but even as she drifted towards wakefulness, and as the sight of Christy's broken, bloodied body began to blur before her, Evi knew she would never quite awake from this nightmare. The world of dreams and the world of wakefulness were no longer so closely defined; her life itself did not feel entirely real. Like her father before her, Evi could no longer distinguish between what was real and what was not; but this was not because she was losing her mind or because the drink was blurring the boundaries of her existence. It was because the world itself was imploding all around her. All those years of violence, all those millions of dead had ripped a hole in the fabric of the world, and they were all falling; they were falling into darkness and oblivion ...

Morning had come to taunt her. Before Evi had even opened her eyes, the harsh, searing light of day had stabbed its way into her room and pressed against her eyelids, daring her to get up and face the world. She lay deathly still, her limbs stiff and heavy, her mouth and throat gritty with thirst, trying to locate the gentle thudding noise she could hear somewhere on the peripheries of her consciousness. Someone was knocking on her door, which irked her because it meant having to get up and communicate with another member of the human race when all she wanted at that moment was to bury herself alive.

As the knocking grew louder and more urgent, Evi felt a cold sweat breaking out across the back of her neck and an all-too-familiar panic sensation of pins and needles creeping up her arms. It was Bela Lugosi. He was coming after her. It was not enough for him to have frightened the life out of her when she had made the mistake of going to see him. No, now he had found out her address. He had come back to finish with her, to finish the story, an obsessive, monstrous man famous for his role as a vampiric virgin violator. She forced herself up, out of bed, and then tiptoed over to the door. "Go away! I'll call for help if you don't leave!" Her voice sounded as weak as she felt.

There was silence on the other side of the door, but the impostor was still there; Evi heard no retreating footsteps.

She waited, counting silently—one, two, three, four ... ten ... Her nerves a little steadier, she made another attempt. "I said, leave. I will, I really will call for help ..." Her voice trailed away.

There was an awkward pause, followed by the sound of a throat clearing. "Evi?" asked a voice in a soft English accent. "Are you feeling quite all right? Might you open the door?"

Evi sank to the floor. It was amazing how quickly a moment of madness could be revealed as just that: Why on earth would anyone have come after her, let alone an elderly man who had no way of knowing where she lived? What sinister reason could there have been for that knock on the door? She looked up at the wall clock and saw that it was shortly after ten, not even an unusual hour for Hugo to have chosen to call on her. "Just a moment," she called back, forcing herself onto her feet. "I'll be with you in a minute."

It was going to take more than a minute, thought Evi bitterly; it would take her decades to look vaguely human, let alone presentable enough to be seen by anyone. "Don't rush," came the ever-patient voice. "I tell you what, why don't we meet in half an hour?"

Evi breathed a sigh of relief. "Splendid, yes, half an hour. It will give me time to finish off some work." She had never been a liar, and this was the wrong time to acquire that new habit. She suspected Hugo knew perfectly well that he had not interrupted her work.

"Jolly good. I noticed a nice-looking restaurant on my way—Cara's, was it? Why don't we meet there?"

Evi floundered. She still felt a certain discomfort about letting a man into her home, but she felt repulsed by the idea of stepping out into the blazing light of day. "I'm not sure about that; I'm not feeling too bright."

There was a sharp rap on the door. "Come on, Evi. I daresay you've not eaten yet today. You could ... you could bring your folder with you. We could talk through the next article."

Evi's fingers went to the painful side of her face. She had not looked in the mirror to see how it looked, but she doubted any amount of makeup would conceal the bruises, another uncomfortable subject to avoid. "I'm not ..." But she needed to speak with Hugo urgently; she would never be able to get through another night if she did not get the truth out of him. "Could we meet this afternoon?"

"Evi, please come out," said Hugo, like the persistent voice of conscience. "Half an hour. There's something I have to tell you."

He was doing it on purpose, thought Evi. She lurched back into her bedroom in search of a change of clothes. It was like the Eccles cakes and Victoria sponges—he knew how to entice her into his confidence, like a strange man offering a child sweets. She rummaged through cluttered, disordered drawers in search of a clean pair of stockings. The analogy had been unsavoury; her mind was still in pieces, or she would never have thought of such a thing. Her body rebelled against sheathing itself in nylon when she still felt hot and clammy from the night, but she somehow managed to find herself in front of the mirror ten minutes later, dressed in a demure floral-print frock, stockings carefully positioned with the seams running straight.

It was her face she needed to work on, Evi thought, looking in disgust at the ghostly face peering back at her like something out of a wartime newsreel. She could have sworn she looked more dead than alive, and it was not just her inability to take basic care of herself that had caused it. When had the blood drained from her face so completely that her flesh looked not so much white but almost transparent? It could not be merely anaemia that made her face look as if the thinnest, poorest canvas had been stretched over a skull to give it the semblance of human features. What mocking artist's brush had painted those smudges beneath her eyes that made them look so vast and empty that they might have been made of glass?

It was yet another of those existential crises that hit her from time to time, she told herself as she attempted to apply makeup. She was alive. She was real; she could feel a pulse beating—albeit weakly—in her neck as she covered her skin in foundation, painting herself with a mask of respectability. Everyone wore masks of some shape or other, and this was hers: the flesh-coloured powder to conceal every blemish, the rouge, the lipstick, the ludicrous efforts to hide behind her clumsy artwork.

Evi thought, as she braced to stop her hands from shaking, that she ought not to have been so harsh with Bela about his profession, since all people were actors in the end and they all assumed a role of some kind. It was just that Evi hated pretence so keenly, she always felt like a child with stage fright, quaking in the spotlight. Inevitably, the act would be unconvincing, and this was one day when she could not afford to let Hugo see through her disguise.

Hugo was sitting at a table leafing through the morning paper when Evi came within sight of Cara's. He had found a place to sit on the pavement outside, which immediately put Evi on the wrong foot as she would have to stay out in the sunshine when she would have preferred to disappear into some gloomy corner, protected by thick walls and a screen of cigarette smoke. Then there was the sporadic noise of traffic she had never got used to, which always left her feeling as though there were insects humming in her ear. Hugo looked up at the sound of her footsteps, making Evi think that he had been watching for her arrival for some time. He stood up to greet her, his face clouding over immediately. "Dear God, Evi, what on earth's happened?" he said, before remembering that he was in a public place. He assisted her into a chair. "Oh Evi, I knew I should never have left it so long."

"It hasn't been so very long," answered Evi, more tersely than she meant, but she was always disconcerted by how comforting Hugo's presence felt. "I have been very busy, and no doubt so have you."

"What happened to your face? Have you had a fall?"

"In a manner of speaking." Evi looked away from Hugo at the boulevard stretched out before them. It was a perfectly pleasant part of town, especially on a sunny day, and there was a sense of energy about the place that would once have suited her. The men and women who walked past them seemed to journey with a purpose and without any sense of trepidation: young people who made her feel world-weary just looking at them, chatting and bouncing along as though they had never met so much as a minor obstacle in life. "I so wish I could go home," she said aloud. "It would be so much easier to hide in England. No one ever asks questions."

The statement was ridiculous, of course. How could she feel homesick when she had no home? Was she aching for the burnt-out ruins of an ancient city the Luftwaffe had destroyed in a single night? Was it truly homesickness when she had had no home there to speak of even before fires had roared through the streets, consuming everything and everyone in their path? What sort of a home was there to be built in a place she had happily fled when life had shown so much more promise than it did now?

"Evi, what happened to your face? It looks as though someone thumped you."

Evi bowed her head. "It's nothing; it was a misunderstanding. I went to see Bela Lugosi yesterday, and I'm afraid I startled him."

Hugo flinched visibly. "You did what?"

"No need to sound so shocked," Evi retorted, looking up at Hugo in sudden annoyance. "I went to do a final interview with him—at his request and the insistence of my editor, I might add—but it all went rather wrong."

"Evi . . ."

"Now, I know this is going to sound very odd, but I'm afraid his house rather gave me the shivers. The door wasn't shut all the way, and I couldn't see his wife anywhere. When I found him fast asleep in his chair, I think my imagination rather got the better of me."

"Evi, no."

"I know, it's ridiculous, but I went to check his pulse, and he woke up to find my hand on his throat. I'm sure he didn't mean to hurt me; he was just taken by surprise. He's still quite strong for his age—"

"Evi, please stop!" The sound of Hugo's hand rapping against the edge of the table stopped Evi in her tracks. They stared at one another across the table. "Evi, whatever are you talking about? Bela Lugosi is dead."

"You mean I was the last person to speak with him before he died?"

"Evi, he died two days ago!"

"Don't be silly; Mr Goldberg would have told me. He would have . . ."

"If your weekly appointment with Mr Goldberg was at the usual time, the news broke a few hours afterwards. He had died in his sleep the night before; his wife found him dead that morning."

"That's impossible. He was very definitely alive and fighting when I spoke with him that very afternoon."

Evi had never seen Hugo reveal any powerful emotion before and certainly would never have expected him to. The years of public school education followed by military life had made him reassuringly inscrutable, a detail Evi had not entirely appreciated until she saw the look of cold fear spreading across his face. "Evi, I don't know what's got into you, but your last interview with Bela Lugosi must have been longer ago than you remember. The man's dead. I have an obituary from this morning's paper to prove it."

"But that's just silly. I was with him yesterday, I tell you. Where do you think I got this?" she asked, pointing at her bruised face. "I was there at his house; I spoke with him." She could feel the tendrils of panic creeping over her, fed by Hugo's strange behaviour. If her last encounter with Bela had not been so terrifying, Evi would have simply scolded Hugo for his ignorance, but she was drowning in her own confusion, and Hugo was pushing her under the water. "You must be mistaken."

"Evi, look." He turned the paper toward her and pointed to an article. "I brought this to show you specially. Look."

Evi looked down at the page before her and saw:

COUNT DRACULA DEAD!
By Vince Martino
Los Angeles – August 17, 1956

The greatest screen Dracula of them all, Bela Lugosi, died in his home of an apparent heart attack. He was 73.

Married for the fifth time, Lugosi was found dead yesterday morning by his wife Hope Lininger, a 40-year-old film studio clerk. The Hungarian-born actor had credited her with helping him to overcome a drug addiction, which had left him a ghost of his former self...

Evi could read no further. She checked the date a second time, then a third, then a fourth: 17 August 1956, today's date.

"I saw him," she said quietly, but her voice was flat. "I spoke to him just as we are speaking now."

Somewhere in Evi's consciousness, she heard an urgent voice saying, "You're not well, Evi. I need to get you home. I think you've hurt your head, but it's only concussion. You're going to be fine."

She was being helped to her feet. Afterwards, Evi had no recollection of how Hugo had gotten her home from Cara's. She had some sense that she had tried to tell Hugo over and over again that she had only just seen Bela Lugosi, that something terrible was happening to her; then she thought she heard malicious laughter somewhere, enjoying her confusion and panic. At the same time, far away, Hugo's voice kept shushing her, telling her that there had to be an innocent explanation.

14

To Hugo's intense relief, he was able to persuade Evi to put herself to bed whilst he called for a doctor, ignoring her pleas that she did not need a doctor, she needed a priest. Hugo was almost inclined to agree with her when the doctor finally arrived, a brusque, dispassionate young man with the bedside manner of a mortuary assistant, whose first question when he stepped through the door was, "Are you next of kin?"

"Mrs Kilhooley has no family. She is an immigrant and a war widow."

"You a friend?"

"A concerned friend."

The doctor shrugged his wiry shoulders, far too disinterested to enquire further, before asking, "Where's the patient?"

"The patient is in that room." Hugo gestured to the closed door of Evi's bedroom. "I should warn you, she's not making a great deal of sense at the moment; that was why I called you. I think she may have concussion."

"How did it happen?"

"She claims she was attacked, but I suspect it was a fall." Hugo hesitated. "I'm afraid she has taken her husband's death rather badly. She ... well, she drinks."

The doctor nodded and entered the room, leaving Hugo uncertain of his place. He walked back into Evi's sitting room, which seemed a more respectable place for him to occupy, then had the idea of making Evi a coffee to fill the time.

The kitchenette was permeated with the offensive odour of bins left to fester. The room seemed more decayed than cluttered. There were no cups and plates piled up in the sink or on the draining board; there were no saucepans lurking guiltily on the hob. Hugo suspected that Evi had not cooked or eaten anything resembling a proper meal in a number of weeks.

Hugo opened a cupboard at random in search of the coffee and was immediately assaulted by a series of empty, unlabelled bottles stacked across two rows of shelves. He opened another cupboard, then a drawer. More bottles. All empty, all unlabelled. On an old-fashioned instinct to protect a lady's reputation, Hugo carefully closed all the doors to conceal what he had found and moved back to the doorway of Evi's room.

Hugo could hear the low murmur of voices in conversation and the sound of the metal clasp of a bag opening and snapping shut. He did not quite have time to back away before the door flew open, and he stood guiltily in the presence of the doctor, like an eavesdropper caught behind the curtain. "She'll be just fine," said the doctor tonelessly, gesturing to Hugo to move out of earshot of the patient. "She's still in a state of shock. I've given her something to calm her for now, but she'll need to take some more medicine this evening."

"Is it concussion?" asked Hugo hopefully.

"Maybe," answered the doctor, with the tone of a man used to hearing that echo of mild desperation in a relative's voice when discussing a sick person's welfare. "The blow to the face wouldn't be enough to concuss anyone. If she was knocked over, then her head would hit the floor. That would give concussion to anyone. I guess her confusion is around the shock she feels at being attacked."

"She wasn't attacked!" Hugo protested. "Who on earth would do that?"

The doctor looked steadily at Hugo. He was shorter than Hugo by a good six inches and had never been taught to stand up straight, but doctors had a level of moral authority Hugo naturally accepted. "You tell me who did it, sir."

Hugo backed away. "I'm not sure I like what you are suggesting. She may not have been attacked at all. I assumed she had had a nasty fall."

"I don't know how she was prior to this happening," said the doctor slowly, "but I bet she was hit by someone."

"How can you tell?" Hugo persisted. "She's not making any sense at all. She keeps saying she was attacked by Bela Lugosi!"

"It's obvious—that is, if you know what you're looking for," the doctor explained. "All down to the pattern, the bruising. Her bruising is about the size of a man's hand span. Some darker, circular patches indicate the use of knuckles. You said she drinks?"

Hugo lowered his eyes. "She can't help herself, Doctor; you must understand—"

"She has to ease up, stop if she can. These drugs I've prescribed are potent, and they don't mix well with liquor. Trust me; it's a lethal combination."

With that, the doctor moved towards the front door and made to let himself out. "You think she's mad, don't you?" said Hugo, forcing himself to ask the question. "That's why you're plying her with sedatives."

The doctor turned to face Hugo, looking every bit like a man still getting used to delivering unwelcome information. "I can't say for sure. If it's shock, if it's just concussion, she'll sleep it off. She needs rest. If the delirium doesn't stop, then she'll become delusional, and that means you'll have to have her committed to a state institution."

With that, he left. Evi was no longer his concern.

Hugo stood in the doorway to Evi's room and let out a soft, low sigh. She was his concern. She had been his concern before she had stepped into the haven of film memorabilia he had created for himself to hide from the world. If conscience could be embodied, it would look like Evangeline Kilhooley: prim, spectral, out of kilter with the world around it, as surely conscience ought to be; capable of being both compellingly attractive and wholly destructive in a single whisper.

The face of conscience looked up at him from the pillow. Evi looked healthier simply because the drugs had relaxed her, but Hugo could see that she was becoming groggy as the effects of the sedation made themselves felt.

Evi looked unblinkingly up at the ceiling, and Hugo suspected that she was staring so hard to keep her composure. "Hugo, I'm not as weak as I look."

"I've never thought of you as weak, I assure you."

"I'm not, at least I think I'm not, but sometimes there are limits to what one may be expected to bear, and I'm afraid I went to pieces. I could almost feel it."

Hugo waited until he was sure Evi had drifted off to sleep before getting to his feet and leaving the room. Christy had told him so much about Evi during their long months together in the camp, that Hugo had fallen into the trap of believing he knew her very well before they had even met. But the woman to whom Christy had promised to return had been ravaged by the long years alone. Hugo was not sure that Christy would recognise his own wife if he returned from the grave to claim her.

Hugo went over to Evi's desk, which was so buried in the morass of papers she had dumped there that he had to clear it just to be able to find the typewriter buried beneath. He simply could not fathom how anyone could live in a mess like this. It was not just the desk that was a disorderly nightmare of screwed-up balls of paper, handwritten notes, half-finished assignments, snacks Evi had barely touched before pushing away. When he opened a drawer in search of pen and ink, thinking that he might at least be able to help Evi by finishing her article for her, he found yet more detritus: torn paper, crumpled paper, documents that looked important bound up with scrawlings long ago abandoned, a man's hip flask . . .

Hugo flinched and closed the drawer, but the reminder that Christy had lived here once had the same effect on Hugo that the sound of a bullet whistling past his ear might have done when he was a soldier. He was immediately jolted back into action. Evi's latest article was still in the typewriter, four large paragraphs already typed up, which meant that it was about half-finished. He would complete it for her and get it to her editor before the deadline.

For ease of reading, Hugo carefully pulled out the page from the typewriter and began to scan what Evi had written:

Bela's terrible decline is well known. After his meteoric rise to fame as Count Dracula, Bela Lugosi would never again know such success at the box office, and he quickly fell out of favour, forced to make low-budget films in ever-humbler roles. His personal life has suffered accordingly, and Lugosi has been forced to confirm rumours that he is a narcotics addict and an alcoholic whose unreasonable behaviour drove his fourth wife, Lillian, to file for divorce.

The City of Angels has always been a hotbed of rumour, and inevitably there are many stories surrounding this extraordinary actor known to millions around the world as the Lord of the Undead. One such rumour is that Bela Lugosi made a pact with the devil which he refused to honour, provoking his long, slow professional death as payment for his failure to keep his side of the bargain. Another is that he persuaded another failed horror actor, Lionel Atwill, to participate in a bizarre ghost hunt to destroy a demonic fiend he believed was hiding in the ruins of an old Spanish mission. Atwill died suddenly, shortly after this supposed encounter took place. Although there is no written record of Bela Lugosi's making any journey to Mission Hills, the rumours persist.

My final interview with Lugosi was as disturbing as his many films. His home almost seemed to be decaying with him. He behaved like a man who had quite literally turned into his own dramatic creation. Lugosi confirmed to me before I fled for my life that the rumour was true: he had been haunted by a fiendish visitor who had demanded that the actor use dark arts to enslave the world ...

"I know what you're thinking," said a flat, lifeless voice, causing Hugo to spring away from the sound. Evi stood before him, having entered the room so quietly he had not heard a sound, which left him wondering how long she had been standing there watching him. "You are trying to decide whether I am mad after all, drunk, or merely a liar. Part of you would quite like me to be a liar, I suspect. But you are sure I am none of those things."

Hugo held up the page he had been reading. "Evi, I don't want to believe any of those things about you. All I know is that what you have written makes absolutely no sense."

"I know it doesn't," she answered, with disarming honesty. "It makes no sense at all, but that is not my fault. I'm a journalist, remember, only a messenger."

Hugo clenched his free hand behind his back to stop himself trembling. There was something so unnerving about the transformation Evi was going through that he was beginning to doubt his own senses. "Bela Lugosi is dead; you are confused. I am in possession of my mental faculties." He said this to reassure himself, only to lose his nerve again at the sight of Evi attempting to smile. He knew it was a trick of the poor light and the effect of the long white nightdress she was wearing that had been made for a rounder, fuller figure; he knew she was shivering only because of the effects of the drugs she was fighting off. Yet she looked so like a ghost, he wanted to reach out and touch the spectral vision simply to prove to himself that she had not crossed over from one world to the next.

"I did see him, Hugo," she said. "You know I did."

"You're a journalist, Evi. Do you expect me to believe that you've never made up a story to suit yourself?"

The ghost stepped forward quickly and dealt him an unexpectedly powerful slap to the face. She was real after all; only a living woman would have responded like that. She was a woman with feelings to injure and a temper to rile and a body she could still use to hurt him. Hugo pressed his hand against his face and breathed a sigh of relief. "That was beneath you," said Evi. "You know I'm not a liar. Maybe this is madness. Why should I pretend to have met Lugosi? Why should I imagine such a thing? I had never heard of him before Goldberg told me to write about him. I had no interest in his life whatsoever."

Hugo put the paper down on the desk, letting it disappear among all the other stray white leaves. "All I know, Evi, is that you are claiming to have interviewed a ... a dead man. Perhaps you could tell me what I am supposed to make of that?"

"I thought you could help me make sense of it," said Evi. Hugo noticed a tear sliding down her cheek, but even that felt unnatural. She was weeping almost without noticing; there was no rage, no distress, just tears, slowly, one upon another, falling, sliding down her face, charting their own course. "I don't feel real anymore, Hugo. I'm not real, or this is not real. I can't decide."

Hugo helped Evi into a chair. He thought she looked more normal sitting down, no longer hovering like a lost soul, and he imagined it might put her more at ease. "Evi, please don't be afraid. I'm sure that this is nothing more than a serious case of shock. I should have done something about this sooner, but it would have been presumptuous to interfere. The years of isolation, the drink, the grief—and there has been so much grief, Evi. As you yourself said, there is only so much even a strong mind can be expected to bear. But there is nothing here that a good psychiatrist couldn't help put right." Evi was shaking her head wearily, but Hugo continued. Part of him suspected he would never get another chance to finish. "Evi, I don't believe you're mad. But watching you is like standing back and watching a friend burying himself deeper and deeper into a grave of his own making. You don't have to live like this. Christy wouldn't want it; he'd never forgive himself."

Evi looked up with a start. "Christy? Since when did you call my husband by his nickname?"

Hugo fumbled for a response. "You know I met him. No one goes by formalities in a situation like that."

"You've admitted you met him, but I know you're not being truthful with me. He told me something to make me believe him."

"Who did?"

"Lugosi."

"Lugosi is *dead*!" shouted Hugo, and immediately regretted it; but uncharacteristically, Evi did not flinch at the sound of his raised voice. "Please, Evi, you must understand. Bela Lugosi is dead."

"Yes," answered Evi softly. "Bela Lugosi is dead."

Hugo heaved a sigh of relief. "Good. I think we may be getting somewhere now."

"I suspected he was dead when I spoke to him last." She reached up and took Hugo's hand, anticipating an interruption. "No, please. I know how it sounds. The more I think about it, the more insane it all feels, but I can't think of any other way to explain things. I did meet him, Hugo, and since all the evidence makes it quite clear that he died before my last interview with him, then I met an imposter or I met a dead man. And I am thinking it must have been the latter."

"Evi, please stop."

"When I went to check his pulse and he knocked me down, it made me think that he wasn't attacking me because he was afraid I was going to hurt him. He was afraid that I wouldn't find a pulse."

Hugo turned his back and stood facing the wall. It was easier not to have to look at her. "Please, please stop. Listen to what you are saying."

"Think about it, Hugo. Even the strength of the man doesn't make any sense. How could a frail old man supposedly at death's door possibly hit me hard enough to knock me down? The force was terrible. He didn't just knock me off my feet, he threw me across the room. No man of that age could do that."

Hugo turned round suddenly, a thought coming to him like an answer to prayer. "Evi, you have said that he always made you sit in darkness. That's correct, isn't it?"

"Yes."

"Then it was an imposter. Perhaps it was always an imposter. He made it impossible for you to get a completely clear view of his face. You'd never met Lugosi before your editor gave you this job, had you?"

"No."

"And one of the first things you told me when we met was that you were not interested in movies. You had never even heard of the man, let alone watched any of his pictures. You had no idea what he even looked like."

"That's true."

"What if this were some sort of elaborate hoax? Someone impersonating the man, perhaps trying to cause you a professional embarrassment? It might even have been some kind of practical joke that got a little out of hand."

It was Evi's turn to look incredulous. "But why on earth would anyone do that? All that time and effort to impersonate a film star no one cares about anymore? What would anyone have to gain by making me falsely believe I was conducting an interview with Lugosi?"

"It's plausible."

"Not at all. The only person who knew about the assignment to begin with was Goldberg. He's an insufferable little man, but he had nothing to gain by sending me on some wild goose chase and employing a man to pretend to be the subject of my feature articles. He is a busy man. If he wanted to destroy me, he had only to send me packing."

Hugo pressed his knuckles into the wall. There had to be a rational explanation. There had to be a rational explanation which did not involve him having to admit that he had fallen in love with a crazed woman who entertained dark fantasies about interviewing the Undead. "Maybe sending you packing was not enough. Maybe there was some reason he had to destroy your reputation, discredit you in the eyes of the public. Were you involved in some private investigation, perhaps? Think about it. Were you working on a story that was in any way dangerous or controversial?"

Evi shook her head sadly. "I know what you're trying to do, but it's no good. I have not produced any work of any significance on anyone for a very long time. I live hand to mouth, writing whatever nonsense I'm commanded to put on paper. I'm not considered a serious reporter anymore. If Goldberg wanted to discredit me, he had only to expose my drink problem. He knew about it well enough; he taunted me about it all the time."

Evi stood up and moved over to where Hugo was standing. He noticed that she was a little unsteady on her feet, which was hardly surprising, but it appalled him to think of how poisoned her body must be if the sedation had such little effect on her. "Hugo, there's something else you should know. He also talked about you. He said I would doubt my sanity afterwards because none of it would make sense, but he said he could prove everything to me, he could make me believe his story that he was destroyed by the Darkness he had served. He said things about my husband he could not possibly have known."

"Evi, it's very easy to suggest things to a person in certain situations."

"Bela said my husband was killed in battle."

Relief again. The cold relief of flawed evidence in an invisible trial. "He was a prisoner. Of course he didn't die in battle."

"I said as much, but he said that battles are fought all over the place, including in camps, and that Christy had been a warrior for the Truth. He said Christy died a terrible, glorious death because he would not submit to the Darkness. He said he knew how my husband died because they were fighting on opposite sides of an invisible war."

Hugo could sense her staring at him and turned to leave the room, but she took hold of his arm with surprising force, stopping him in his tracks. "A terrible and glorious death because he would not submit to the Darkness. Hugo, please tell me what that means!"

He could not bring himself to look at her. "Evi, I owe you an apology," he said flatly, but he could not risk any emotion taking hold of him or he knew he would break down, and he would never forgive himself for such weakness. He continued, in the same flat, rapid tone, "I owe you many apologies. I should have known you were too intelligent to be taken in; it was only a matter of time before you realised that I had known your husband. But I think you know now that I witnessed his death. He didn't want you to know. He didn't want you to know how he died. I made a promise, and I didn't want to break it. It felt like the greatest dishonour to break an oath made to a dying man. But I don't believe he ever intended this. He never imagined what it would do to you to be left in the dark."

"He told you to keep the truth from me?"

Hugo forced himself to look down at Evi's reproachful face. "Please, Evi, he was trying to protect you. You ... you have no idea how terrible it was."

"Terrible and glorious?"

The case was hopeless; Hugo could feel himself drowning. It was as though he had been sheltering from a cataclysmic storm, only for a tidal wave to smash against the windows of his shelter, shattering the glass to smithereens and sending him spiralling under freezing water. He staggered back against the wall, too overcome to speak, praying she would take the hint and leave him alone. "Please ..."

"Is that how it happened, Hugo? Was Bela Lugosi right? You don't have to answer; I know he's right, about the murder anyway. I dream about it. I wake up screaming in the night."

Hugo felt himself sweating. He remembered the sensation well, the sweat brought on by unadulterated terror, not the heat, though he had struggled with the heat of the Korean summer far more than the deadly chill of the winter—and those winters had been so savage, when they had been forced to march for days in their shirtsleeves and bare feet, their winter coats and boots having been confiscated.

There had been agony and death whatever the season, men dropping and dying, shivering with hypothermia, their feet frostbitten and gangrenous. In the summer, with the blistering sun bearing down on them and the murderous thirst, he had been forced to watch men ravaged by disease, tormented by maggots and blowflies that infested their untreated wounds as though the men were already corpses to be eaten by parasites. Hugo would always remember the summer as the harshest season, with the stench of death everywhere, but perhaps that was only because the one death from which he could never recover had happened on a summer's day. The worst of deaths. A terrible, glorious death. Hugo always wondered whether Christy would have been in a less volatile temper if the cold had been leaching the life out of him rather than the sun burning his flesh. Hugo had never been at his best in the heat either.

"I hardly know what to say to you, Evi," said Hugo, but his throat was taut with stress. "I have no idea whom you have been speaking to; I can't make sense of any of this now. Perhaps we are both mad, I don't know, but your Angel of Death was right, whoever he was." He let himself sink to the floor. It was all wrong, but he doubted Evi cared if he sat on the floor. "Christy was murdered, and I saw it. He was killed in front of my eyes, and I could do nothing to stop it."

Evi stared at him, more out of curiosity than reproach. "And you didn't tell me? You know I've been tormented all this time wondering what happened to him, and you had the answer all along?"

Hugo looked up at the ceiling, focusing his eyes on the long crack that splintered its way in a diagonal jumble from one corner to the next. If he looked hard enough at something inconsequential, he would not see Christy lying dead in the dust, riddled with puncture wounds. He did not have to hear his own voice screaming at his friend, in the last fraught moments before the guards turned on him: *For God's sake, do what they want! Do what they want, you stubborn Irish bastard!*

"Hugo, did they shoot him?" Evi did not belong where Hugo was; the sound of a female voice startled him. "Was he shot? I've often thought that must have been how it happened. I've dreamed he was full of holes. That was why I thought Lugosi must be telling the truth. If he was shot, it might be martyrdom; it was a terrible death."

"He wasn't shot, Evi," Hugo managed to answer, but he still could not look at her. "It might have been easier if he had been." That had come out all wrong. Hugo summoned up every scrap of courage he still possessed and looked steadily at Evi. "Would it be enough for me to tell you that he went to his death without fear, his dignity intact, his head held high? And that he died surrounded by men who would happily have died defending him if we had had the chance? Is that enough?"

Evi moved closer to Hugo, brushing tears away from her face as though they were an embarrassment. At least she was aware that she was weeping, which felt a little like a return to sentience. "Would you have died for him, Hugo?"

Hugo took a risk and drew Evi into his arms, as much to hide the shame the question provoked as to comfort her. He felt the weight of her head resting against his chest and let his hand press lightly against her hair, as though he were sheltering her from a downpour of rain. "I would have gone anywhere with him, Evi," he said quietly. "If they hadn't dragged me away, I would never have left his side."

"Bela said Christy died as a witness to the Truth. Did he?"

Hugo felt the blood draining from his face. He heard himself shouting at Christy, pleading with him to do as he was told, to give in, to betray everything he believed ... "Yes, he did. I'm afraid I didn't understand what he was doing at the time; all I could think of was that I couldn't let him die. I wanted him to do whatever was necessary to stay alive."

Evi disengaged herself from Hugo and looked up at him with the steely determination he remembered from their first meeting. "I want you to tell me precisely what happened. Neither Christy nor you had any right to keep the truth from me; neither of you had any business deciding what I was capable of bearing."

"Evi, please. You don't have to know the details," said Hugo. "He did die a terrible death, and yes, he was killed because of his beliefs, so some might say it was also glorious. That's all you need to know."

Evi gave Hugo a shove, causing him to hit the wall with an ignominious thud. "I have not come this far to be fobbed off by you!" she raged. "He was my husband! Bad enough that he died far away from me, but to be deceived and kept in the dark?"

"He didn't want you to know!"

"As you yourself admit," Evi continued relentlessly, "Christy could never have known how much it would destroy me not to know. You are released from your promise."

"It's not as easy as that," Hugo protested. "I can't speak of it. I've never been able to talk about Korea; the words just won't come out of my mouth!"

"Don't be such a bloody coward," snapped Evi. "We've both been to hell and back. Are you honestly telling me you can't look me in the eye and tell me what happened?"

Hugo felt his temper flare; the anger was misdirected, and he knew it was, but he could not help himself. "Would you like to look me in the eye and describe your worst memory to me? Come on, now; it's not that hard. Describe to me the moment you found out your family had perished in the Coventry blitz; describe to me the first time you saw a dead body. Don't be a coward; tell me in lurid detail about the first time someone hurt you. Don't spare yourself; tell me how it felt to be helpless, humiliated, crying with pain. You're not going to tell me you can't bear it, are you?"

Evi turned her back on him; she was furious now, but it was infinitely easier that way. Anger was a cheap anaesthesia for two broken lives that had come crashing together, connected by horrors, both real and imagined. "I think you have made your point. But you have no business demanding to know the details of my worst memories. My husband's murder *is* my business."

"I can't! Don't you understand? I just *can't*!"

Evi's temper cooled a moment before Hugo's did. "Could you write it down, then? You could sit at my desk and write an account of what happened. Sometimes it's easier to put things on paper."

Hugo shook his head. "I've tried before. I shall sit before a blank sheet of paper all day."

But she was walking over to her desk as though she had not registered his concerns. Evi had the brutal efficiency of a chaotically untidy woman with a good memory, and she rapidly picked up handfuls of paper, clearing a decent-sized space across the front of the desk. "I stopped believing that every problem has a solution a very long time ago," she said, opening a drawer and sticking her fingers into the far corner. Evi retrieved a small brass key which she inserted into the lock of a cupboard Hugo had barely noticed, though he could not help registering that it took her three or four attempts to get the key into the lock before opening it. He moved close enough to look inside, only to see a sight to gladden the heart of any archivist.

"Good heavens, where did you get that?" he asked, staring at the perfectly preserved Dictaphone sitting in neglected splendour at his feet. "Dictaphone" did not do the machine justice; it was practically an antique, the type that still used wax cylinders. "It looks like something out of—"

"Bram Stoker's *Dracula*, I know … an unfortunate coincidence, I suppose," said Evi, reaching down to lift it. It was a heavy old dinosaur, impossibly awkward and cumbersome, which no doubt explained why she never used it. "What's the name of the doctor who records all his notes on wax cylinders?"

"Evi, I know what you're thinking, but ..."

"I found it years ago in a junk shop. Seward—that's his name. It was one of the few things I brought with me. I suppose I imagined it would be terribly useful, but it doesn't fit in the pocket like a pen and paper, and my shorthand was good enough."

"It won't make any difference whether I'm speaking to a machine or to you; it can't be done."

Evi ignored him and began setting it up. "That's not true. Machines don't cry. They have no feelings to hurt; they don't stare at one and interrupt with hundreds of questions." She turned to face him. "I'm asking you to try, Hugo. Lock yourself in here and imagine that you are sitting in the confessional with no witnesses except a priest who can't see your face, has no idea who you are, and can't repeat anything you say. When I play it back, you don't have to be anywhere near the room."

Hugo sat down at the desk, shrugging off the feeling that he was in an interrogation room. There was something about the poor light and the presence of an anglepoise lamp that suggested a threat, besides that infernal machine waiting to record every nuance of his juddering voice. In what other setting was there recording equipment in evidence than in a place where a man's words could be used against him? *You have the right to remain silent, but anything you say may be taken and used in evidence against you.*

"Leave me," he said. Hugo watched as Evi slipped noiselessly out of the room, before getting up to lock himself in. He should have asked for a glass of water before she left, but Hugo thought better of it as he settled himself down. It was better for him to feel a little uncomfortable, a little anxious, if he was to re-create the worst event of his entire life. He had been thirsty then too ...

15

[Transcript begins] I have never spoken of this before or been required to do so. Many returning soldiers have given evidence about the terrible crimes committed against prisoners of war by the Communists. I witnessed many such crimes, none of which will be unfamiliar to you. We had our personal effects stolen from us, including winter coats and boots. We were forced to march many miles in freezing temperatures, and I saw dozens of men perish from exhaustion and cold. In the camp, we were subjected to a relentless barrage of Communist propaganda, which they called "reeducation". I have been told subsequently that the starvation we suffered had no malicious intent; it was the result of the poverty suffered by the entire region. I do not believe that that was ever the case. We were starved and abused as part of a deliberate attempt to break us and so make us more amenable to the grotesque ideas being forced upon us.

Challenging anything was dangerous. Religious observance was, for the most part, forbidden. I witnessed men beaten and subjected to the most degrading punishment for praying or possessing religious objects. I was not a religious man. This gave me a modicum of protection, but I know that for others, this suppression of their right to religious observance was the cruellest torment suffered in that place.

I cannot put a figure on the numbers who died as a result of disease, hunger, or mistreatment. Likewise, I cannot say with any accuracy how many of us were left behind, but it still fills me with horror to consider that so few of us made it home.

I first met Christopher Kilhooley not long after my arrival at the camp. He already had something of a reputation as a hothead, but he was extremely popular among the men. He was [unintelligible] for all his reputation for getting into arguments and challenging everything with a reckless disregard for his safety; he was also known for his kindness. There were men like that, who would gladly share their last scrap of bread, and he was just such a man. People sometimes imagine that hardship brings out the best in men, but anyone who has been through a war knows that is simply not true. A selfish man will not be less selfish in a prison camp, a criminal will still be a criminal, a man who bullied when he was free is likely to be a bully in captivity. It is not always the case; some no doubt go through that trial and come out purer. I'm too hardened by experience to believe that this is a common event, though. In the middle of it all there are always found saints: one or two truly great men who make the rest of us retain some belief in the best of humanity. [six-second silence]

Things first turned bad for Christy during one of those ghastly classes. It was freezing cold, even harder than usual to concentrate, and we had been sitting for over an hour listening to some idiot droning on and on about how we had all been the slaves of capitalism, risking our lives to protect the rich and powerful. Tempers were fraying, as there was no sign of it coming to an end. Then the teacher—let's call him the teacher for now [laughs]—he pointed at Christy and ordered him to stand up. Then he asked him to tell the rest of us how important Marx was to him, and he said, "Which one? Harpo or Groucho? I do love a good comedian." We all burst out laughing. It didn't seem so funny when the guards attacked him. I rushed in without thinking, and before I knew it, we were in the middle of a fight we were never going to win. [Transcript ends]

It was no good; Hugo felt half mad talking out loud in an empty room with just the sound of the machine whirring gently in the background. Somehow he would need to tell Evi the story after all.

He felt himself being held on the damp, chill floor, his lips split and bleeding, wondering what had possessed him to come to the defence of that stupid bastard in the first place. It was a bloody stupid comment, designed to provoke a violent reaction—and it did. The man must have had a screw loose. It was a little late to change allegiances, though.

The two of them were hauled to their feet, arms twisted behind their backs, and he could hear an order being shouted in a language he did not understand. If they were going to hang together, Hugo thought he should try not to resent the man for landing him in trouble.

If Hugo had been in a state to be fair (which he was not), he would have reminded himself that nobody had forced him to leap forward in defence of an unarmed and outnumbered man; he had made some sort of choice himself even if he could not remember it. Hugo exchanged a fleeting glance with Christy as they were forced to remove their shoes and socks and stand barefoot on the frozen ground. Hugo felt the shock jolting through his body and was ashamed to discover that his teeth had started chattering almost immediately. He did not want them to think he was afraid; he did not want Christy to think he was afraid either, since he was not shivering at all. It was anger serving as an anaesthesia, Hugo said to comfort himself: Christy was too hopping mad to feel anything yet.

There would be plenty of time to feel the cold. Guards stood over them, shouting at them to undress. Hugo remembered the sense of black despair that came over him as he struggled to unbutton his shirt, his fingers already numb with the cold; he could feel the first patter of snow falling against his neck and knew what was coming. This was an execution by the elements. They were going to be made to stand out in the gathering blizzard until they froze to death. "Leave him alone," said a voice on the other side of the vast wall of despair Hugo was busily constructing. "It wasn't his fault."

Hugo wondered afterwards whether he had been meant to feel grateful to the other man for attempting to save him; instead, he felt an unusual surge of petulance rising in him, all the more so when the guard answered Christy's plea for clemency by spitting in his face. He waited until they had been left alone before offering a word of thanks. "Get lost, Kilhooley; I wasn't obliged to come to your rescue."

Christy looked straight ahead. They were standing next to one another, just a foot apart, but neither man was sure that they had permission to speak, so they did not risk turning round. "Thanks awfully for defending me, then," he answered, mimicking Hugo's plummy accent. "Much obliged, old chap."

"We all make mistakes," Hugo retorted with the shadow of a smile. His friend gave a faint laugh before falling silent.

Neither of them had the strength to speak unless it was absolutely necessary. Within minutes, Hugo was shivering so uncontrollably, he felt as though his body was convulsing. His joints began to throb with a dull, aching pain that quickly took over every muscle in his body. "Stop rubbing yourself down!" commanded Christy. "You'll kill yourself!"

Hugo wondered whether it was already too late. His mind was beginning to drift. He was drowning; he could feel himself sliding down into the death-dealing darkness, the icy water bearing down on him, crushing the life out of him as he struggled to find his way back to the surface. He could see light peering through the rippling gloom, but his head would never break through to the world of air and all its promise of life. He rose up through the water, his head slamming repeatedly against the crust of ice, but there was no way out. He was being buried alive, condemned to die in this water-filled chamber from which there was no escape ...

He never heard the sound of ice being smashed. Hands grabbed his arms and pulled him to safety; he felt his body grazing as he was dragged away from the frozen lake and onto the chalky bank. "It's all right, lads; he'll live," said a man's voice Hugo did not recognise, speaking in a lilting Wiltshire accent. A passing farmer must have helped the boys smash the ice and get him out. Hugo felt himself being turned over onto his front, then the sudden shock of a blow to the small of his back, then another and another. He began to struggle. "Hold on, sonny; don't move," said the farmer who was pummelling him. "Just getting the nasty water out."

Hugo coughed with the sensation of water coming out of his mouth, then blood. His body convulsed, causing the farmer to desist; then he started vomiting. Someone had put the lights out. It was so dark, who had put the lights out ... ?

"Wake up!" A harsh voice with an accent that did not belong to home. Christy's voice.

Hugo stared through the grey blur of falling snow, unable to recall how he had come to be there. "My father's going to kill me," said Hugo blankly. "I shouldn't have done it."

"You're drifting. Wake up!"

"Where the hell am I?"

"Watch yourself. You're going crazy. Focus on something."

He was in a prison camp. He had got himself into a fight, and he had been condemned to a slow death by hypothermia. With his head clear, the pain returned, and he could feel the cold leeching its way into his bones like a cancer. Hugo searched his mind for some mental distraction.

If I should die, think only this of me . . . No, not death on a foreign battlefield. He tried again. *Into the valley of Death rode the six hundred . . .* Worse, wartime death again, in full Technicolor detail.

> I stretch lame hands of faith, and grope,
> And gather dust and chaff, and call
> To what I feel is Lord of all,
> And faintly trust the larger hope.

Hugo felt despair crushing him again and an almost overwhelming urge to scream. Just to scream, to open his mouth and let out some wild, primeval roar of desperation for the whole world to hear. He looked sideways at Christy, but his fellow belligerent was standing with his eyes closed, whispering unintelligible words under his breath. Hugo noticed that he seemed to be counting off something on his fingers, working his way through very slowly to ten, pausing and then starting again. Whatever he was doing, Christy had found some way to keep going, leaving Hugo floundering for the strength simply to keep quiet.

"You know he was praying the rosary, don't you?" said Evi, when Hugo had sunk into one of the many silences that punctuated his narrative. "Without his beads, he was counting off the prayers on his fingers."

"Yes, I guessed that," said Hugo wearily. "Unfortunately, so did our captors. Things became very bad for him after that. He was a marked man."

To look at the two of them, an observer might have thought that they were a married couple miserably discussing the possibility of divorce. Hugo had been unable to sit alone, talking at an aged Dictaphone. It had felt far too much like a police interview or the recording of a confession under duress, and he had eventually found Evi and begged her to turn the wretched thing off. He needed her company, he needed to be reminded of why he was dredging up such a story; but when she had obediently sat down with him to listen, Hugo had felt the words being strangled out of him.

In the end, they had positioned themselves on chairs, sitting back-to-back, close enough to touch but well out of one another's line of sight. Hugo could not help thinking that the whole scenario was mad, but it fitted his sense that they had both lost possession of their mental faculties somewhere along the line. "They let me off after half an hour," he said tonelessly. "He stood there for three. Never protested, never said a word."

Hugo swallowed a wave of nausea. When the Communists had finally relented, the other prisoners had wrapped Christy up in their own coats and huddled around him to warm him up, but he was already suffering from severe frostbite. Across the years, Hugo heard his old friend shouting with pain as his body went through the agony of warming up when it was already halfway to breaking down altogether. Evi did not have to know that Christy had had to pull off two of his frostbitten toes because he could not bear it anymore. Hugo clenched his fists by his sides to stop himself from retching; it was such a ridiculous detail to feel squeamish about after all he had seen by then and had yet to witness, but he could not get the sight of those mangled black stubs out of his head.

A hand wrapped itself around his fist. "I'm so sorry, Hugo," said Evi anxiously. "I know this is hard."

Hugo opened his fist and held her hand gratefully. It was the closest he had ever felt to her—to any woman, for that matter. "I should have told you this a long time ago. Are you okay?"

"Yes." Her hand shuddered in his. "I'm so glad you were with him. I'm sorry you went through that, but I'm so glad he didn't have to suffer alone. Not that time, anyway; I know he died alone."

Hugo had watched the long, exhausting months of that most diabolical year slipping away before his eyes—that slow, torturous process of being broken down, the encroaching belief that they had been abandoned and would never go home. Christy had been a great believer in hope, if hope could be believed in. Hugo had wondered whether it was Christy's faith that kept his spirits up or the thought of the wife waiting for him that made him so eternally optimistic that freedom would come one day. Hugo, who had neither faith nor family, had found some shelter in Christy's determination. Christy: one of the few fixed points as men grew weary and sick, as friends and companions had died.

"I'm sorry, Evi. If I could have stood with him, I would have done so, I assure you."

"In my dreams, he is always standing alone, and Bela Lugosi said he died alone. Well, he must have, I suppose. You're here."

The mention of Lugosi made Hugo flinch almost as much as the unintentional accusation. He was here; he was alive—the man who had not stuck his head above the parapet; the prisoner who had not chafed against every attempt at controlling him; the survivor who had not got himself a reputation as a religious degenerate prepared to sacrifice absolutely everything rather than betray his own conscience ... "He was a marked man, Evi. After that incident, they grabbed every opportunity to hurt him. Every bully knows that the best way to hurt a man is to seek out the part of his life that matters to him the most and attack it. I sometimes wondered what they were really doing—attacking him or attacking his religion."

"Christy would not have seen a difference," said Evi. "You don't understand; it was like the blood flowing in his veins. He was not at all pious—he never made a great fuss about it—but I know he would never have abandoned it."

"Evi, may I ask a question?" said Hugo, shifting in his chair. "I don't know whether this will mean anything to you, but did Christy take a crucifix with him when he went away?"

Evi turned around to look at him. "A crucifix? I don't think so. I suppose there was the crucifix on his rosary beads, if that's what you mean."

Hugo shook his head. "It hardly matters. I always wondered where they got it from. Sorry, would you mind moving back?"

Evi almost smiled. The situation felt a little like a child covering his eyes and convincing himself that no one else can see him. "If you prefer," she said, turning back-to-back again. "Are you going to tell me what happened?"

Hugo shook his head. "Well, I don't know where it came from; maybe it wasn't even his."

There were so many details that he found impossible to remember; the shock had had the effect of shattering his memories of the time directly before and after, so that the moment of Christy's last stand hung before him almost like a tableau. There were a series of images he replayed in his mind repeatedly during the long nights when sleep refused to come, some quite disconnected and not always viewed in the correct order. Flashbacks had a tendency to happen that way, scattering themselves around his consciousness with no sense of continuity or chronology. He would see Christy dead, and then he would see him arguing with his aggressors. He would see him crumpled up on the ground, fighting for breath . . .

Hugo could not even remember what misdemeanour Christy was supposed to have committed to find himself in trouble; he simply remembered his being separated from the rest of them, standing alone as though awaiting sentence. Hugo was so accustomed to seeing Christy on the wrong side of their captors that his initial feeling was one of mild exasperation and the hope that things were not going to go too badly for him this time.

A second tableau—but now Hugo was not sure if he had made a mistake. Where had that large crucifix come from? Hugo remembered it as belonging to Christy, some pious object he had been hiding that had been discovered by chance and dragged out as evidence with which to damn him. Evi's comment unsettled the memory; of course it could not have been Christy's crucifix. It was a massive object, sculpted from a single piece of wood, something one might find hanging in the side chapel of a church, not in the hands of a soldier. They must have looted it from one of the churches they had destroyed and laid it down on the ground in front of Christy as a taunt, not an accusation.

Hugo felt sick with fear. He felt again that surge of panic as when it dawned on him what they were going to force Christy to do and how likely he was to resist, whilst a hand was holding his very tightly, and a reassuringly female voice said, "It's all right. Tell me what happened. Just tell me what happened. I know how it ends."

"As soon as they put that crucifix on the ground, I knew they were going to tell him to stamp on it. It's the sort of thing they would do. I knew he'd refuse."

"And all hell broke loose?"

"An interesting choice of words. That's what it felt like."

As the agnostic Protestant Englishman he had been back then, Hugo would have simply called it rage, but he had no difficulty using the word "diabolical" now.

Christy stood with his hands behind his back, shaking his head slowly to make absolutely sure his refusal was registered. "Never."

"It's only a piece of wood! It's just a carving!" someone shouted, but it was not a guard shouting at Christy. Hugo heard his own voice—the voice of reason—calling out to a friend who was surrounded by enemies and seemed more concerned about offending an invisible deity than the large number of angry Communists spoiling for a fight. "What does it matter?"

Christy looked across at him, silencing him immediately. "Come on, now, buddy; you know better than that."

"He's right; it doesn't matter," said the guard who had put the crucifix at his feet. "It's just wood."

Christy's face flushed with anger. "Go to hell."

Hugo leapt forward instinctively, but he felt hands snatching hold of his arms and pulling him back. "Take your hands off me!"

"Stay back; they'll shoot you!"

"Let go! Whose side are you on?" But he was asking that question to himself far more than to his fellow inmates. Another tableau frozen in memory: Christy curled up on the ground in the foetal position with two men standing over him. It may have been guilt, but Hugo could not stop struggling to free himself. He could hear the thud of fists and boots, but the only sound coming from Christy was the crack of his own bones fracturing. Hugo was the one shouting. "What the hell do you think you're doing! Stop!" The men restraining him refused to let go; in desperation, Hugo aimed a sharp kick behind him, hitting his minder squarely on the knee. The shock caused the man to let go, sending Hugo tumbling head over heels. He looked up in time to see Christy being hauled to his feet, but Christy was struggling to stand up straight, and the blood trickling out of his mouth and nose was making him cough.

Let it end here, thought Hugo desperately, getting himself up. *They've made their point; let it stop now.* Christy could recover from a beating. It was not the first time he had found himself on the receiving end of behaviour like that. *Let them be satisfied with that ...* But the guard was gesturing to the untouched crucifix, saying again, slowly, to emphasize each word, "Just a piece of wood."

Christy was silent much longer than was normal for him, especially when he was under pressure; and to anyone who did not know him, it must have looked as though he were softening, hesitating to find a way to back down without losing face. For that reason, the guards were unusually patient, waiting for him to give an answer. Finally, when his breathing was under control and he felt strong enough to speak, Christy raised himself up as tall as he could and said, loud and clear, "You want me to stamp on a piece of wood? That's fine; I can do that."

Hugo heaved a sigh of blessed relief.

"Find me something else made of wood," said Christy. "If you just want me to stamp on a piece of wood, find me another piece of wood. Your head will do just fine." Fortunately, the insult appeared to have been lost on the guard, who simply looked confused. "Go ahead; find me something else made of wood, and I'll stamp on it, if that's what you want. But that is not what this is about."

There were enemies everywhere. Hugo could not remember afterwards where they had come from, but he was suddenly aware that Christy was being surrounded. "Do it now," ordered the guard, deliberately standing a little too close to him, but Christy refused to take a step back.

"Go to hell."

The seconds that followed seemed to happen in slow motion. Hugo saw the guard strike Christy in the face with the full force of his strength. The guard was much smaller than Christy in stature, but in Christy's already weakened state, it was enough to knock him off his feet. Somehow, Hugo found himself standing over his friend, moving too quickly to be held back. He could feel spittle against his face that was not directed at him and looked up to see the men in uniform he had noticed before, closing in around them in a semicircle. He had noted before that they were armed only with bamboo canes, which had at least reassured him that they did not intend to kill Christy over this, but now that they were much closer he noticed that the sticks were sharpened at the end into points. Spears. Many small, thin, razor-sharp spears.

"Christy, for pity's sake," pleaded Hugo, crouching beside him. He wondered whether the seriousness of the situation could have failed to dawn on him; perhaps he was simply unable to think clearly. Christy looked so far away, lying on his back, eyes half-closed where the lids were beginning to swell. "They're going to stab you; this isn't worth dying for."

Christy gave no answer.

"You've made your point; please stop. Think of your wife. God wouldn't want you to die like this." Hugo looked up and gestured to the guard to give him a moment longer, watching as the guard signalled the others to step back one pace. "Christy, *please.*" But Christy was not even looking at him. Hugo felt his temper flare: "For God's sake, do what they want! Do what they want, you stubborn Irish bastard!"

Christy's face broke into a smile. "Never." He reached up to take Hugo's hand, but his fingers were broken from being stamped on, and he could barely hold him. "Friend, if you were given a picture of the king of England and told to stamp on it and spit on it, would you?"

Hugo shook his head slowly. "No," he said, almost inaudibly.

"Don't ask me to insult my King."

Hugo had not wept since he was in the nursery, but he felt tears tracing incriminating lines down his face. There had been so much death, so much violence; during the last war, he had seen men killed before his eyes whom he had known all his life, with whom he had gone to school, played rugby—friends he had watched grow from boys to men in the squalor of a theatre of war. But this was a death he was not prepared to witness. He rose to his feet as though reporting for duty. "Leave him alone," said Hugo, placing himself between Christy and his enemies. He knew it was futile—laughably so—but he said it anyway: "This man is your prisoner. You have no right to do him any harm."

"Stand aside," said the guard. "Go back with the others."

Hugo could feel panic rising in him, but he knew he could not stand aside now. "Leave him alone."

"I tell you to go back with the others."

Hugo looked back at Christy, but Christy was shaking his head. "It's okay; you can stand down now. It's all okay." The semicircle was closing in. Hugo fell to his knees, calculating that it was the best way to protect his friend from what was coming, but in an instant, he felt himself being pounced upon again, and he was being dragged out of the line of fire. He fought like mad, screaming at the top of his voice to be left alone, for the men to let go, for it all to stop. He fought off the rescue so violently that in the end, the others held him facing away from his friend so that he would not be able to see him being killed.

Hugo heard once again the thud and slam of a body being broken; the low, barely audible noise of clothing and then flesh punctured and torn; then the long, savage cry of a man in excruciating agony, who believes that he will never draw another breath. Hugo was the one who was screaming.

Silence. The weary, uneasy silence when a battle has ended; the surviving men march away, and the dead lie unburied wherever they fell, shrouded in the dissipating smoke. Hugo felt himself being released, but he could not lift his head, and he ignored the well-intentioned efforts to make him sit up. Hugo could hear the discordant sounds of grief and rage all around him, but he could not bring himself to rise, and the other men quickly left him to himself.

No effort Hugo had ever made was greater than the strength of will it took to get himself up. There was a childishness about shock, the way it rendered a person as helpless and irrational as an infant. Part of him wanted to lie where he was forever, to lie there until he wasted away and died. He rebuked himself—or tried to—for his moral cowardice. Christy was the one who was dead, not he, and his foolish screaming and struggling had served only to draw attention away from the torturous death his friend was suffering. There had never been any chance Hugo could have saved him, and it seemed quite obvious to him now, as he heaved himself onto his knees, paused until his head stopped spinning, and stood up.

Christy's body lay just a few feet from where Hugo had been held, and his stomach lurched at the sight of him. For a moment, he thought Christy's killers had done him a final macabre insult by laying out his body the way they had, almost as though they had been trying to turn his corpse into the crucifix he had refused to smash. His arms were stretched out as though he really were nailed to a cross, but Hugo quickly realised from the state of Christy's injuries that he must have stretched his own arms out as his killers descended on him. It had either been the pride of a man who could not bring himself to cower and curl up like a child even in the face of murder; or perhaps his last gesture to the world had been to embrace the death he knew was coming.

Christy's killers had set upon him so violently that his clothing had been torn to shreds and hung over him in frayed, jagged strips, revealing dozens of abrasions and puncture wounds, none of which would have been enough to kill him outright. But whoever had thought this up had never intended Christy to die quickly. Hugo knelt by Christy's head. He could see now that Christy had had his teeth knocked out, which explained why he had struggled to speak when the guard had questioned him, and his face was still in the process of swelling and discolouring. As it was, Hugo could see blood seeping down from the crown of his head, where the spear-like points of those bamboo sticks had been driven repeatedly into his scalp. *My God, how was he not screaming when they did this? By what super-human effort did he keep his mouth shut?*

It was the strangest instinct, but Hugo could not bear the sight of Christy's bloodied face and felt overwhelmed by the urge to look after him in some way even though he knew it was too late. He reached into his pocket and pulled out the cloth he used to wipe his own face whenever the sensation of sweat dripping over him became unbearable. It was not at all clean, but he very carefully ran it over Christy's face, closing his friend's eyelids to avoid having to look at his staring, dead eyes again.

Hugo jumped out of his skin. It had not been his imagination—Christy had blinked, once, twice, and his lips moved. He attempted to search for a pulse in Christy's neck, but the area beneath his ears was so mangled that Hugo did not dare touch him for fear of hurting him. Not that it could make much difference. If Christy really was alive, and he clearly was, the agony he was going through did not bear thinking about.

"Christy, can you hear me?" asked Hugo, but there was no response; not for the first time, he wondered whether his imagination was playing tricks on him. He carefully took hold of Christy's left hand, which looked less damaged than the other. "Christy, if you can hear me, squeeze my hand."

Almost immediately, Hugo felt the slightest pressure of fingers attempting to curl round his. Christy was too weak to do any more, but that fluttering movement assured Hugo that Christy really was alive and conscious. A sound like the growl of a dying animal resonated from deep in Christy's chest, and Hugo tried not to notice that Christy's ribs were so badly broken, he could see the pattern of splintered bone beneath the taut flesh. Christy's lungs must have been punctured; he was dying of slow suffocation, fully conscious, tormented by all those many injuries and by the terror, surely the worst horror any human being could endure, of breathing becoming ever more painful and impossible until the last whisper of oxygen was squeezed out forever.

"I'm sorry," said Hugo, and he did not even understand what he was apologising for, other than that he was one who would survive, and that seemed shameful enough. "I'm so sorry."

Christy's mouth was moving again. Hugo leant as close to him as he could, desperate to catch any word he spoke. When the words came, they were whispered in a rush, all spoken in the same short breath. "She mustn't know I died like this. Mustn't, mustn't know. Don't tell ... her ... it'll ... kill her."

"Christy, she's your wife. Surely she—"

"Please." Hugo nodded, but he would surely have promised anything to Christy at that moment. "Pray with me."

Hugo felt himself blushing with shame. "I don't know how to."

Christy made a noise that sounded suspiciously like laughter, and Hugo suspected he would have found himself on the receiving end of a witty retort if Christy had still had the breath to waste on such an answer. "Watch with me, then."

For the ten longest minutes of his entire life, Hugo knelt in silent vigil, watching as the life slowly trickled away from his friend. Christy did not communicate with him again except to stop him from moving his arms when Hugo attempted to make him more comfortable. Hugo watched as Christy's lips moved in what he could only suppose were prayers, but the only words he heard were in Latin. Out of some sense of solidarity, Hugo tried to pray himself, but the only words that sprang to mind were a desperate plea to a God he was not even sure he believed in: *Take him, God; for mercy's sake, just let him go.*

Then he was dead. Hugo continued to kneel at his side, unable to bring himself to abandon his post, even though he knew without a shadow of a doubt that Christy no longer needed his comforting presence. It was terrible to live alone, Hugo had always thought, but so much more wretched to die alone; and though he had not been able to save him, he had at least spared Christy that. He should have died peacefully in his bed, his white head bearing witness to a long, fruitful life; he should have died in the arms of his doting wife. By what madness had a young Irish American soldier come to die behind barbed wire in a country he could not have picked out on a map before he was sent there? How could a man not brilliant or gifted, not privileged, unlikely to cut a great figure in the world—a man indistinguishable from any other—have come to die in this way?

Hugo had no idea what happened next. He was aware that he could no longer hear Christy's laboured breathing; he thought he remembered trying desperately to think of a prayer to say, because it seemed like the proper thing to do at such a moment, but not being able to think of a single word that would make any sense. The next thing he was aware of, he was lying under a covering, drifting in and out of consciousness. He thought someone must have helped him to his feet and led him away, but his head rang with discordant noises, and his mind was a blank fog. The intervening minutes or hours had melted away.

16

They were adrift. Like two children huddled together for warmth in a lifeboat, Hugo and Evi clung together, spinning and bobbing across a vast, hostile sea in the wake of a disaster they had miraculously escaped. The minutes ticked away, but they were drifting beyond the reach of time and space, two lost souls wandering through eternity together. Neither of them had the strength to speak or move, but for the hour that followed, there was no need to say anything.

Evi's head rested on Hugo's arm. She felt the weary sense of peace that only utter emotional exhaustion can bring with it; she was not sure how long she had cried, only that she had stopped when she simply could not weep anymore. She no longer had strength or tears left to expend. In the stifling silence of the aftermath, Evi felt only the ache of her body feeling the effects of her breakdown and the listless fatigue she might have experienced if she had spent hours caught up in a ferocious battle she had only just survived.

"Thank you," she said finally. She meant to add that she was glad Christy was not alone at the end, but she was exasperated to discover tears choking her again when she had thought it impossible. "It's almost the way he would have wanted to go."

Hugo stroked Evi's moist, hot cheek. "I'm so sorry, my dear. I've gone about this the wrong way. I wanted more than anything to find you when I came home from the war, but I knew I could never trust myself to keep my promise. Of course you would want to know how he died—it's only natural you should want to know—but I have never broken a promise in my entire life. And I could not have refused to honour a man's final request. He was thinking of you right at the end, Evi. Let that be comfort enough."

"Hugo, I could feel him near me in Lugosi's room. When Lugosi said he could not harm me, it wasn't just that Miraculous Medal around my neck stopping him. It felt as though there was some force holding him back."

Hugo sighed, too exhausted to argue with this madness any longer. "You must rest," he said, resisting the urge to spend the rest of the day sitting on the floor with Evi in his arms. "Come, now, doctor's orders."

He walked her to her room with the utmost care, helped her into bed, and tucked her in, unable to shake off the awkward feeling that he was treating her like a child again. She closed her eyes without further protest, reaching out to him as she began to doze off. "I'm falling," she murmured. "I can't stop falling."

Hugo knelt by her head and held her. "You're not going to fall; I'm holding you. It's just the drugs."

"I'm always falling."

"Listen, I should have been here a long time ago, but I'm here now. You have a good sleep. I'm going to finish your article. I'll take it to your editor myself. You need have nothing further to do with this horrible business. In a few weeks' time, all this will feel like a bad dream."

Hugo waited until he was sure Evi was asleep before he tiptoed out and busied himself with the act of salvaging Evi's work. He had to rewrite the article completely to remove any reference to an interview Evi believed she had had with a dead man, but it did not take very long to finish, as he was knowledgeable on the subject of Lugosi's rise and fall. He did a quick word count, took a last look round Evi's door to ensure that she really was fast asleep, then tiptoed out.

He was amazed by how unreal everything felt as he walked along the boulevard with the warm air touching him almost in blessing. He was still in a bit of a daze, mechanically hopping on board a bus, getting off at the wrong stop, and having to take a rather longer walk than he had planned to the unimposing offices of the third-rate magazine Evi had found herself scribbling for in her penury. She could do so much better than this, he thought, as he made his way through the newsroom, with its maddening clatter of typewriters and the toxic cloud of cigarette smoke. She had to be able to do better than this; she was worthy of a more considerate employer than the vile little man to whom he handed her articles in exchange for a small brown envelope.

He owed it to Christy to take care of her. He could get her back on her feet, get her well again, encourage her to use her writing talents for loftier purposes than writing sensationalist copy on subjects that did not even interest her.

On the way back, Hugo stopped at the sight of a familiar word he thought he had read out of the corner of his eye. He turned and found himself facing a pair of gates, and he realised he was standing at the entrance to a convent. Behind the gates was a small courtyard—or was it a cloister?—with a statue of the Blessed Virgin and some narrow, well-attended flower beds. Next to the gate was a notice board containing various handwritten signs drawing the public's attention to the times of Masses and dates of charitable events, but it was the most prominent sign that drew his attention. An exorcist had come to lead the sisters in retreat, and the sign invited members of the public to hear him speak that evening on the subject of the devil.

Hugo did not recognise the priest's name—there was no reason why he should, and it sounded Mediterranean— but "exorcist" was one of those words that tended to leap off the page, especially at an agnostic Anglican like him.

He would never have admitted it to Evi—or dared broach the subject with Christy—but when he was a child, the images evoked by the very word "Catholicism" consisted almost entirely of swirling clouds of incense, nuns and monks swooping about in black like bloodsucking bats, and crazed exorcists chanting Latin incantations. And here in this very convent, in 1956, there dwelt an exorcist, ready to do battle with the evil one.

Hugo thought that he ought not to leave Evi alone for long, as he had no idea how she would sleep. In any case, Hugo had never entered a convent before—he was not sure he had even spoken to a Roman Catholic priest, for that matter—but he had some residual belief that there might be such a thing as Providence after all. He could not help noticing the coincidence that had led him to a place where a man was speaking who believed in the devil and the forces of darkness, precisely at this moment of his life when he was attending to a woman who believed she had been conversing with the dead.

Hugo was still hesitating to ring the bell when he caught sight of an ethereal-looking woman crossing the courtyard in his direction. Before he could run away, Hugo found himself staring into the face of a strikingly beautiful young sister, dressed from head to toe in white. She could have been anything from seventeen years old to thirty-five; it was so impossible to tell the age of a woman with her hair covered and none of the identifying features of clothing styles and colours or makeup, and her eyes held his gaze without a hint of nervousness at the sight of an outsider peering into her secluded home. "May I help you?" she asked brightly.

Now Hugo really had no idea what to do. He looked away, pretending to examine the intricacy of the iron-work. "I'm frightfully sorry to trouble you," he began, aware that he already sounded like a walking cliché. He might as well have been at the border of a foreign country, wondering whether he had the right entry visa. "Sorry to disturb you, but I couldn't help noticing a sign on your notice board about a priest visiting your convent."

"That is correct," confirmed the sister with a little smile. "You are welcome to attend his lecture; it is open to the public."

It was all going to go horribly wrong, thought Hugo. He was tempted to give her a polite nod and agree that it would be a splendid idea to come along to the talk, but he thought of Evi sleeping fitfully in her home, pursued by some shadow or other that he did not understand. "Yes, I should like that very much, but I wonder if it would be possible for me to speak with him?"

The nun hesitated. "He's busy ..."

"I know, I don't mean to inconvenience anyone, but it is a matter of the utmost importance. I can't think of anyone else who can help her."

He could sense that she was weighing up in her mind whether the stranger was to be trusted. "Is there someone in need of his help? I can send for a priest to go to the lady's home, if you like. Or is she in the hospital? It makes no difference, of course, but I need to—"

"There is someone in need of help, but only he can help her." Hugo braced himself, though he thought it unlikely that the woman would scream or burst out laughing, and that was some consolation. "She ... well, I'm no expert on these matters, but I think she needs an exorcist." He ignored the look of alarm that momentarily crossed the nun's sweet face. "Please, if I could just have five minutes' conversation with him, it would be enough."

If the nun thought him mad or ridiculous, she showed no further sign of it. Giving him a little nod, she opened the gate and ushered him inside, leading him wordlessly through the courtyard to a narrow wooden door.

The interior was just as Hugo had imagined a convent would look. The angelic figure in white led him down a corridor so silent that his footsteps clattered along the tiled floor like the percussion section of a symphony orchestra. He noted a picture (or was it an icon?) of a girl in some sort of nun's habit, holding a bunch of roses and a crucifix, painted in sentimental, pastel shades. There was a smell that reminded him uncomfortably of school, the fruity odour of floor polish, though he never remembered the corridors of the academic prison camp he had inhabited for ten years feeling quite so fresh and airy. He was shown into a pleasing little parlour overlooking a small, enclosed garden and waited alone whilst enquiries were made.

Left to his own devices, Hugo's doubts began to creep in again. What on earth was a self-respecting Englishman doing sitting in the parlour of a convent awaiting an interview with a complete stranger on the subject of his girlfriend's tragic but undeniably mad behaviour? "Girlfriend"? Where had that come from? Hugo clutched his head to support the weight of too many contradictory thoughts and speculations. His friend. Evangeline Kilhooley, a professional acquaintance. A friend about whom he was concerned.

The sound of the door opening caused Hugo to stand up instinctively, in time to see a man dressed in black entering. Hugo tried desperately to get the thought out of his mind that the priest looked like he belonged on the set of a horror film too—but it was only his attire, unfamiliar to Hugo, that suggested such a thing. Hugo was looking at a well-preserved man in his sixties, displaying the strong features and friendly expression that would have looked quite striking on the silver screen.

Hugo had no idea how he was supposed to greet him; he should have asked the nun about it. Fortunately, the priest noted his discomfort and proffered a hand. A hand-shake. Order restored, the men sat down.

"I'm terribly sorry to disturb you, sir," Hugo began, pushing aside the thought that he had got the man's title wrong, "but I saw on the notice board out there that you are an exorcist, and I thought you might be able to help." Hugo groaned at how badly it was coming out, but it was a start. "I have a lady friend I am very concerned about. I'm not a Catholic, and I've no experience of ... well, I have no knowledge of the supernatural ... well, I'm not sure how to help her, and I thought you might be able to advise." There, he had said it.

The priest smiled reassuringly. "You may have more knowledge than you realise," he said in the English of an educated European, "but you are quite right to seek help. Your lady friend is a Catholic?"

"Yes. Well, I suppose she is. She's ... well, I'm afraid her life has been a bit of a mess for some time, but it's not her fault. Her late husband was terribly Catholic."

The priest smiled graciously once more, this time, Hugo thought, at his expense. "Terribly Catholic?"

"She's a war widow; her husband died in Korea." Hugo paused; he could already feel the roaring darkness of the memory coming back to get him, and this was not the moment to go to pieces. "I suppose that's where all this began. I was friends with her husband; we met in the prison camp."

"I see. He shared his faith with you, then?"

"He died for it." Hugo had no idea where those words had come from; he backtracked immediately. "I mean, he was murdered, Father. They wanted him to stamp on a crucifix. He wouldn't, and they killed him." He knew it sounded heartless, but he could not pore over all those details twice in the same day. He could already feel the bile rising in his throat. "That was what I meant by *terribly* Catholic."

"A martyr, perhaps?"

Hugo could almost hear Christy's raucous laughter. "There were no halos in Christy Kilhooley's vicinity, Father, I assure you." Where was this irritation coming from? "Look, he was a stubborn Irishman, always getting himself into trouble. They were always baiting him so that he'd lose his temper and give them a reason to hurt him. It was no different this time." Anger again; it was almost as though he were angry with his friend. "I'm sorry, Father, but it was all so horrible. They wanted him to stamp on a crucifix. He wouldn't, so they beat him. He still wouldn't, so they stabbed him with bamboo sticks. It was a horrible death, and we all had to stand back and watch."

"That sounds like martyrdom to me. Maybe you don't fully understand why he did it?"

"I do, I understand the principle, but I ..." Hugo shifted in his chair. He should not be here, he thought; he should not be in this room. "Look, this is entirely beside the point. The fact is, he left behind a young widow. She's English like me, a GI bride."

"I see."

"She'd already been through a great deal of suffering before she came to America to start a new life. Like many in England, she lost her family in one of the bombing raids. Then to be told that her husband was missing, to wait for years to be told he was dead ... well, you can imagine, I'm sure ..."

The priest nodded sympathetically. "Was that why you sought her out? You wanted to care for your friend's widow?"

Hugo felt himself reddening at the man's assumption that he had done the right thing. "I'm afraid not. Christy didn't want her to know he had died like that. It was a terrible, lingering death; he thought it would destroy her if she found out, and I couldn't trust myself to keep his secret if I met her. That was what I told myself, anyway." He hesitated, but some invisible force nudged him forwards. "To be frank, Father, I think I used that as an excuse because I was afraid to find her. I wanted to pretend that none of it had happened, and a connection with a dead friend's widow would have made the past inescapable."

Hugo sank into silence. He was aware of standing at a crossroads between the tragic and the outlandish. The first part of the story was easy enough to convey in a manner that he had known would gain the sympathy of any clergyman with an ounce of compassion. The second, though ... "Do you believe in the devil?" asked Hugo desperately, as though he were asking if the priest believed in fairies at the bottom of the garden.

"Yes," he said calmly, "I do."

"Do you believe in demonic possession, then?"

"Of course."

"Ghosts? Vampires? The dominion of the Undead?"

The priest blinked as though a small boy had set off a firecracker at his feet. "Please explain exactly what you mean."

"I knew this was a mistake!" wailed Hugo, all propriety going out the window. "You must think me stark staring mad!"

The priest chuckled under his breath. "Tell me the rest of your story, and then I'll judge."

Hugo sat up. "If what I'm saying really is stark staring mad, you will tell me directly, won't you? It would be reassuring to hear you say it."

"Tell me first how your paths crossed if you did not seek her out."

"She's a writer, Father. She was commissioned to write a series of articles about the late actor Bela Lugosi." Hugo could have sworn that he noticed the priest start ever so slightly, but if he had, the reflex was quickly suppressed, and he continued listening intently to Hugo's story. "Evi has no interest in films, especially horror films, and knew nothing about the man. Her editor referred her to me because I'm something of a film enthusiast. I run a small film emporium."

"You think it a coincidence that you should meet like that? What were the chances of two English meeting in a country as big as America?"

"It was an extraordinary coincidence," Hugo agreed. "I might almost say that I felt as though somehow we'd been brought together. Of course, I couldn't resist meeting her. I rather enjoyed it. We met for afternoon tea; I had all the cakes specially made for her. All very English. You see, I knew an awful lot about her; Christy used to talk about her all the time. Absolutely all the time—funny habits, her likes and dislikes. If you think about it, he'd been away from her for so much of their short marriage. I suppose he was still in that infatuated stage."

The priest sat back in his chair as though pondering the situation. "I see no alarm with any of this. Providence has brought you together. But that was not why you came to see me, was it?"

Hugo stared miserably into the corner of the room. "Look, this is all going to sound like a mountain being made out of a molehill. The poor woman's ill; that's all. She's lonely and sad, a young widow all alone in a foreign country. She took to drink; it could happen to anyone. But she also seems to have started to lose her mind."

"Sadly, all too common."

"Quite. I noticed that her work was getting out of control. Her articles have been of fairly good quality for a woman with no interest in film. I used to proofread them for her. I'd have to correct some details, but that was all. Then she claimed she met the late actor about whom she was writing after he died."

"Bela Lugosi?"

"Yes." Hugo paused, trying to get a read on the priest, but he saw no traces of condemnation. "She is clearly delusional; that, or she's been hoodwinked by an impostor."

"Possibly," said the priest, after a long silence. "What did she say about him, the dead Lugosi or the man she believed to be him?"

"She claimed he attacked her. The strange thing is, there were bruises on her face, and she was showing signs of concussion. The doctor was sure she'd been struck; he said that was the way it looked."

"Did she tell you how it happened?"

"She arrived for an interview with him and found him slumped in his chair. She said she thought he was dead, so she went to take his pulse. She was obviously frightened very badly, but it was what she claimed he said that brought me here to you."

"Ah, a message. Interesting."

"You must understand, I had kept my promise to Christy. I didn't tell her how her husband died until I had absolutely no alternative. I wouldn't even admit to her that I'd known him in case she might attempt to make me break that promise. But she forced the details out of me; she practically told me how he died. She said Lugosi had told her that her husband died a terrible, glorious death, just like his master. Something about him being a witness to the truth as Lugosi was a witness to the darkness. Or something like that."

The priest was suddenly on his feet. "Where is she now? This woman, where did you leave her?"

Hugo stood up, flustered. "I left her fast asleep in her home. She was completely exhausted, and the doctor gave her some sedatives. She'll be out for the count for hours."

The priest was throwing the door open and marching out, leaving Hugo to scurry after him. "Do you have the address of the house where she used to visit—where she used to meet Lugosi?"

"I can find it for you," promised Hugo as the two men thundered down the corridor. "It will be in her work folder, back at her flat. Sorry, apartment."

"Very well. We have little time."

Hugo knew better than to ask any questions and followed his guide to a waiting car.

Evi was going to prove she was not mad if it killed her. She knew she had seen him, met him, talked with him. Unlike Hugo or the doctor, or anyone else who took it upon himself to interfere, Evi knew the difference between her grief-stricken dream worlds and reality. She was the captain of her own—admittedly troubled—mind, and she knew she had not imagined Lugosi the last time she had visited him.

When sleep once again deserted her, the sedatives being next to useless, Evi forced herself out of bed, changed her clothes, and left for Lugosi's house. It was not going to be easy to find evidence of his existence if he really was dead—if creatures like that had no reflection in a mirror, she could assume that he would not show up on celluloid if she attempted to photograph him. So she would have to find some other way to prove she had seen him. It occurred to Evi, as she neared her destination, that he might even be persuaded to help her. If he wanted his story to be believed, the public had to know that she had not simply dreamed it up. He would have to give her the means to persuade a sceptical readership that she was not out of her mind.

There was the house. A boringly ordinary little house, indistinguishable from all the others on the road except for its dilapidated state. The house was most definitely real, and a part of her felt relieved. She had been so unsettled by the whole business, she would not have been surprised to arrive and discover that there was no house there at all, just a crater or ruin like the House of Usher. So far so good.

Evi rapped on the door with forced confidence. She waited a discreet interval and gave the door a push. As she entered, Evi acknowledged that she had made an elementary mistake on her last visit. It had been her own fault for creeping about in the darkness like that; it had allowed her imagination to play tricks on her. It was time to let in some light. Nothing was ever so very frightening in broad daylight, not even a creepy old man running rings round her, and she would not allow him to frighten her this time. Evi was carrying a knife in her bag simply to deter him, should he become aggressive again. It had been all very well to hear that her dead husband was protecting her, but she suspected that Christy would expect her to take a few added precautions.

Evi stood in the dark hall, leaving the front door wide open. She called out his name, but there was no answer, as expected. She noticed a door immediately to the left, which she guessed must lead to some sort of living room or dining room. She threw it open before stepping cautiously inside. Nothing but the furniture. She stuck to her plan, went over to the large, thick drapes and threw them back, releasing a massive cloud of dust. Here too the old actor must have insisted that the curtains remain drawn.

She noticed an interconnecting door at the other end of the room and moved towards it. Her fingers strayed to the Miraculous Medal around her neck as she opened the door and looked inside. It was so dark that Evi could see nothing beyond the thin square of light in the doorway, cast by the light in the room she was leaving. She stepped gingerly forward and searched the inner wall for a light switch, until she felt one under her hand and flicked it on. To her surprise, a lightbulb came on above her head, revealing an unkempt kitchen. Poor Mrs Lugosi, she thought, who had been not only nursing the old man during his decline but, in their impecuniousness, working to support them both.

She returned to the entryway, and with light streaming through the open front door and the sitting room, it looked perfectly ordinary. She started up the stairs, throwing open the curtains that covered the large window on the landing. She knocked at the familiar door behind which she had conducted her interviews, and awaited an answer.

Evi was sure she heard something, a grunt or a whispered word. She put her ear to the door and heard the sound of someone getting to his feet. There was someone there, then; she had not dreamed it all up. And since Bela Lugosi was dead, he must be an imposter after all. "Mr Lugosi?" she called brightly. "It's Evangeline."

Before she could open the door herself, it was opened sharply from the inside, and the man Evi had known as Bela Lugosi stood before her. A squeal of horror stuck in her throat, and Evi could no longer breathe. Lugosi's skin was not so much pale anymore as barely flesh at all. She could see every bone, virtually every muscle, of his face. His eyes were so bloodshot that the whites had completely disappeared.

He recoiled from the light as though he found it physically painful. She was about to step towards him, but he glared at her with such savage rage, she could never describe it afterwards in words that felt adequate. It was not so much a look; she felt as though all the rage and hate in the world was bearing down on her, and the sheer intensity of it would burn her alive if she could not escape.

She snatched the knife from her purse, but she was shaking so violently that in her clumsy state she succeeded only in slashing her own forearm. Evi looked down and saw blood pumping out of her wrist, and a second later she heard a terrible, demonic shriek inches away from her head. She dropped the knife and staggered back to the top of the stairs.

The man, the creature, stood spellbound in the light, his eyes transfixed on the blood flowing from her arm. Evi was sure she could smell smoke. As she took a last look at the being before her, they were separated by a sudden flash of blinding light, and Evi was thrown back by a wave of intense, searing heat. She was falling, her body spinning and turning as she crashed against the many hard wooden steps down to the corridor below.

For a moment, crumpled on the hard, dusty floor, Evi was too stunned to move. She heard that shriek, that dreadful otherworldly scream of despair—and something even more sinister: the unmistakable roar of a blazing inferno. She felt pieces of the wooden banisters raining down on her as the heat caused the wood to crumble and fall; then she saw a wave of flames above her head, greedily engulfing the landing and the whole of the top of the house. She tried to get up, but the staircase had begun collapsing as she fell, and something heavy and unyielding covered her legs. Even though she knew that nobody could hear, that nobody could possibly reach her in time, she opened her mouth and screamed for deliverance.

"Christy!" she screamed. "Christy!"

And she drew up her arms across her face to shield her eyes from the fire that was about to claim her.

Hugo and his companion saw the flames from the other end of the street. "That's Lugosi's house!" shouted Hugo. The priest slammed his foot on the accelerator, sending the car speeding towards the burning house, then transferred his foot from the accelerator to the brake with equal violence. The car lurched to a halt, and the two men threw themselves out of the vehicle and ran towards the building. The front door was hanging open, and smoke was billowing out, but Hugo hurried inside with the instincts and the training of a military man.

As soon as he entered the corridor, his eyes and nostrils stung with the smoke, which was much denser than he had expected. Crouching down, he saw a figure on the floor just ahead of him and dashed over to pick her up, but Evi was trapped beneath the wooden beams that had collapsed over her. He could hear and feel the fire raging above his head, but he did not dare look up as he began battling to free her. If he were going to be buried by burning debris, he did not have to see it.

The priest appeared at his side, and between them, they were able to lift the last remaining beam. They carried Evi out of the house as the fire truck pulled up in front of it. "They will not put out that fire," said the priest grimly, turning his attention back to Evi. "It will burn itself out." He pulled back Evi's sleeve, noticing the source of the bleeding. "Quickly!"

It had been years since Hugo had had to save another person's life, but without a thought he removed his belt and looped it around her arm, tightening it until the blood flow from the wound slowed down. Hugo said, "You need to make a bandage," but before he could finish the sentence, the priest pressed a folded handkerchief against the wound. "Did he stab her?" asked Hugo desperately. "It's a bloody strange place to wound a person if he did."

"An accident," said the priest. "It's never good for a person to carry a weapon he doesn't know how to use. The blade must have been unsheathed, and she panicked. The Darkness causes accidents like this."

The men from the fire truck and the ambulance came running up, and took control of the situation. As Evi was carried to the ambulance, the priest said to Hugo, "Get in the car, I'll drive you to the hospital. I'll need to speak with her when she wakes."

It was only as Hugo sat back in the car that he noticed the blood on his clothes and began trembling with shock. "She will be all right, won't she? She's lost so much blood."

"Your friend has gotten herself into a situation she does not understand. If she'd known the danger she was in, she would never have entered that house alone, and not with a knife as her only protection."

"What started the fire?"

"Not what, who. She started the fire—unintentionally, of course," said the priest, turning the key in the ignition. "I suspect she started something she couldn't stop. Of course, I'll have to question her on the details since the fire will have left little evidence of what happened. The fire confirms my suspicions." He glanced quickly away from the road at his pale, trembling passenger.

Hugo tensed every muscle in his body, but he still could not stop himself from shaking. "I'm sorry, you must think me a frightful coward. For the life of me, I can't stop myself!"

"Not a coward. You ran into that burning building. You knew you might never come out again. Her husband made the right choice when he sent you to her."

The shock was making Hugo irritable. "He didn't send me! Christy did nothing of the sort!" Hugo turned to look at him, but the priest was looking fixedly at the road ahead of him. "Forgive me, but I wish you'd make some sense."

Hugo's companion smiled. "Don't you remember what you told me? That the man said he could not harm her because her husband protected her."

"Father, she came within a whisker of being burnt alive or bleeding to death. I fail to see how she was protected from harm!"

"Do you still believe in coincidences? Do you still believe that it was purely chance that led you to meet your dead friend's widow at precisely the moment she was set upon a dangerous path she could not survive alone?"

Hugo closed his eyes. The trembling was slowing down now, but he could feel exhaustion taking over. "My head hurts," he said to the world in general.

"Close your eyes and rest. Soon you'll need your strength again."

17

Evi could feel herself being carried. She had no idea where she was, but it had been a long time since she had had any certainties at all. Christy had always said that the only difficult thing about being married to a writer was never knowing whether she was living in the same universe. It was in her nature to drift from one reality to another at will, returning to the static realm of household chores and deadlines only when Christy called her back, usually in comical fashion: "Evangeline Kilhooley, please apply for a reentry visa to planet Earth."

Perhaps that was all this was about. In the absence of a mischievous voice to call her home, and with no home worth returning to, she had drifted further and further away until she could not find the way back or work out where she was going. There was nothing to anchor her, nothing that made the real world seem, well, *real*. Evi had some confused recollection that she had been imprisoned in a burning building, trapped like the heroine of some bad horror movie in a perilous state, the flames creeping ever closer to her with no hope of deliverance. Then she had found herself in a noisy, bright corridor, full of light and human company. Somehow or other, she had gone from that lonely house of death to a maelstrom of activity. She felt something soft wrapped around her wrist.

"Don't touch, honey," said an authoritative female voice. "We've stitched your wound. You're gonna be okay, trust me."

"Where am I going?" she asked.

"The doctors have finished with you for now. We're just going to get you comfortable."

Evi closed her eyes. The rest of that day and the days that followed were a series of untidy, disconnected fragments, as though the life she had been hopelessly trying to hold together had been shattered by some overwhelming force. She opened her eyes again to find herself in a private room, in a comfortable bed positioned near a window, but she never saw what was on the other side of the glass. She drifted again, aware only of a vague sense of safety.

Then there was fire everywhere. She saw a figure, half man, half monster, blundering through the flames, his hair and cape ablaze, reaching out through the fire to her, determined to drag her in. She felt the ground disintegrating beneath her feet. She screamed, screamed until her lungs were empty, screamed for the sake of this wretched creature being slowly destroyed before her eyes, screamed for her life . . .

Two faces came into focus. Hugo, a face so familiar to her now that she could have painted its every detail had she had the gift, and a stranger. For a moment, she did not notice the stranger's Roman collar; she saw a grey-haired man swathed in black and recoiled in horror. The man seemed to expect such a response and smiled. "It's quite all right; I'm not a vampire. I just look like one."

Hugo held Evi's hand. "How are you feeling?"

"Did they find his body? The fire brigade, I mean."

The priest sat down beside the bed. There was something businesslike about his manner that Evi found strangely comforting. It offered the possibility that the conversation would not become personal. "There will be no body to find, but perhaps you knew that," said the priest gently. "Now, I need to ask you some questions—that is, if you feel strong enough."

Evi nodded, watching as the priest took out a notebook and pencil. She had almost come full circle.

It was the kindest and harshest interview of her entire life. The questioner was clearly well versed in the art of getting answers to painful questions, and there were so many questions—questions about details she had barely thought about, seemingly idle words spoken by Bela Lugosi and his preference for darkness, for example. The priest refused to let any question go unanswered. If she broke down or struggled to speak, which happened many times during the lengthy interview, he would reassure her, offer her a momentary distraction such as a sip of water, and then get straight back to the question she had not yet answered.

Finally, there were no more questions. The priest sat in silence, looking slowly over the pages of his notes—so many pages; had she really had so much to say? Evi lay still, too troubled to fall asleep, too weak to move. She could feel the sensation of her own heartbeat, a strong, rapid rhythm in her neck, beating out the pattern of her life as though she needed to be reminded that she still belonged to the land of the living. The priest looked up at her. "Well, my daughter," he said solemnly, "you've had an extremely narrow escape, and I don't mean your life. You have a very powerful intercessor, but then martyrs usually are." He put the notebook away, slowly and deliberately to ensure that she noticed he was no longer taking notes. "You have been very patient with me; I have asked you a great many difficult questions, and you have answered well. Is there anything you wish to ask me?"

Evi tightened her grip on Hugo's hand. "Was my husband really a martyr?"

"Yes, without doubt."

"Did I interview a dead man or am I crazy?"

"The phantom you saw did not originate in your own mind."

"Will the nightmares ever stop?"

The priest hesitated for the first time. "In time, but that depends on many things. Imagine that you have suffered a long illness, you have passed the crisis point, and you are now recovering. The danger may be over, but the infirmity and pain may continue a long time until you are fully healed."

He stood up. "For now, you must rest." His hand rested briefly on her forehead in blessing; then he left the room wordlessly. She turned to face Hugo, who had been silently holding her hand all the way through the interview. "It was you who carried me out of that building, wasn't it?" she asked.

"I had some help," he answered, bending forward to kiss her lightly on the cheek. "It's all going to be all right now, I promise."

Sleep, long rest in a calm, quiet sanctuary where the only interruptions were Hugo's visits and the comings and goings of nurses and doctors. There were the peaceful hours of rest when she slept like a baby and felt strength slowly returning to her; there was the tormented sleep when nightmares returned and she woke screaming and shaking, begging for something to drink, desperate for the anaesthesia she needed to silence the storm within her.

The outside world might have disappeared into eternity, and Evi would never have known. During her weeks of convalescence, she was sheltered from the hustle of everyday life, from money worries, from the battle to finish her work on time, from newspapers filled with the chaos of human existence. Hugo visited whenever he could, bringing cakes and books in equal measure to keep her spirits up. She grew stronger, able to sit up in bed, then occupy an easy chair, then take short walks around the hospital garden with the assistance of a nurse or Hugo if he was there. Evi initially chafed against, then quickly submitted to, the strange experience of being looked after, and that unnerving sense she always had that she was being kept under constant observation.

When the nightmares became less intense and less frequent, she was moved from her private room to a ward shared by seven other patients, though she felt little inclination to get to know any of them. Her thoughts began to move towards home and the need to try somehow to return to normal life. She knew she could not hide out here forever. She was eating better and putting on weight; the doctor had said her blood count was improving; and the hankering for alcohol, though the subject was rarely broached, was lessening to the degree that she thought she might have the willpower to fight it on her own. "Not yet," was all the doctor would say whenever she asked about returning home. "Discharge you too soon, and you'll be back again within the week."

Then there was the conversation she could never forget. Hugo was at her side with a thermos, because Evi's only complaint about the excellent treatment she received in the convalescent home was that nobody for love or money could produce a decent cup of tea. "Do you know when they're going to let me go home?" she asked. Hugo pretended to be occupied pouring the tea. "Well?"

"Not yet, my dear. You mustn't rush these things."

"The doctors are very pleased with me; they say I'm getting stronger every day." Evi waited for Hugo to answer, but he was apparently not listening. "Hugo, what are you not telling me?"

Hugo feigned confusion. "I'm really not sure ..."

"Don't bother," she retorted, a sure sign she was back to her old self. "What are you trying to hide from me this time?"

Hugo blushed with embarrassment. "Your landlord's thrown you out."

"What!"

"I'm awfully sorry to say it like this, but you already owed him several months' rent before you became ill. You've no money, and you haven't been working, so he said you had to leave."

Evi stared openmouthed. "Don't be too delicate about it, will you!"

"Well, I'm sorry, but if you will ask these things. I wasn't even supposed to tell you."

Evi gave a roar of frustration. "For pity's sake, I've apparently done battle with the Undead, and you still feel the need to patronise me! What happened to my belongings? Did he just throw them out of the windows or something?"

"No, no, it's all right; your belongings are safely stored away in my shop."

Evi sank back against the crisp white pillow. No husband, no children, no job, no home. It was as though an invisible blitz had ravaged her life, leaving her cowering in the ruins, possessing only the clothes she wore. "So I'm homeless," she said calmly.

"There's something else I need to tell you," said Hugo, oblivious to the thought that he might need to stop the flow of bad news, at least to allow Evi some breathing space. "I've decided to return to England."

Evi felt something similar to the sensation of being hurled across a room. "But . . . but what about your shop?"

Hugo sighed. "I'm selling up, Evi; there's no future in it. The fact is, business has been terrible for months. I specialise in horror, and there's no appetite for horror films any longer."

Can't think why, thought Evi dryly, but she could feel her hard-won energy draining away. "And what will you do?"

"I've been offered a position at my old school," said Hugo. "I wrote to a chum who works there, and he said they needed a history master." For the first time, he noticed the effect he was having on Evi, who had descended into silence in front of him. "Evi, I'm not sure I'm making myself very clear. I want to take you with me."

Evi glared at him. Confusion and desolation turned into anger, an emotion Evi had not felt for so long that it was like the return of an old friend. "Of course you're not making yourself clear. I thought you were saying good-bye!"

The two of them were suddenly aware that they were in a public place and were drawing a great deal of attention to themselves. As if by magic, a plump, middle-aged nurse appeared at the bedside. "Is this gentleman bothering you?" she asked Evi.

"No, not at all," Evi said, floundering. "I'm terribly sorry I raised my voice."

"I shan't stay long," promised Hugo, mortified. "I know she needs to rest. Five more minutes."

The nurse nodded reluctantly and stepped back without leaving the room. "This isn't the place to discuss this, Evi, but please consider it," he said quietly. "I love this country, but I'm a fish out of water here, and so, I think, are you. The priest I spoke to warned me that it would be safer for you to leave Los Angeles after all that's happened."

"He said that?"

"Yes. His advice was that we should go somewhere far away and put all of this behind us. Live quietly."

Live quietly.

No child in the history of mankind had ever longed for a quiet life; the dreams of the innocent always gravitate towards adventure and fame. Every child believes that he will grow up to set the world alight and cherishes that hope until adulthood and the shades of the prison house bring him to his senses. It is the dream of the wise to live in obscurity. When Hugo kissed Evi good-bye, leaving her to think things over, she did not feel wise, but she knew what answer she would give him when he returned.

EPILOGUE

My life since the events recounted has been as contented as I could have expected. One good man carried me across the Atlantic to a brave new world; another good man carried me home again. I took on a new identity and a new name—not Hugo's pretentious stage name but the name he left behind when he first left England. We followed the instruction to live quietly and have done just that. Hugo's old school—like so many boarding schools—is an isolated community of its own, separated from the rest of the world by rolling hills and misty woodlands.

It is a happy-enough hiding place for a weary soul who has stared the devil in the face and lived to tell the tale. As that good priest promised, the nightmares have lessened over the years, but not a day goes by when I do not feel the Darkness at my heels. We have one living son whom we called Christopher and four others lost before birth. After the fourth miscarriage, we resigned ourselves to the realisation that we were not meant to have any more children, and we both hoped our son would forgive us for leaving him alone with only two troubled parents for family. Christopher's schoolmates are his brothers, but I know it is not the same, and I have hated my damaged body for failing to nurture my own children.

In time, Hugo embraced the faith, though I suspect that had more to do with Christy than with me. He works, and I write. I write to fill the hours and to allow my mind the guilty privilege of wandering back into the past and its dark memories, which I can never entirely escape. I owe it to my husband and my son not to give in to the Darkness again, but the past and all those horrors are a cross I struggle to carry—especially when the shadows lengthen and night falls all around me, so much bleaker and lonelier than I remember from childhood.

Strange to think that my eldest son will soon be the same age Christy was when I first met him, a charmer in an ill-fitting uniform, surrounded by friends he left behind forever on the beaches of Normandy. I retain the hope that the Darkness that devoured my generation, leaving a trail of dead and wounded in every continent of the world, might leave my boy in peace. Neither Hugo nor I have ever spoken to him of the memories that haunt us— the loved ones who perished in the fires of Coventry, the stubborn Irishman murdered behind barbed wire in a far-away land, the demons we fought and who haunt us still.

I have always been tortured by fear, and perhaps it is my mind tormenting me yet again, but I sense something drawing my son away from me. Perhaps he is merely growing up, so nearly a man that he thinks he has no need of me anymore. It is just that I see shadows everywhere. I am afraid. There, I have said it. I am afraid. Afraid of the Darkness returning. This time it will come for my son, not for me. Please let it come for me. I have faced it once; I can face it again. I shall go out from my hiding place and seek it out. Among the shadows and nightmares, I will let it take me, but not my son. If the Darkness calls me, I am ready to fight it once again.

E.